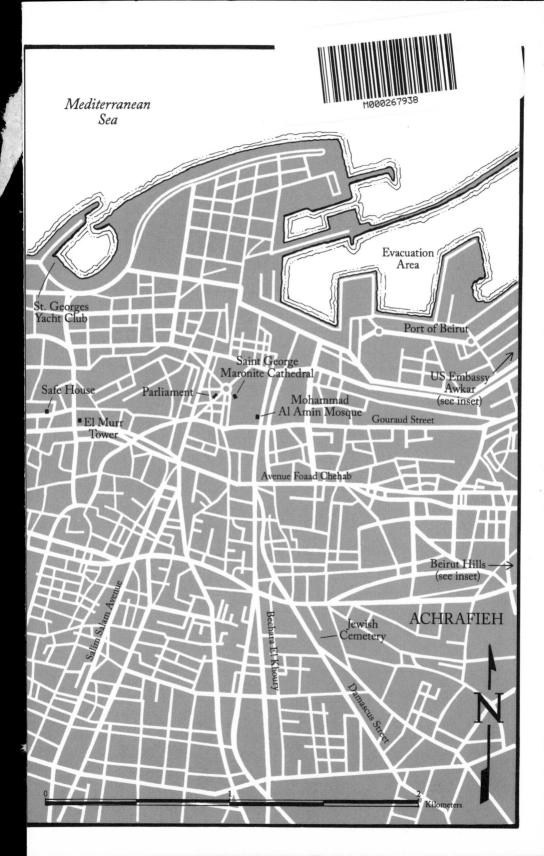

BEIRUT STATION

BEIRUT
STATION

TWO LIVES OF A SPY

PAUL VIDICH

PEGASUS CRIME

NEW YORK LONDON

BEIRUT STATION

Pegasus Crime is an imprint of
Pegasus Books, Ltd.
148 West 37th Street, 13th Floor
New York, NY 10018

Copyright © 2023 by Paul Vidich

First Pegasus Books edition October 2023

Interior design by Maria Fernandez

Beirut–Lebanon map copyright © 2023 by Rick Britton

Library of Congress Cataloging-in-Publication Data is available.

ISBN: 978-1-63936-511-1

10 9 8 7 6 5 4 3 2 1

Printed in the United States of America
Distributed by Simon & Schuster
www.pegasusbooks.com

For Linda

"The spirit lives within me,
our savage ancient spirit of revenge."
—*Agamemnon*, Aeschylus
Robert Fagles, translator

PART I

1

Beirut

July 2006

Beirut's heat wave made the evening air in Analise's apartment oppressively warm, and she was glad her hardship tour was ending. The last bit of agency work, and the most dangerous part, was coming in the morning. She rehearsed what she had to do, going over the details—the vehicle, the bomb, and the face of the targeted man. She closed her eyes to summon a memory of his photograph, but a whispered question interrupted her thoughts and her mind returned to the man lying next to her in bed. He had said "What's troubling you?" and was waiting for her answer. When she could no longer stand the silence, she crossed the bedroom and threw open the window for the weak Mediterranean breeze. Nearby pop music and laughing voices came in with the cooling air and relieved her sense of confinement. She smelled the tobacco of his cigarette and felt the sea air on her skin.

"It's nothing to do with you," she said, returning to bed. She knew the mistake that men made, thinking that silence after coitus was a woman's way of expressing dissatisfaction. She stretched her hand up toward the ceiling fan, her wrist moving one way, then the other, watching how light from the half-closed blinds carved ribbons on her small hamsa tattoo. She clenched and unclenched her fist, letting the dim illumination deepen the red markings.

"Why did you have it done?"

"This?" She lowered her hand. "It brings good luck and wards off evil, if you believe in that sort of thing."

"How long does the henna last?"

"Three weeks. Maybe a month. Then it fades. Like everything."

"Something is bothering you. You're not the type to depend on luck."

She turned on her side and looked into Corbin's eyes—wide, mysterious, and content. She felt no obligation to respond to his comment, which she knew was something he'd said to fill the silence. The tattoo was there to be done, and she had done it on a whim, feeling vulnerable, wanting to avail herself of whatever powers it offered. Little of her life was spontaneous then, and she had done it because she could. She wasn't going to tell him that, or anything else, and certainly not what troubled her. She had trained for what was coming the next day and prepared her mind to be ready if everything suddenly changed, her life at risk. Her non-official cover with the United Nations High Commissioner for Refugees wouldn't protect her from an angry mob.

Their eyes lingered on each other—hers dark and almond-shaped, his green and round but darker in the dim light. Her long, olive-complected legs were next to his pale white form, and for all their intimacy she felt the distance of their different backgrounds.

4

She took his cigarette and put it to her lips, brightening the end, and exhaled from the corner of her mouth. She handed it back.

"You said you quit."

She thought of the ironic comment she could make, but it was not the time or place to hurt him or be insincere. "You need to leave soon."

Car honking and the whine of a motorbike came in the window. Lebanese voices argued in the street, a woman's rising in shrill protest.

"What's she saying?"

"She is pleading with her husband to leave the city. She says that it isn't safe now and they will be stuck when the war reaches Beirut." Analise saw that his interest had drifted to her knobby knees.

"What's your view?" she asked.

"It's late. I don't have a view."

"It's not like you to pass up an opportunity to give your opinion. Your sources are big shots in Tel Aviv. All I have are the wild rumors from refugees who show up at the UN fleeing the fighting." She respected his work, which made it easier to put up with his behavior. She had consented to sleep with him that night because he had shown up at her door with alcohol on his breath. They were two people in a war zone who had fallen into a pattern of casual sex.

He raised the cigarette above his head, watching the ember burn, and in doing so revealed the small serpent tattoo on his wrist.

"When did you get it?"

"This?" He flexed his wrist so the serpent moved. "I had it done after I discovered my wife was cheating on me."

Her eyes narrowed. "That explains why you've picked up tourists in bars and fucked prostitutes. A frenzy of promiscuity to lighten the burden of your betrayal."

She rounded the word's vowels to soften her sarcasm and looked at him tolerantly. She saw his eyes move across her body, and she knew that he was mildly smitten with her. There was a pause between them as she accepted his interest, her eyes trying to look into his mind. She indulged his talent for casual womanizing, and against her better judgment she found him oddly sympathetic. She allowed his fingers to travel along her thigh.

"What's so important that you have to get up early?" he asked.

"Work."

"The job you say you're quitting?"

"Refugees don't suffer nine to five."

He smiled and his hand moved to her knee. "There will be more."

"I won't be the one to process their papers. It's hard to look into their eyes and see desperation. It's easy for you. You sit at your laptop, listen to the other reporters, file stories, and then drink at the bar. Or come here."

She removed his hand. "It's late." Her brisk tone was meant to shut down his flirting. Suddenly, she rose from the bed and moved to the sliding door where a large X of masking tape protected the glass. She looked south but saw only Beirut's hills and rivers of headlights on nearby streets.

"What is it?"

She pointed.

He was at her side, Blackberry in hand, looking into the night. Darkness provided a curtain of modesty from the many people who had moved to their balconies, drawn by the distant sound of jet aircraft. Everyone's attention went to the canopy of night, looking for Israeli warplanes, but clouds obscured the sky.

"Where will they strike?" she asked.

"It's probably a false alarm."

"Do you believe that? The IDF crossed the border with tanks. Don't you read your own stories, or do you just hand them in? Words on the page?"

She watched him dial a number on his phone. Her eyes moved back to the view south. A brilliant flash lit the sky, and it was followed by a massive fireball that rose into the night, billowing smoke. Startled cries in the street mixed with murmuring voices, and an eerie quiet followed.

Analise counted the seconds until the sound of the concussive blast arrived. "It's the airport or Hezbollah headquarters in Bourj al-Barajneh."

Another bomb hit in the distance and lights in tall apartment buildings flickered before electricity was lost. Sirens wailed, and then the gravity of the bombing sank in, the quiet summer evening becoming a chaos of calm unease. A hurrying couple with a baby stroller sought shelter in a building lobby, an elderly man with a cane looked up at the sky, and everywhere barking dogs. Anti-aircraft bursts cast little yellow smudges on the dark canvas of night.

"It's me, Corbin," he said, when his call went through. She was beside him, but he was indifferent to her presence. "Israel is bombing the southern suburbs."

His head was turned away and he had lowered his voice, but she overheard fragments of the conversation. She was careful not to show interest, but took note of what he said. She met his eyes when the call ended.

"They want a story for New York's morning edition. I have to go back to my hotel."

"Take a shower while there's still hot water."

"I don't have time."

He grabbed his pants from the floor, where they lay in a heap, and shoved one leg in the trousers and then the other, cinching the belt over his abdomen. She had found his body attractive the first time she saw it, and that was one reason she continued to see him despite being warned to call it off. She gave him what he came for, and she took whatever information she could winkle from him.

When they stood at the apartment's door, she fussed with his collar, straightening it, and kissed him briskly. A shadow crossed her face. "There may be roadblocks. Be careful."

At the balcony, she stood wrapped in a sheet, arms across her chest, and watched him flag a taxi. He waved at her and called out something she couldn't hear. *This has to end*, she thought.

She gazed at gray smoke pluming into the starless night. The air was warm but she felt cold. It was always that way the night before an operation, particularly one in which a man's life would be taken. She was glad to be at the end of her tour and glad to be moving on. There was a plan in place, and what mattered was that the plan kept her from thinking too much about her role. She merely had to maintain cover and do her part. Most intelligence officers needed to be trained to compartmentalize their lives, but Analise's instincts had sprung from her chrysalis fully formed. She never hesitated to close down a concern, and she could give a dozen explanations for what she was doing, or where or why, each more convincing than the truth.

2

Somewhere in Haret Hreik

Analise was there at the agreed-upon time and place, but the Mossad agent hadn't shown himself. She paused to study one man's reflection in the clothing store's display window, half-shuttered to protect against the bombing. A scarf covered her head and her focus on the mannequin in the window disguised her interest. Oversized Prada sunglasses hid her concentration as she followed his movement across the street.

She had noticed him after passing Al Qaem Mosque, and he was there each time she moved up the street and stopped at another closed shop. He was behind her in a long queue of men that snaked toward a Coral gas station selling liters of rationed gasoline in plastic jugs. His face was hidden by a keffiyeh, and he wore a Western-style sport jacket and tan cargo pants. *Bauman?* she wondered. Her Mossad counterpart hanging back? Or Hezbollah surveillance?

She glanced around for more surveillance—the appearance of one man augured the presence of others. She adjusted the wireless earpiece hidden under her headscarf and tapped the mic, speaking softly. "I don't see him."

She walked toward the man, looking past him, but her peripheral vision noticed his shoes, the ring on his finger, the make of his wristwatch—seeking one confirming detail. She had moved past him when she stopped and searched her string bag, mumbling in Arabic, "Damn it. I forgot the bread." From the corner of her eye, she saw that he had stepped out of the queue and followed her.

Crackling in her earpiece carried a broken conversation and then a command. "What do you see?"

Dust billowed where workmen clawed at the rubble of an apartment building destroyed by the Israeli air strike. Laborers' cries mixed with the whine of passing motor scooters, and anxious mothers with tissues over their noses shooed children away from the tangle of fallen electrical wires. Western journalists, some wearing gauze masks against the stench of death, watched as workmen dug for bodies, wary of unexploded ordnance. At the far end of the street, girls lined up at a crude pipe, filling water bottles from a broken spigot.

Analise whispered every detail, knowing that she was the eyes and ears of the men in a panel van parked a kilometer away.

"Surveillance?"

"One maybe. I can't be certain."

"Guards?"

She looked at a three-story house guarded by two young bearded men with AK-47s. They stood by a parked Jeep Cherokee and scanned the street with the diligent scrutiny of sentries. "Two." Then curtly, "Where's Bauman?"

"No names!"

She cursed the rebuke. How had she gone from blessed monotony in the final week of her tour to this adrenaline punch?

All she wanted to do was close her eyes and open them when it was over. It was happening again, the doubt, the fear, the feeling that she had forgotten her training, and the irresistible impulse to flee. *Breathe*, she told herself.

Her eyes darted across faces in the street.

"He's there. Sport coat and trousers. Behind you."

She glanced up at the drone, realizing she was being watched from the van, and then turned. She raised her eyes, looking past the tall man in the keffiyeh and then right at Bauman. Their eyes met, a brief moment of recognition passed, and then the caution of two people falling into the practiced regimen of covert work.

Analise walked toward the Jeep, noting the license, glancing at the house's wood door, but she kept moving close to the shops to avoid debris in the street. Her head was down, eyes looking past her footfalls, ears a tuning fork for danger. Beads of sweat on her forehead moistened the edges of her headscarf.

Intelligence was always exactly wrong, but if she was lucky the intelligence for that day would be generally correct. She and Bauman were ground spotters tasked with observing what was hidden from the overhead drone, and she instinctively slowed as she neared the Jeep. Time became elastic, stretching as she waited for the one detail she needed.

When the door opened, a burly man in a polo shirt with a pistol stuffed in his belt walked to the Jeep. His aviator sunglasses glinted in the sun, and he wore the smug attitude of a man of little stature entrusted with work of great importance. He pulled one driving glove tight onto his hand, then the other, and after nodding to the guards, he waved at the door.

Qassem stepped into the sunlight. Analise recognized him at once; he matched the photograph she'd committed to memory. She had been instructed to approach Qassem's grandson and find a way to earn his trust, so she had become a volunteer teacher at his school. Once a friendly relationship had formed between student and teacher, she had gathered intelligence on the grandfather. The notoriously secretive Hezbollah militant was a man as much as he was a jihadist, and she looked for a way to exploit his humanity, knowing that every man had his weakness. Some men succumbed to greed, others power, a few to addiction or carnal urges. The trick was to find the right bait to compromise the man. Qassem was a tough case. He was surrounded by an insular group of clan members, and he moved frequently, which made it difficult for the dogged intelligence officer to track his whereabouts. But Analise used his affection for his grandchild to locate him.

Qassem lit a cigarette and drew deeply, smiling at his driver, exchanging a careless remark that Analise was too far away to hear. He was a heavyset man in his mid-fifties with short silver hair that matched a coarse graying beard, and he joked with his driver. A lighthearted moment of a confident man who was completely unaware that he was being watched.

"Talk to us. What do you see?"

"He's outside," she whispered. Street sounds were all around, but she concentrated on the two men by the Jeep whose attention had turned to the group of Western journalists touring the night's bomb damage. Qassem watched impassively with the confidence of a patient fighter comfortable in his neighborhood.

"Two men."

"Who's the other?"

"His driver." Crackling on the line. "Can you hear me?" She turned her head away from the house and spoke louder. "Target and driver."

"You're sure?"

"Yes."

She recognized the Israeli accent and knew it must be Gal. He was the Mossad lead and mission architect. She'd confirmed Qassem's location in the neighborhood the week before, and the bombing had trapped him until the operation could be assembled and the Pajero positioned. Weeks of careful planning and they were arriving at the moment when the best intelligence of the combined efforts of the world's top spy agencies would be tested, their reputations put at risk.

Suddenly, Qassem's two grandchildren—a skinny teenage boy and his sister in a hijab—emerged from the door and were hustled by the driver to the Jeep. He pulled the sullen girl by the arm, hurting her, and the boy protested loudly, but the driver responded indifferently. The mother was at her children's side, consoling them, waving off the driver with a dismissive gesture, but then she calmly encouraged them to get in the Jeep, kissing them, giving each a warm pat.

Analise turned to keep the boy from recognizing her and veered toward an alley. As she moved, she encountered the press group standing before the crumpled apartment building. Journalists and photographers gathered around a slender man in a red military beret who gestured toward a limp hand protruding from the rubble. Cameras' whirring clicks were a counterpoint to the man's accented English, but over it she heard her name shouted.

"Analise."

Her head didn't turn and she remained oblivious, as if the name belonged to someone else. Her name, again, louder and more strident. Corbin had pulled away from the Hezbollah press guide. His dark glasses were propped on his head; he lowered them and stared.

"Analise!"

Without breaking her stride, or giving Corbin the satisfaction of a confirming glance, she slipped into the alley. Once around the corner, her pace quickened. She listened for running footsteps.

Jesus fuck, she said to herself. Her training kicked in and she continued on with her string bag of vegetables like a woman returning from market with the evening's dinner. *Fuck, fuck, fuck.* The curses were a loud drum beat in her ear as an image of Corbin filled her mind's eye. All the gnomic briefings, all the concentrated thinking about escape paths and contingencies didn't account for the operation of chance. Her mind was numb to the random connections that had fallen into place to bring her and Corbin to the same patch of earth that afternoon. What were the odds?

She gripped her handbag and continued apace without hearing footsteps behind her. Corbin wasn't following, and then he was gone from her thoughts. There was only pulsing in her ears and the soft padding of her shoes in the narrow alley. She brought the microphone to her lips and whispered to the men in the van.

"Two kids," she said.

"What?"

Louder. "Two kids in the vehicle. Abort."

"We lost you. Where are you?"

"An alley. Coming to you."

Analise emerged from the alley and walked past a ruined mansion, doubling back when she was certain it was safe and opening the door with a strong shoulder push. The shortcut avoided Corbin. She listened for the telltale sounds of danger and then she rose through the interior well's staircase, open to the sky, taking steps two at a time, almost flying up like a bird, quiet and swift, until she came to a wood door that guarded the top-floor apartment. A bomb had punched a gaping hole in the roof, but the door into the apartment stood intact, still attached to the crumbling walls. She moved through the ruined living room to the fire escape, taking in the damage. She stepped around broken glass from a tall parlor window that had blown in. Wall plaster was cracked and streaked with water damage, and a child's doll had been left behind in the rush to flee. An orange western sun flooded the once magnificent room with a warm glow that made the russet sofa burst with flames. Electricity was gone, but the sea breeze coming in the window turned the ceiling fan in squeaking rotations. A trespassing rodent scrambled out of sight.

She crossed adjoining roofs and entered another stairwell further on. A central atrium connected the buildings, and at the base there was a courtyard with shattered pieces of fallen cornice. She descended the stairwell two steps at a time, passing rooms now open to the sky. Unexploded cluster bomblets lay scattered on the landings, but over successive visits planning her route she had come to ignore the danger. Analise hurried down to the dark lobby where she saw a tall man silhouetted in the front door. At the sound of her footsteps, he turned.

"What held you up?" Bauman asked. He'd removed his kaffiyeh so his tanned face was clearly visible—a coarse-blond South African in baggy fatigues with his press credential in a plastic keeper now around his neck. His thin lips were pursed and he stood tall and brooding.

"Corbin saw me. I had to come a different way."

"Did he recognize you?"

"He called my name."

A tremor of silence followed and the whole fraught history between them was punctuated by Bauman's quick judgment. "That's unfortunate."

They heard the muezzin's amplified call to prayer, which did little to empty the street. Then a shouted command came through their earpieces. Together they moved across the street toward a white Agence France-Presse panel van. She slipped in and Bauman followed, closing the door.

Rick Aldrich, Beirut's station chief, was already there, as was Gal, his Israeli counterpart on the operation. Upon hearing the door close, they looked up from the monitor showing a drone image of the Jeep. Aldrich had the brisk irritation of a man whose concentration had been interrupted. Tall, in his early sixties, he had a rugged face paled by sleepless nights, and intense blue eyes. He had the impatient gruffness that came with dangerous covert work, but she knew that he thought of himself as a CIA officer who took the risks he assigned to others. He was a man of discretion and nerve who rarely raised his voice, but his fierce gaze could vanquish. He was part of the old guard new to the war on terror and he occasionally slipped into the heroic anachronisms of the Cold War, making him sound out of touch.

"There are two kids in the Jeep," she said. "Abort!"

Gal was mildly annoyed by her tone. The Mossad agent was older, his body frail with age, but he was clear-eyed and had the quiet expression of a man who listened patiently but formed his own judgment. He had delicate hands with manicured nails. They were not hands that could strangle a man or point a gun. They were the hands of a bookkeeper who recorded debits and credits against his adversaries with tick marks in a ledger book. No one would look at him and think he would start a fight in a bar.

Gal turned back to the monitor, watching closely. The screen showed the Jeep avoiding a bomb crater, moving through the maze of narrow streets toward the parked Pajero. They all knew what was coming, and they understood that one step was taken and the next would fall soon. A powerful explosion would engulf the Pajero, sending shrapnel from the shaped explosive into the passing Jeep. Semtex was a precise explosive but its lethal blast killed indiscriminately, friend and foe, young and old, guilty and innocent.

"Did you hear me? Two kids." She remained frozen before the three men, who looked at her with collective skepticism. Men at the moment of victory being asked to stand down. The taste of blood, and the satisfaction of revenge hot on their faces.

"Fuck it," Gal said. He turned back to the screen and waved to the quiet technician who operated the monitoring equipment, taking the cell-phone detonator in his hand.

The drone's camera closed in on the moving Jeep, enlarging the flat image to show the SUV from above. It enlarged again, moving closer in. A child's hand was clearly visible hanging out the rear window, playing with the air.

The late-model Pajero had accumulated a fine layer of dust and looked like any other SUV popular among Hezbollah militia. The license plate was dirty and the cover of the spare tire attached to the rear was shredded in one spot. Great effort over several weeks had gone into making the new vehicle look old and weathered from long use on Lebanon's harsh roads. Nothing had been overlooked. A particular yellow dirt from the Beqaa Valley had been flown to North Carolina and embedded in the wheels and chassis to imitate the appearance of wear. Only the VIN had been removed to prevent determined investigators from tracing the vehicle's origin.

Images from a second drone appeared on another screen, and the monitors vied for the attention of the five people in the van. The overhead shot alternated with a low-angle front view from a drone hovering in place somewhere along the street.

"Bag him," Bauman said, his South African accent at its gentlest and most appealing.

Analise looked from Aldrich to Gal and then glared at Bauman. "We had an agreement." A human silence lingered amidst the electronic hum of monitors and communication devices controlling the drones. Analise put on the face of superhuman tolerance. "What are we doing?"

"It's going down."

"I was seen. He'll make the connection."

"It doesn't matter. Your part is done."

"There are two children in the Jeep."

She felt the insult of their patronizing indifference, and all the old anger at her treatment in the agency welled up. Catcalls in training, male camaraderie that excluded her, and crude sexual advances. The whole weight of her struggle to be respected. They were the senior male officers who would get the glory and she was the junior female colleague who would suffer the sting of knowing she had ginned up the boy with appalling lies to earn his trust. *This isn't happening*, she thought. Her parting gift from the agency would be a lifetime of resentment.

"This whole bloody thing is what exactly?" She looked around. "So exactly what are we doing here?" She had grabbed Gal's neatly pressed sport jacket and swung him around. They were the same height, but he was older and weakened by asthma. Everyone's attention moved from the monitor to her violent confrontation.

"And you?" she asked Aldrich.

"Two blocks away," the quiet technician announced, an imperturbable cog in the operation, and everyone's gaze was briefly drawn back to the monitor, where the drone's camera showed the Jeep moving up a deserted street, then taking the required detour created by a bomb crater and moving toward the Pajero parked further on.

Faint staticky voices from the second drone and then dead silence until an American's voice somewhere off camera in Haret Hreik came on, shrill and petulant.

"Kids in the vehicle. Do you hear?"

Gal spoke patiently. "He is a wanted terrorist, a high-value target with blood on his hands, and this mission has been planned for months. For me, it's been years."

"This isn't right," she said.

Gal's eyes narrowed. He said nothing. No anger. No remorse. No defense against the indefensible. The technician's countdown of the Jeep's rapid approach to the Pajero created an urgency in the cramped space.

"You made the bomb," Gal said, wheezing. "We take responsibility. Your hands are clean. You've made your concern known and I'll be certain to note your objection in my report." He turned to the monitor.

"They're kids."

"There are no innocents," he said. "Only casualties." He nodded at the technician who held the cell-phone trigger.

Analise turned to Bauman, appalled by his silence. She saw the impassive face of a man condemned to heartless extra-judicial murder. He was reluctant, but not so reluctant that he spoke up. She had begun to wonder about his indifference. The cold vacant expression on his face was something that she wouldn't forget.

Aldrich's jaw clenched and his eyes narrowed—an angry bull. He was at the technician's side in one long stride and his entire body vibrated with indignation. He took the cell phone and shut it down.

"Kindly note that I am the senior field officer in this situation. A final decision to proceed is mine, as you are aware. You may recommend; however, I decide."

"That's not how we cooperate," Gal said.

Aldrich's arm rose in a long arc across the top of the van toward the scream of low-flying Israeli jets. "Next time, have the courtesy to warn me you're starting a war so I don't have to look like a god-damned idiot when Langley asks what's going on."

"The White House knew. It's their job to share the information, not mine."

Everyone was aware that during the argument the Jeep had passed the Pajero and was now beyond danger, traveling through the maze of streets. No one needed to say the obvious. The mission was over. Ended. All that remained was the filing of competing after-action reports that put an anodyne gloss on a catastrophe.

Gal took his eyes off the image of the Jeep on the monitor, now escaping its fate. He breathed lightly and shrugged. Disappointment and acceptance: the twinned emotions of a patient hunter.

"So that's it. We plan again, but let's not kid ourselves that it will be easy. They have learned how to play the game. Hezbollah has created its own protective covering, moving between houses, changing cars and escape routes, shutting off cell phones that we can intercept. Never patronizing the same restaurant. We won't get another easy chance."

Gal put a comforting hand on Bauman, accepting the unwelcome disappointment. "We are all human beings. I have children, they have children, we all have grandchildren, and we all want a simple life to live in peace with other families. It is true for us and for most of them, but there are among them loud voices who want blood for blood and will never let peace live. Qassem is one such voice. So he can't be allowed to live."

Gal looked from Analise to Aldrich and then at Bauman, who hardly contained his anger. "We will try again. A new plan." He looked at Analise. "Suggest something."

He nodded at the van's driver, who had turned his head and looked through the small window into the rear of the van. The signal to leave. Gal sat on the bench against one wall. All eyes were on him. The storied Mossad agent had joined Israel's National Intelligence Service in the sixties and had risen in its ranks. Each person in the van knew he had made a career of hunting Qassem.

"Am I disappointed? Of course." He added, "I have been disappointed before and I'll be disappointed again. I see a question in your faces. What's next? It is not a question I am prepared to answer. It's the same question since the destruction of the second temple. The gift of prophecy is given to the fool."

Failure behind them, a new exhaustion settled on the five people as they sat in silence, bumping along the unpaved street, a bitter loss after a well-played match.

"What do I tell the Knesset?" Gal asked. "To save two children we let our number one terrorist go? And then tomorrow he kills again?"

"You have it backwards," Aldrich said. "Better one hundred guilty go free than one innocent life is lost."

Gal grunted. His hand made a weak, dismissive wave. "You are in the wrong job if that's what you believe."

3

Rue Gouraud

Analise's surveillance detection route had begun two hours
earlier, and she was confident she was clean, having passed
Mohammad Al-Amin mosque's blue domes twice, circling back
to confirm no one followed. Her scarf wrapped her head and
oversized Prada sunglasses hid her face from casual passersby.
She removed her cell-phone battery before entering Achrafieh's
glass-domed shopping mall.

The old souk of her grandmother's memory, with its narrow
streets of covered awnings and displays of fragrant flowers and
ripe fruit, was destroyed in the civil war; the new mall was soulless
with brand-name retail shops. She stepped off the escalator and
moved patiently from one store to the next, an elegant shopper
looking for a bargain. In one, she fingered a Ferragamo scarf and
smiled at the price, high even by the new standards during the
war. She haggled, enjoying the shopkeeper's game, and played
along until she heard a loud cry from a group gathered around

a large-screen television. News coverage of ambulances racing to hospitals was interspersed with graphic images of buildings collapsed by Israeli bombs, and suddenly the shopkeeper cursed the West, staring suspiciously at Analise. Part of her hated the stress of the work, constantly alert to being recognized or followed, and always needing to repel suspicion. Another part of her was exhilarated by the danger and enjoyed retreating into the mind of a calculating intelligence officer. Two lives, one open and known, a lady working for the United Nations, the other an agent known only to Mossad and the CIA's station chief.

Analise paused at a narrow alley just off Rue Gouraud, where a music store projected loud hip-hop onto the sidewalk, nearly empty from the war. Once more she dawdled; once more she took stock of the people nearby, looking for surveillance.

She joined several passing stylish Lebanese women, acting like one of them, but she cleaved off when they passed an alley where the second-floor balcony of a pink Ottoman-era home was graced with a trio of arched windows. Houses didn't have identifying numbers, but Aldrich had described the recessed front door. Analise ducked under the lush jasmine that cascaded from the balcony and approached the door, knocking three times, as instructed.

The woman standing before her was tall and attractive dressed in a long skirt and silk blouse that left her arms uncovered. Two shrewd eyes appraised Analise's dusty boots and tan trousers, and the woman briskly offered a hand. "*Marhaba.*" Analise found herself in a lofty central hall filled with dim sunlight that seeped through mashrabiya latticework. The air in the dark hallway was as cool as a vault. She fell in behind Aldrich's friend, climbing the wide stone stairs, and wondered what type of Lebanese woman would accept this type of arrangement. Aldrich's first marriage had been to a glamorous, intelligent American journalist who chafed under the demands of his long hours and secret work. She left him during an overseas posting for one of her several lovers, and Aldrich, no longer a young man with the stamina for adventurous romance, had found it convenient to take up with a Lebanese woman who was unlikely to betray him in bed.

Analise entered the second-floor parlor, where Aldrich was across the room drinking a martini from a stemmed glass. His graying hair was casually swept back on his forehead, and his rumpled linen suit loosely fit on his trim form. He turned to her with the trained calm of a cautious spy, but confirming it was her, he smiled courteously and invited her in.

"Vodka martini straight up? Two olives?"

"No thanks."

Aldrich turned to the woman at the door. "*Shukran.* That will be all." She retreated to the hall, closing the door.

He looked at Analise. "There is a risk meeting like this, but what I need to say has to be said in person. Hama is discreet, but I don't take unnecessary risks. I told her you volunteer at the International College middle school, so if she asks around, she'll get the same story."

Aldrich moved to the arched balcony doors, motioning for Analise to join him, and pointed at two white sport utility vehicles parked at the end of the alley. A tall American woman in tan fatigues stood alertly by the lead vehicle, scanning vigilantly for threats. She dressed the part of a security detail—dark glasses, side arm, and a grim face, listening to chatter on her wireless earbud.

"You know Helen?"

"We trained together. She's helping get the boy's sister out of the country."

"I stopped holding meetings in Beirut Station's secure conference room in Awkar. My sensitive conversations found their way to Langley and then to Gal. The Awkar compound has watchtowers and concertina razor wire, but there are people on the inside who I worry about. When I want a private conversation, I have it here."

Aldrich nodded at the SUV. "I told Helen that I couldn't do my job from Awkar. My assets wouldn't risk being seen walking past the marine guards. When I moved here, she insisted that I have a double." Aldrich nodded at a tall man who stepped out of the decoy SUV—Aldrich's height, similar graying hair, and an identical rumpled linen suit. "He has a vague idea who he is impersonating and how dangerous it is, but he is well paid and probably sees it as a good alternative to retirement in the States."

Aldrich directed Analise's attention further along the street to an Arab-looking man on his cell phone. "Mossad. They follow us too. We need to work together, but he'll play us if it's in his interest. Gal kept us in the dark on the invasion."

He looked toward a narrow slice of harbor view where a glistening white cruise ship and gray navy cruisers were assembled to evacuate foreigners stranded by the war. Acrid gray smoke from bombed fuel tanks at the airport rose in the distance and darkened the sky. Aldrich's entire body vibrated with irritation. "They played Washington. The White House was alerted, but they didn't know it would be like this. Bombed bridges, roads, and villages. Airport runways cratered. An exodus of desperate refugees that has overwhelmed Beirut."

Aldrich turned to her. "And for what? Two kidnapped Israeli soldiers?" He looked at her. "Gal's response, 'the White House knew.' Arrogant crap. We'll work together because we have to, but I have no illusions about them. This war is a mistake. It complicates our job."

Aldrich's bluntness distinguished him from other high-ranking men in the agency who avoided taking sides by perfecting opinions that were elaborate compromises, expressing conviction and doubt in the same sentence.

"Two kids were almost killed," she said.

"It was unexpected and inopportune. You wouldn't be human if you didn't feel terrible." Aldrich had been looking at the harbor's armada when he turned to her. "We remind ourselves that we're honorable men and women who cling to our principles. It's how we like to think of ourselves when we go to church. We like to believe we're better than the Russians, or the Syrians, or the Israelis. Maybe we are. Maybe we aren't."

Aldrich wore the heavy burden of his job. "We go forward. Make another plan to get Qassem. Work with Mossad."

He moved back inside. She recognized the tricked-out leather attaché case that he put on the table. He turned the key counterclockwise, opening it. Had he turned it clockwise, the usual way of opening a lock, gas jets inside would have incinerated the contents. He lifted the sandwich that was on the top and handed her a manila envelope marked "Confidential: Charles Corbin."

She scanned two pages.

"Did he tell you he has a wife?"

She stared at the color photo of the woman. Blond hair, gentle smile, full lips. Her physical opposite. "Yes."

"It's easier for him to earn your trust if he's not hiding things, but don't be fooled by his answers just because he appears to be open. He's a reporter and happy to play us." He paused. "I need to know what he is hearing about Israel's plans. What Mossad is not telling us." He looked at her. "Did you get into his Blackberry?"

"I didn't get a chance."

"Don't let him get too close."

"I won't." She was ready to defend her lie as a misunderstanding of the different meanings of the word *close*, but there was no need. Aldrich had opened a second folder and presented cables with the latest intelligence on Najib Qassem.

"It's the update I requested. It will help us figure out the next step."

"My tour is over."

"You're exhausted." A beat of silence. He met her eyes. "It's tough, I know. Lonely. How's your marriage?"

She thought a half-truth would answer his question without telling him anything he didn't already know. "We're talking."

Agency work had put a strain on her marriage. Her first overseas posting came several months after her wedding. She was sent to Iraq working the non-official cover of an Arabic-speaking Iraqi antiquities dealer to penetrate the ratline Saddam Hussein's generals used to escape Baghdad. Dirty, treacherous work, and a hard spot for an attractive woman fluent in Arabic. The violent death of a one-eyed colonel had been the finishing touch to a bad assignment—squalid, nasty, dangerous, without any satisfying outcomes except that it kept her away from desk work. The crouched Iraqi colonel had leapt from a hiding place with fierce eyes and a long blade, slashing her shoulder, and she'd killed him with one shot from her Glock. Her cover was blown, and the reward for the kill was to return to Langley and the bleak prison of desk work. She pored over classified cables from diplomats, foreign intelligence agencies, and field operatives, and then synthesized the best stuff into briefs for the DCI and the White House. Meticulous, highly analytical work. The stateside pleasure of time with her husband hadn't worked out. She discovered that the fondness she'd harbored in his absence became intolerable irritation in the sustained intimacy of domestic life. Twelve months in, her request to return to the field was approved and she was sent to Beirut to join Qassem's targeting team as a deep-plant HUMINT source, working the non-official cover of an interpreter assigned to the United Nations High Commissioner for Refugees. She left behind her husband and placed her wedding band in a jewelry box for safekeeping.

"We booked a weekend in Paris before I start in Cairo. We'll see what happens." She looked at him, irritated. "I'm not supposed to be here."

"And the kids weren't supposed to be in the vehicle. But they were. We need to finish this," Aldrich said. "The boy trusts you. He expects you to evacuate his sister. If we'd gotten Qassem, this would be moot, but we didn't. You can't leave. Not yet."

"I did my part. I found Qassem." She shook her head. "My cover may be blown. Corbin left three voice messages. He's curious why I was in Haret Hreik."

"What did you tell him?"

"I haven't returned his calls."

"Avoid him. Keep your distance."

"I can't avoid him," she snapped.

Aldrich heard the change in her tone of voice. "Give him a reasonable story that will hold up for a couple of weeks. I've extended your tour two months. I'll make Paris up to you."

"So that's it? I'm being put out there."

"You're already out there."

Some part of her annoyance showed on her face, and Aldrich's expression softened. He was quiet for a moment and turned to the open balcony doors where the setting sun glowed warmly on his face. Visible beyond the rooftops, the Mediterranean was an endless canvas of deepening blue. The wind had settled with dusk, and the surface of the water was still, which brought a pleasant calmness to the tension between them. Aldrich had gaunt cheeks, a tanned complexion, and the ascetic aspect of a man who had spent his adult life thinking about an unrepentant enemy. His arms hung at his sides, and his quiet face had the brooding mystery of a Buddha.

"I also thought of leaving the agency in my early thirties. I was fed up with Langley's politics, everyone a Cassius waiting for a Caesar. If you didn't use the knife in your hand, you found it in your back. I resigned and walked out the turnstiles at Langley Headquarters, giving my badge to the security officer. I passed through the sliding glass doors that I'd crossed thousands of times, thinking that I was free. A chapter in my life was over. I was proud of my work, but happy I was leaving."

His eyes came off the rooftops and looked at her. "Those are the feelings you're having—that I had—but I didn't know how hard it would be to reenter civilian life. I couldn't talk about what I'd done, or who I'd worked for, or why there was a gap in my resume. There was no job on the outside that offered the same satisfaction. Nobody tells you this and it's not in the recruitment brochures. We spend our careers in hot zones, always aware of the danger, and we become addicted to crises. We become adrenaline junkies."

He smiled. "I wanted my life back. I wanted the future that I'd imagined when I joined, but my marriage was already over. We tried valiantly to save it, pretended we could pick up where we'd left off." Aldrich popped the last olive in his mouth and threw back the dregs of his drink. "My drinking didn't help." He looked at her. "It was worth fighting for when you joined, and it's worth fighting for now."

"It doesn't have to be me."

"In this moment, in this circumstance, it does. I have cleared the boy's sister to be evacuated to Cyprus. We need to play this out until we have another plan." Aldrich nodded. "If you want out when this is over, I'll write letters and make calls."

Analise shook her head.

"You are the only one the boy trusts," Aldrich said.

"He'll bolt if he suspects anything."

"But he trusts you?"

"For the moment."

"I need you to do this." He was pensive. "I have a story to tell you." He pointed west toward Ras Beirut. "Bill Buckley lived on California Street on a hill overlooking AUB. Qassem was across the street waiting for him to emerge with his briefcase. It was one morning in March 1984 as he was headed into the office. Bill was station chief and an odd duck, even by our standards, but he was a good friend. He lived on the tenth floor of the building and it was his three hundred and forty-third day in Beirut. He was posted here after the truck bomb destroyed our embassy in 1983. It was one of those sublime mornings that you see here, the ones that make Beirut an attractive posting. He would've been awakened early by the muezzin's call to prayer.

"Bill was untidy and he didn't have a housekeeper because he hated the idea of anyone snooping through his personal things. I led the team that investigated. I found dishes scattered in the living room, a huge bag of laundry, and endless pairs of socks and underwear. He hated doing laundry. He preferred to keep buying new things. He had his unbreakable habits. For thirty years he had bought his suits from Brooks Brothers. Whenever he passed through New York, he bought lightweight navy-blue suits, size 38, and that was all he ever wore. He had a lot on his mind, as you can imagine, and habits made it easy to go about his day without having to think too much about clothing, or food, or travel. He lived by routine.

"He knew that routines make you vulnerable, and maybe it was for that reason he broke his routine that morning. Normally, an embassy driver waited outside his apartment building in his armored vehicle, but that day Bill drove himself. It was a short distance to the British compound where the American embassy was temporarily housed. He left the underground garage in a gray Renault and was cut off on the street by a black Mercedes sedan. Three men approached and one struck him on the head. Bill was shoved into the Mercedes and kept on the floor under the weight of his abductors.

"He was held captive for fifteen months. His kidnappers released videos of him, and in each one his condition was worse. The videos were hard to watch. His words were often incoherent. He would suddenly scream in terror, his eyes rolling helplessly, and his body shook. We believed that he was blindfolded and chained at the ankles and wrists and held in a cell the size of a coffin. Hezbollah kept him somewhere in Beirut's sprawling southern suburbs. No one should suffer as he did. Tortured. Drugged. Incoherent. In the last video, he was a broken man, suddenly aged, his voice dull and monotonous, a living dead man."

Aldrich turned to Analise. "No one should die like that. It was difficult for the agency and hard for me." He looked off at the harbor. "Imad Mughniyeh organized the kidnapping, but Qassem tortured Bill and ordered his execution. That's why I want him. I don't give a shit about Condoleezza Rice." He looked at her. "I need you to finish this. Work with Bauman."

"What about Rice?"

"What you don't know, what I learned from Gal, is that Qassem plans to strike again." Aldrich paced the room, hands behind his back. "Bush is sending Rice to broker a cease-fire. Gal has intelligence that Qassem is planning to assassinate her."

He paused to let the information sink in. "To keep her safe, we have to remove the threat. Taking out Qassem was important; now it's urgent."

Aldrich's face darkened. "There's a risk the boy gets hurt, but there's a greater risk if we fail. Hundreds, perhaps thousands, will die if this war gets out of hand. One boy's life is precious, but—I don't have to finish the sentence. The assassination of the American secretary of state poses intolerable risks for an escalation of the war."

He paused. "We have ten days, maybe two weeks. State is working out the logistics of her visit. How bad could this situation get? Qassem works with Syria but he takes his orders from Iran. A proxy war will draw us in and the Russians would follow. Brilliant agency analysts are writing turgid memos with options and scenarios for the White House, but you know as I do that none of their gnomic speculation gets them close to the truth of what we know, what we wake up to every morning, the dangers we face on the ground. Beirut can be a kill zone."

"Who knows about Rice's visit?" she asked.

"Her visit is classified but the logistics have to be arranged with the Lebanese president. If he knows, then Speaker of Parliament Berri knows, and it is certain that the head of Hezbollah, Hassan Nasrallah, knows."

Aldrich looked up when there was a knock at the door. Hama stuck her head in the room, motioning toward the wall clock, and he raised his hand, acknowledging the reminder.

Analise put on her dark glasses and wrapped her scarf around her head, tying the ends into an ample fold. She held up her Nokia. "Don't call my cell again. Hezbollah tracks cell-phone calls made by IDF soldiers calling their wives. Wireless circuits aren't secure."

"How do I contact you?"

"Use the draft folder of this email account." Analise wrote down the username and password for a Hotmail account. "Go to the drafts folder, leave a message for me, but don't send it. As long as it stays in drafts, email intercepts won't detect it."

4

Evacuation Con Brio

Doubt wasn't an emotion that Analise permitted herself, but that morning she felt its first stirrings—a nagging voice in her head. She knew the plan, but things change, and even the best plans encountered unexpected difficulties that required adjustments and workarounds. She had not foreseen the consequences of her student-teacher relationship with the boy Rami. The way to Qassem was through his grandson, whom she'd arranged to meet as a volunteer English teacher at the IC middle school. With the boy's eagerness to learn had come trust and with trust had come complications. She had not known the boy hated his stepfather, nor could she have predicted that Rami would ask her to help his twin sister escape an arranged marriage. Their abusive stepfather had promised the girl to an older, wealthy man to curry favor.

Analise was explaining a little of this to Helen that morning. They stood on the balcony of Halima Monsour's apartment overlooking the shuttered St. Georges Hotel and the armada of evacuation ships assembled around Beirut's harbor and along the coast to the north. Helen looked the part of a toughened agency security officer in cargo pants, dusty boots, utility vest, and glinting aviator sunglasses, but her appearance was softened by a blond ponytail and a pretty face. Helen's eyes came off Halima Monsour, who was inside the apartment helping dress the girl.

"Who does she think I am?" Helen asked, nodding at Halima.

"American consular officer."

"And the girl?"

"Her name is Nafeeza. I told her the same thing. I told her you're here to get her on board the ship and there will be more people like us waiting for her when she gets to Cyprus."

"How old?"

"Thirteen."

"Jesus Christ. How did this fall to you?"

Analise had told Helen only what was required to enlist her help. Non-official cover was a complicated layer cake of shifting deceptions and wavering truths that became a constant dance with the people she dealt with every day. She needed to keep in mind what she had said to whom, who knew what, and which dark secrets she kept locked in her vaulted consciousness. Overseas agency officers hid behind false identities and made-up jobs, but non-official cover was a deeper deception where the agency could disavow an officer's existence.

"You don't need to know," she said. It was the old question: What could one colleague working a mission say to another colleague working a different mission? "You don't want me to tell you, so let's do the awkward thing and shut down this conversation."

"Confidential?"

"Over our heads." Aldrich's caution came to mind. "You know the rules. I don't want to put you in a position where you'd have to answer to the review board if shit happens. One day we will open a beer and kick back. For the moment, let it go."

Helen said nothing for a moment, then nodded at the girl. "She has to be nervous."

"Frightened out of her mind. Being sent off with people she's never met and traveling to a country where she hardly speaks the language. I can only imagine what she is thinking. It's worse if she stays. She spat at her stepfather and was beaten. Rami came to school and told Halima that his sister would kill herself if she was forced to marry. Halima came to me because I'm UN."

"It can't be legal."

"Heroin smuggling isn't legal either. The law in Beirut is in the street."

Helen nodded at Halima. "What does she know?"

"The UN is helping."

"Do you trust her?"

Analise had another doubt—the lingering doubt that came with the fear that followed every covert intelligence officer to her grave. Namely, that a breached non-official cover would identify her to the enemies she'd made and one of them would eventually find her and settle a score.

"I'm a volunteer teacher. That's it. She introduced me to Rami."

The balcony's sliding glass door opened and Halima put her head out. Her reading glasses had slipped to the end of her nose, and her face was overspread with concern. She had bronzed skin and thick hair braided into a crown. Her eclectic dress mixed the flair of a Paris salon with Muslim modesty, and the ochre tint in her hair matched her blush-red lipstick. Abundant silver rings graced her knuckled fingers, and a heavy necklace of precious stones hung around her neck. Trim for a woman in her mid-fifties, there was also something rebellious in her appearance—her colorful, ankle-length skirt cinched tightly at the waist with a broad leather belt.

Analise had heard her life story in bits and pieces over the six months that they'd been teaching together in the IC middle school, getting to know each other over coffee, on lunch breaks, becoming Halima's confidante. Halima was gregarious and easily fell into the role of older woman happy to tell stories of her youth. She had moved to Paris as a young woman and fallen in love with the city's sophistication, art, and relaxed attitude toward young Muslim women dating men. So different from Beirut. Halima's easy warmth put strangers at ease and drew attention from suitors. In time, she learned to push men away. It was her warmth and wide, friendly face that attracted Analise. Her eyes sensitive and questioning one moment, and excited the next. Analise was drawn to her eccentricities, her expressive hands, and her bravura openness. She asserted equality with men by holding on to old ways—giving Lebanese men the deference they demanded but then turning the power of their expectations into a weakness she exploited. Her appeal wasn't in her legs or face but in her intelligence—talking of life in her charming way, weaving a web around the listener. She knew that there was nothing more seductive than the sharp wit of a mature woman.

"We're almost ready." Halima pulled Nafeeza forward, careful of her bandaged wrist. The young Muslim girl was dressed as an American teenager and her arms were uncovered. "Look."

In her mind's eye, Analise saw the Pajero explode and the girl's bloody mangled body in the street. She grimaced.

"You look pale," Halima said, concerned.

"It's warm out." Analise drew Nafeeza close, embracing her, and surprising the two women with her sudden show of emotion. Analise was trained to hunt jihadists, but no one had instructed her how to live with the guilt of an innocent girl's murder.

"Beirut swelters in July." Halima nodded to the east. "We should be in the hills with everyone who's fled the bombing."

A loud horn blast from the gleaming white cruise ship drew their attention to the harbor's chaos of evacuation vessels. The French frigate *Jean-de-Vienne* cruised a mile outside the port, and closer in, anchored in formation, were several British navy ships. Tandem-rotor helicopters rose from the aircraft carrier *Illustrious*, hovering momentarily before leaning forward in flight toward the docklands and the *Orient Queen*, where Americans were boarding. Further north, on a beach near the embassy compound, soldiers from the 24th Marine Expeditionary Unit helped Americans board landing craft.

"Hurry." Halima moved quickly into the apartment. "Two more blasts and the boat will depart. Hurry."

Halima looked Nafeeza up and down, evaluating her transformation into an American teenager: hip-hugging blue jeans, sneakers, loose T-shirt, and hair that was streaked with green. Halima fussed with the hair, moving it one way, then the other, trying to make the girl, who'd removed her hijab, comfortable displaying herself. Fretting, cooing, soothing, and encouraging Nafeeza with the pleasant confidence of an older woman.

Analise watched Helen guide Nafeeza along the harbor toward the *Orient Queen*. Halima was at her side on the balcony, watching the girl be hustled to an uncertain future. A second blast of the ship's horn filled the air, and a tremor of anxiety stirred the rear of the queue. Waiting evacuees snaked from the pier's chain-link fence to the ship's gangplank. Family groups with roll-on bags stood in the sweltering heat next to businessmen condemned by the sudden order to leave. Adults clutched toddlers' hands; others held babies in their arms. Scattered among the evacuees were tourist groups dressed in Bermuda shorts, straw hats, and flip-flops who arrived from assembly points by commandeered buses—stunned to find their vacations interrupted. From the balcony, the scene was a surreal landscape of unfolding chaos.

A third horn blast further unsettled the crowd, and those near the rear of the queue pushed forward toward the battle-ready marine guards who controlled the crowd.

"There!" Halima pointed to the top of the gangplank. Helen stood beside Nafeeza on the second deck of the *Orient Queen*.

"If she's lucky, she'll get to her aunt in Detroit."

"And if she's not?"

"They'll discover a Lebanese girl with an American passport who hardly speaks English. They'll hold her in Cyprus until the UN intervenes."

Halima gazed at Nafeeza leaning on the ship's railing, a young girl headed to a foreign land. "She is like me. She will leave and never want to come back. She will breathe freely for the first time. Of course, I came back, but I had to leave Beirut to be able to return. We Beirutis have complicated feelings toward our city. We love Beirut when we are away and we hate it when we are here. We are happy only when we are leaving or returning."

Halima turned to Analise. "Your face? Are you frightened?"

Analise smiled. "The sun is playing tricks on your eyes."

Analise found herself alone on the balcony when Halima went back into the apartment. Her thoughts drifted as she looked down at the St. Georges Hotel. The squat, shuttered shell was a reminder of the old Beirut with its gambling and scandals. Its pink façade was blast-scarred from the suicide truck explosion the previous year that killed Prime Minister Hariri in his passing motorcade.

She had studied the blast to plan her mission against Qassem. Hariri had been traveling in an armored Mercedes limousine with a security detail of two lead cars and two follow cars, with an ambulance staffed by trained medics bringing up the rear. The motorcade used sophisticated electronic countermeasures to jam remote-controlled improvised devices along its route. They hadn't counted on an inelegant but effective vehicle-borne suicide IED that investigators estimated contained one metric ton of military-grade TNT. As the motorcade passed, the suicide truck driver had triggered the bomb, killing himself, Hariri, and twenty-one others. Analise's challenge was different. Only one man should die.

The sun was out and cabanas on the lawn of the St. Georges Yacht Club and Marina were occupied by a few Arab tourists indifferent to the latest war.

Halima called Analise to come inside, but Analise was restless and said she needed a moment. She needed to be alone to ponder a plan, settle her thoughts, and to efface the image of the girl she had almost killed.

Analise looked at the horizon, where the sea and sky were welded in a joint. The fear Halima had seen on her face had a grip on her heart. Was Aldrich right? Had she become an adrenaline junkie? Every day she confronted the usual dilemma—she couldn't go forward, but she must.

5

Commodore Hotel Pool

C orbin looked around the Commodore Hotel's pool for Analise and, not seeing her, turned back to the morning's war news on his Blackberry. The *Hanit*, an Israeli navy ship patrolling the Lebanese coast, had been hit by a Hezbollah anti-ship missile. He typed a message to his editor about the escalating hostilities, knowing that the old gray men in the *Times*'s newsroom would be yelling for war updates.

Then he drafted a second note, fiddling with the language. "Where is the information I requested on Bauman? It's been a week. Have you heard back from Agence France-Presse?"

He reread the note and was satisfied with the tone. This was the second time in a week that he'd made the request. It was early morning in New York, but his editor would see the email when he got into the office. War news got everyone's attention, but the editor had taken an interest in Corbin's suspicions.

Corbin raised his eyes to the pool's shimmering surface, looking again. The remorseless late-morning sun had evaporated the puddles left by the overnight sprinklers. Some stranded foreigners sat under wide umbrellas, sipping cool drinks and smoking nervously, but several others had given in to their involuntary confinement and were sunbathing. Waiters in penguin black and white moved among the guests, handing out small fans and taking orders.

"Good to see you this morning, Monsieur Corbin. Hot day. Will you be one?"

Corbin looked up at the brightly smiling waiter.

"Two."

"Of course."

Corbin stood suddenly and yelled, "Analise."

Analise was across the pool by the hotel door when she heard her name. She turned at the urgent cry of his soprano voice, his hand gesturing wildly. She had rehearsed an answer to the question she knew he would ask, planning to give her lie a grain of truth—knowing that it would make it more believable—but in the moment of seeing him, she vacillated. Paltering with his memory would lead to one question and then another, and she didn't want to find herself backtracking. An outrageous lie fit better with his exaggerated view of the world.

She waved back and was then at his table, standing before him.

"I left twenty messages," he said.

"I got them. All three. You're a dog with a bone."

"A personal failing that I put to good use as a reporter." He sat and leaned back in his chair. "What were you doing in Haret Hreik the other day?"

She laughed, dismissing his question. "I wasn't there."

"I saw you."

"You imagined you saw me." She looked at him. "You get dull when you get curious." She wasn't certain if he believed her or pretended indifference.

"How about a beer?"

The waiter caught Corbin's eye, and in a moment, he was at the table with a tray holding two Almaza beers.

"They know you here," she said when the waiter was gone.

He lifted the chilled glass and pressed the cool surface to his flushed cheeks. "The drinks are cold and the electricity predictable. There is an emergency generator. People drop by to chat, order a beer, and charge their cell phones."

"That's what I hear. You make friends easily. Waiters. Journalists. Girls at the bar."

Corbin went to defend himself but changed his mind. "Tell me why you were in Haret Hreik. Try me. See if it's a story I'll believe."

She centered her beer on the coaster and looked at him. "When we started this, whatever you call what's going on between us, I said you had an annoying habit of asking too many questions. How would you react if I started doubting what you said?"

"I'm an open book."

"An open book and a closed mind," she said sarcastically. "I don't know if the things you say are an act, the truth, or if you know the difference."

He smiled tolerantly, amused. He pointed at her Prada sunglasses propped on her head. "You were wearing those."

"You saw someone who looked like me. I'm a common type. Tall. Middle Eastern. Female. Wearing sunglasses."

"I have a witness." Corbin whistled at a photographer taking cell batteries from a tangle of power cords by the lobby door. "Bekker," he shouted. "He was with me in Baabda District."

43

The photographer was tall, heavyset, with unkempt hair, rumpled desert fatigues, and a utility vest that sprouted batteries. His collar was loosened against the summer heat, and two 35mm digital cameras dangled from his neck. He wiped perspiration from his forehead with a stained handkerchief and acknowledged Corbin with a vaguely dismissive gesture.

He crossed the pool area, moving like a man of bulk without weight. "G'day, mates." He nodded at Corbin and let his eyes drift to Analise. "Have we met?"

"You saw her on the press tour," Corbin said. "She was running from us."

"Right." He looked at her. "I was looking at the poor bastard being pulled from the rubble. The woman I saw had a hijab."

His soft, rolling accent left her thinking. *Afrikaans?* "Who are you?"

He lifted the plastic keeper around his neck. "Simon Bekker. AP, *Reuters*, the *Guardian*. Whoever pays." He nodded at Corbin. "Now him. Thinks he's God's gift to the news but he can't spell to save his prick. He is the superior kind of war correspondent. Writes what's poured in his ear."

Bekker hitched his canvas bag on his shoulder and nodded toward the cloudless sky. "Perfect weather for Israeli pilots. Hezbollah hit an Israeli warship. We've got ourselves a beastly fokken little war."

Analise watched him walk away. Her blouse was stained with perspiration from her walk across Hamra and she billowed the fabric to cool off. "What rock did he climb out from under?"

"I should have given you a health alert on him."

"He didn't see me."

"Maybe it wasn't you." He studied her. "Why didn't you return my calls?"

She bent over and retied her bootlaces, her mind searching quickly for an answer. "My cell phone was hacked," she said, looking up. She pulled a cell battery from her bag. "I removed it so I'm not tracked. I replaced it yesterday and got your messages."

"The first half-truthful thing you've said."

"Or maybe it's the first thing you're willing to believe. Sometimes you have to look inside yourself and realize that the choice you struggle with has already been made for you."

"What does that mean?"

She looked around the crowded pool, at Bekker huddled with other journalists and at the hotel guests—an English couple sitting opposite each other in sullen silence, carefree young children frolicking in the pool's shallow end, and a young woman in a bikini sunbathing, who happened to be looking at Corbin.

"Her too?" Analise said, turning to Corbin.

Corbin shook his head, amused.

"We are all prisoners of something," she said. She sipped her beer. "You might not condone the war, but you enjoy reporting on it."

"I like my job."

The startling closeness of low-flying jet aircraft rattled hotel guests around the pool, and waiters went from table to table reassuring nervous patrons, explaining that the presence of foreign journalists would keep the hotel safe. Analise saw the pair of F-16 fighters fly low over the hills east of Beirut and carve an arc toward the Mediterranean.

"Reconnaissance patrol," Corbin said. "They want to make sure Hezbollah doesn't try to move the captured Israeli soldiers under cover of the evacuation. They want to unsettle Beirut and force a truce that will push Hezbollah aside."

"What else have you heard?"

"About the war?"

"About Mossad."

"They hide their mistakes behind a reputation of infallibility." He handed her the front page of the morning's *Herald Tribune* with his byline. "Bush called the invasion 'a moment of clarification.' He said it's now clear why we don't have peace in the Middle East."

Corbin's face wrinkled in a comical expression of exaggerated disbelief. "He's the president of the fucking United States of America. He's either an idiot or manipulated by Cheney." Corbin leaned forward, eyes wide. "The White House knew about the war before it started. They were involved in the planning of the Israeli military strikes. Mossad is in bed with the CIA?"

It was the way he said the agency's name—abruptly, carelessly, thrown out without any conscious dissembling at the end of a sudden thought—that convinced Analise her cover was intact. She looked for a small sign to doubt her judgment—a tightening grasp of his glass or a wary shift in his eyes—but saw none.

She finished her beer and put down Lebanese pounds.

"Leaving?"

"I have to meet Halima. I'm an English tutor today."

"What is she up to?"

"Teaching. Complaining. Making do with the shortages."

"Charming woman. Reminds me of Simone Signoret—a big heart with brave opinions. Wears a lot of heavy jewelry."

It always surprised Analise to discover what men noticed about women. She thought it an incurable gender illiteracy. "She's fond of you, or at least that's what she says. I haven't tried to change her mind."

"Dinner tonight? There's a male belly dancer Bekker told me about."

Analise stood. She tried to imagine a man's undulating abdomen imitating a woman's seductive curves. She stared. "Don't you have a story to file? Or a deadline to meet?"

Analise had turned to leave when she heard him. It was the tone of his voice that got her attention, the abruptness in it suggesting that he had finally gotten to the point of the meeting.

"General Hammadi said the Forces de Sécurité Intérieure want to speak with you. They're asking about Bauman." He added that they'd sent the request to UNIFIL, thinking she worked there, and when the mistake was pointed out, someone remembered they knew each other and offered him up. "I was identified as your friend."

"Which branch of the Internal Security Forces?"

"The intelligence side of the ISF, the Information Department. Inspector Aboud."

"What about Bauman?"

"I don't know. He's a cipher in the press corps. A lot of rumors, a lot of speculation, some jealousy. All the usual professional courtesies." He smiled. "I told Hammadi I had nothing to add, but you were close to him."

6

Parliament

Analise knew there was no point in putting off the meeting with the Information Department of the Internal Security Forces. The innocuous name put a mysterious gloss on the only reliably professional directorate in the ISF. Police professionalism was established in the French Mandate and survived independence along with the language, particularly among the Beirut elite, but it became weak and corrupt during the civil war. The Information Department was the trusted intelligence unit established to investigate the assassination of Prime Minister Hariri.

ISF's interest in Bauman was worrying, but a part of her no longer saw the world through the lens of what could surprise her but as a continuum of problems that stood in the way of her work. Each day increased the risk of Qassem's threat, and the continuing chaos of war provided a good cover for a Hezbollah attack. Sitting in the back of the taxi, moving through the honking traffic, her imagination opened up to every workable plan, however oblique, that she could assemble with the limited resources available. She worried there wasn't enough in her larder to feed Mossad's hunger.

"Why are we stopping here?" Analise had looked up when the taxi stopped, but she didn't recognize police headquarters.

The driver showed her the address on Corbin's handwritten note and said, "It is written."

Analise had given Corbin's note to the driver without looking at it, and she saw that they'd arrived at the Parliament building near Place de l'Étoile. A stern policeman in a dark blue uniform opened the car's door and ushered her to a young man in a tailored suit with a Lebanese flag on his lapel. The policeman was a burly man with a thick neck and a moustache. His colleague had a grim smile and nodded, bending stiffly at the waist.

"Inspector Aboud *réclame le plaisir de votre compagnie.*"

She thought the two men didn't look anything alike, but they had the same implacable indifference of authority. The younger man was clean shaven and polite and the other had a hatchet face and narrow eyes.

"What is this about?" she asked as she was escorted into the building. She knew the old stories about the ISF that reinforced its reputation for ignoring police protocols in the service of resolving a crime. When Shia militia kidnapped a wealthy Druze merchant who was the close cousin of an ISF colonel, all that needed to be said was communicated through the arbitrary arrest of a prominent Shia cleric, and the merchant was released unharmed without the ransom being paid.

"My name is Fares," the young man said. "Follow me. *S'il vous plaît.*"

Analise passed through a wide vestibule and found herself in an arched marble corridor with pink colonnades and heavy crystal chandeliers hanging on long chains. At the end, she climbed wide stone steps to the second floor, where offices lined a wide hall. She was escorted to a corner office with grand proportions that signaled a prominent minister. Brass wall sconces were mounted on lacquered wood paneling that accented the rose-and-eggshell walls. There was a framed photograph of a politician, and, next to it, shadow lines where another photograph had recently hung.

"Our current president." The man who spoke was pudgy and middle-aged, but he had the confidence of a man sure of his status. "I hope we won't have to replace his photograph as quickly as the last one."

"General Hammadi," Fares said, nodding at the man.

Hammadi waved off the introduction. "I'm no longer a general. An honorific title like ambassador that follows you to the grave. You may call me Adham Hammadi."

He had a trim, graying moustache and dark round eyes that brightened with a friendly smile. His white linen suit was set off by black cloth wrapping his upper arm, which he raised, touching her elbow in a courtly manner to draw her into the office. A carved wood desk sat at one end facing a French Empire sofa, bergère chairs, and a low table set with a repeating pattern of black-and-white stones. A water cooler sat on one side of the room opposite tall windows with sheer curtains that softened the harsh midday light, but did nothing to silence the honking from the street. The room, with its high ceiling, felt cool, and a fan rotated with slow, creaking turns.

Hammadi indicated another man, who rose from the sofa. "We were just speaking of you. Let me introduce Inspector Aboud." Aboud's blue uniform was crisply starched, his cravat perfectly knotted, and his black shoes were highly polished. He had dark skin and the severe expression of a man for whom politeness was an inconvenience and not an obligation.

"Thank you for coming," he said.

"Did I have a choice?"

"There is always a choice. But the consequences differ. You have honored us with a visit and I can offer you coffee. In the police station you would get tap water."

Hammadi directed Analise to sit in a bergère chair and asked Fares to bring coffee. He tapped the black armband. "I had hoped to meet earlier but there was a funeral this morning. My good friend Amir Siniora."

Hammadi pointed to an easel that displayed a dozen photographs of middle-aged men. Red Xs were drawn across all but one of the faces.

"It was a sad occasion this morning. He left a wife and two young children. He was outspoken against Israel and a patriot who offended many people. A brilliant journalist, a scholar, and people listened to what he said in his editorials. And now he is another face in my gallery of immortals."

Hammadi took a red felt-tipped pen and drew an X on the remaining unmarked photograph. Hammadi returned to his desk and lifted a typed document. "Have you seen this?" Having waved it toward her, he withdrew it. "Perhaps you don't read Arabic. I can translate."

"I read Arabic well enough." She reached for the document, but Inspector Aboud intercepted it.

"It's privileged. For the moment."

The office door flung open and Fares entered, pushing a cart with coffee, silverware, pastries, and porcelain cups. He poured fragrant coffee into her cup and then did the same for the two men, and silence ensued while he served sweets. Analise felt that she was an invasive specimen being subjected to careful examination by the two men.

Hammadi waited for Fares to move out of earshot, then turned to Analise. "My nephew is studying law, but for now he is my driver and bodyguard." Hammadi paused and touched his ear. "Listen."

Somewhere outside, mixed with the street noise, there was the pleasant sound of a melancholy song drifting up to the office. When the song ended, Hammadi spoke. "The beautiful lament of Fairouz's songs touch all of us—Shia, Sunni, Christians, Druze. She is our Édith Piaf. You know that we are one country with many faiths, but a country with one destiny. We all share one fate. Our enemies are from the outside—Syrians, Iranians, Israelis."

He added three spoonfuls of sugar to his demitasse cup and stirred slowly in one direction and then the other. He drank the sweetened drink in one quick motion and sat back in his plush chair to observe her.

"Journalists are not well liked by men with guns and grudges. Beirut is kind and gentle. But also tough and cruel." He pointed at the new photograph defaced with an *X*. "He was a voice for Lebanon—writer, scholar, philosopher, and clever in six languages. A friend of celebrities and beggars in the street, a man respected by many, which made him dangerous. He wrote passionately about terror, the PLO, and about the Lebanese malaise, but he reserved the full power of his eloquent pen for an independent Lebanon, and because of that, he embraced Hezbollah.

"Murder is an art here and murderers turn the manner of death into a warning. We all thought Siniora would be kidnapped, shot in the head, his typing fingers cut off. That is the mafia's way. But no. He was killed in his Peugeot with a car bomb."

Hammadi dismissed his nephew, who stood guard by the door, speaking in Arabic, but when he turned to Analise he continued in English.

"We appreciate the work of the United Nations High Commission for Refugees. Beirut is overwhelmed by families fleeing the south. Foreigners are evacuating—leaving Lebanon to the Lebanese." He added with mordant sarcasm, "We have always wanted the country for ourselves, but who knew it would happen this way? Once again, we find ourselves at the mercy of outside interests. Romans, Ottomans, then the French and the Syrians, and now the Israelis."

Hammadi leaned forward. "Why does the West hate us? We look at the West and see how they think of us. An Arab mafia. The West sees us through the lens of a crime novel."

Analise was surprised to find herself the object of his lecture, and she wondered why she had been brought to the office.

"How well do you know Bauman?"

"What is this about?"

"I'm told you know him."

"He's a journalist with Agence France-Presse. He reports on the war."

Hammadi's lips pursed in contempt. "He is no different than the others. Only his French gives him a gloss of sophistication. They write for their newspapers without understanding Lebanon. They are too full of themselves to see what is happening, or too stupid. They get people to talk, preying on their ignorance or their vanity. I consented to be interviewed about the war, but he used the time to ask me who among my colleagues in parliament is for Hezbollah. I learned my lesson. I berated him when I saw what he had written—embarrassing me—and he had the temerity to justify his treachery with pompous talk of the public's right to know. His answer to me when I raised an objection: 'You are naïve.'"

Hammadi had become agitated, but after a moment he smiled. "You can understand why I don't like him. It might not surprise you that I asked Inspector Aboud to investigate him. We have a few questions for you."

Inspector Aboud folded his hands on his lap. "Bauman. An interesting case. What can you tell me?"

"Is this an interrogation?"

"An interview. If it was an interrogation you'd be in handcuffs. An interrogation measures guilt but an interview obliges me to treat you with respect."

"How is he connected to Siniora?"

"We don't know that he is. Beirut is a complicated city. How long have you known him?"

"Is he in trouble?"

"You sound like his friend."

"I am happy to answer your questions, but this conversation is beginning to make me feel like a suspect. What is going on?"

"These are difficult times," Inspector Aboud said, smiling. "You look tired," he said. "We won't be long. It's impossible to sleep these days with the bombs and the sirens. Everyone is on nerves."

"Nerves fray," she said, correcting him. "We are on edge."

"Fray, yes. My English is not as good as my French. *Mes nerfs son à vif.*"

"We can speak Arabic if you prefer. *Fina nihki Arabi, iza bit faddil.*"

"Your Arabic is very good. Where did you learn it?"

"My father and my grandmother."

"Your accent is from the Beqaa Valley."

She nodded. "A small village." Analise was surprised when Inspector Aboud leaned forward and lost his patience.

"He's not a journalist."

"Bauman?"

"Did he ever tell you that he carries an Israeli identity card?"

"No. Why would he? He's South African."

"That is what is on his press credentials. We are trying to confirm he is who he says he is and that our information is in error. I thought you might know."

She let out a shallow, frustrated breath, but said nothing.

"The car bomb by the Commodore Hotel was in an SUV. It was very well timed. It killed Siniora instantly. We believe it is similar to the bomb that killed Rafiq Kassir last week. It seems that it is a new kind of explosive device."

Analise's surprise was real, her interest genuine. "Who is responsible?"

"We went to Bauman's hotel room and found his South African credentials. We contacted our friends at Interpol and learned—and this I found surprising—that he was once picked up in Belgium with an Israeli identification card, also in the name of Bauman. What is an Israeli working for Agence France-Presse with false South African press credentials doing in Beirut?"

"I would only be speculating."

"How well do you know him?"

Analise knew that he wouldn't repeat the question unless he already had his answer. "He's a reporter. We share information. War brings people together."

"Friends?"

"We were friendly. I work for the United Nations and he reports on the war."

"Were?"

She shrugged but didn't elaborate.

"We don't know who is responsible for Amir Siniora's murder, or Kassir's, or the others in the past month, but we believe the method used in each attack is the same. These politicians had many enemies—the PLO, Syria, Mossad, the Arab mafia. The list of dead is long and the list of suspects short. Attention to these murders is lost in the distraction of the war."

"No one likes war."

"Some like it less than others." Inspector Aboud looked at Analise. "Where were you yesterday morning?"

"How is that relevant?"

Hearing the irritation in her voice, Hammadi raised his hand to pause the questions.

"I was teaching. Then I went to the office." Then she remembered. "Don't bother speaking to my colleagues. Most left Beirut for their homes in the hills."

"You teach at the International College middle school?"

"I volunteer one day a week. My job is with UNHCR. I see tragedy on the faces of refugees whose applications we reject every day." She looked at him narrowly. "Is that enough?"

"What do you teach?"

"English." No good would come from being argumentative. They knew the answers to the questions they posed and she would only make things difficult for herself with uncooperative responses. "I also teach Arabic to the children of Lebanese families who have returned from London and don't know the language. You can speak with the administrator, Halima Monsour. She will confirm it."

Hammadi smiled. "I know her. She enjoys a good party and makes lamb meatballs that I don't get to enjoy often enough." He smiled. "She is an old friend. I offered to marry her years ago and she had the good sense to decline."

Inspector Aboud leaned forward. "I'd like to make this a weekly meeting. To keep us informed about Bauman."

"Say hello to Halima for me," Hammadi said. "Who knew that we would be having this conversation? But that is Beirut. Without real information, the wildest rumors circulate as authentic truths."

She heard his lugubrious wisdom, but what he said next fell on her like a gloomy prediction.

"Tel Aviv and Washington believe that if you remove the head of Hezbollah, somehow, miraculously, democracy will rise like a phoenix from the ashes of war. The same errors that America made in Iraq are being made here." He folded his thick, stubby fingers, yellow with cigarette stains. "Do I want to live with Hezbollah? No. But you don't destroy it by cutting off the head. Sayyed Hassan Nasrallah and Najib Qassem are just the men who got in front of the parade and waved the crowd on. One leader is killed and another comes forward."

Later, when she thought about the meeting, she realized how absurd the whole episode was and became aggravated when she thought about what they had tried to do. She saw in the encounter enough of her own naïveté, but she understood that it had protected her from exciting their suspicions.

As she walked out of Hammadi's office, she felt the hot whips of panic. Her acquaintance with Bauman, until an hour earlier secret and inviolate, was drawing dangerous attention. Worry made her step more quickly through the marble corridor with the twinned goals of warning Aldrich and finding a workable plan for the attack on Qassem.

7

Drones

In its dangerous moments, Analise knew that covert work was an ordeal, and like most ordeals, it had the power to bind her to it closely. When the ordeal was over, she remembered the triumph broadly as soothing relief. Far more vivid and terrible were the moments of fear that came suddenly in the midst of an operation when things began to go wrong. There was no one to come to her rescue—and no one to protect the lives that she put at risk. Fear settled in, and with fear came panic.

Analise had been staring at the computer monitor in her UNHCR office when she felt panic stir. Inspector Aboud's interest in Bauman was an unexpected complication that jeopardized the operation. She closed her eyes and tried to banish the thought, breathing deeply to settle her nerves. She looked at the computer screen again, exhausted by a long day of reviewing seemingly irrelevant details in search of a workable plan.

She stood, leaned over in a long stretch to loosen her muscles, and then moved across the darkened office to the balcony. She opened the sliding glass door and felt the cooling breeze from the evening sea. She shook her head to clear it of the clotted thinking that came from staring at data that didn't give up its secrets.

A curse slipped from her lips.

Beirut's summer evening helped settle her mind, and she watched Beirutis escape from the confinement of their homes to walk in the night. She heard laugher below in the darkness, and the whispered conversations of couples stealing a moment of romance in the intimate shadows. A dog barked nearby.

The view before her was an unavoidable picture of a threatened city and a reminder of what she needed to accomplish. Food had always been a comfort, and her return to Lebanon had brought her back to the food she remembered from visits to her grandmother—savory *shish taouk*, bowls of *fattoush*, and confectioned almonds. As she gazed into the night, she ate *halloum* cheese with paper-thin *khibz markouk*. The distraction of food helped free her mind from its rut. She was stuck in surveillance video data overload. Exhaustion and eye strain had brought her to an impasse that made it impossible to unlock the mystery of the footage.

God, it's hard, she thought. No one expected Bauman to be the mission's weak link.

Her UN colleagues were surprised and offended by the scale of the Israeli attack, and the ones not dispensing aid in makeshift shelters had decamped with relatives in the hills east of Beirut. With everyone gone, UNHCR's offices were dark and quiet, except for the concussive blasts to the south, which rattled windows facing Abdallah Mashnouk Street. Evening had come and with it another wave of bombing.

Analise was back at her desktop computer doing her best to ignore car alarms set off by the high-explosives' shock waves. She signed in again to the secure web application, entering the numeric code from the digital fob around her neck. It connected to servers in Langley through a secure Internet Protocol router that would show up to anyone following the web address as a duty-free shop in Milan. Drone video footage was paused and she picked up the sequence where she had left off, an SUV, targeted with a white crosshair, traveling slowly through the maze of narrow streets in the southern suburbs. The video was taken from high above and had a flat perspective with almost no depth of field. The black-and-white footage showed the vehicle's roof, but no details of the people inside, or along the sidewalk. It vanished down one alley but then materialized a block away, appearing and disappearing in an evasive maneuver. Without sound or color or context, the images had a distracting monotony, and details were washed out by bright sunlight.

Analise toggled the mouse to slow the motion. A man emerged from a doorway and slipped into the SUV and the vehicle drove off. She replayed the sequence, enlarging the image to study what she could of the man who briefly appeared. She believed it was Qassem, but she couldn't be certain.

She rewound the footage, slowing it further, and stared when the man emerged. He hesitated briefly and he seemed to know the drone was above. She peered at the footage, but eye fatigue and mental exhaustion played tricks on her—she thought she knew his face, then replayed the video and was not certain it was Qassem.

She sat back and rubbed her eyes. Closed her mind. Shut out the car sirens. Hours of reviewing days of drone footage had given her little to work with. A terrible frustration rose within her. Some days Qassem's SUV arrived in the morning, other days in the afternoon, and there were days when it didn't show up at all. The route his vehicle took also alternated, some days approaching from the highway ramp by the Coral gas station, and other days from a nearby alley by a vegetable stand. There were dozens of permutations and there was the possibility that the patterns she was observing were not his current patterns.

The vehicles that brought him to the house also varied. One day it was a Jeep Cherokee, the next a GMC Envoy, or a Toyota 4Runner, a Chevy Tahoe, and on one occasion he had arrived in a food delivery van. Many times, two identical vehicles arrived and he stepped from the rear vehicle while the decoy drove off.

Analise came to appreciate that Qassem's movements were the sophisticated maneuvers of a man who knew he was being watched and had learned ways to subvert surveillance. She recognized the mind of an intelligent adversary who knew there were drones in the sky.

Hours of vigilant work hadn't provided enough information to allow her to predict a route. A predicable route determined where they could park the Pajero. She had been trained to study video footage in Iraq—looking for clues in a wilderness of images. Early in her Baghdad posting she had been assigned to a team tasked with finding three kidnapped American missionaries being held for ransom. One, an older man who'd gone unshaven in captivity, had been killed to prove the kidnappers' seriousness. The video footage released by the kidnappers was grainy, and it began with the bearded missionary sitting on a white plastic chair in front of a green wall. He wore an orange jumpsuit, his hands bound with rope and his ankles shackled. Behind him stood three men in black hoods and camouflage uniforms crossed with bandoliers. The tall man in the center held a butcher's knife. He spoke in Arabic that Analise had translated for the two other intelligence officers watching with her. The missionary was directed to read a statement that was put in front of him in which he confessed to crimes that bore no relationship to his work in Iraq. When the missionary finished, two hooded men held him down, and the taller leader stepped forward. He pulled the missionary's head back by his hair, revealing his neck, and then carved through until he'd beheaded the man. The missionary's screams haunted Analise, but she put the horror into a closed-off part of her mind.

Analise had watched the video over and over in the following days and weeks, studying frames grid by grid, shutting out the gruesome killing to concentrate on telltale clues to the prisoners' location and the killers' identities. She had compared background street noises that could be heard on the video to audio samples of street sounds collected in neighborhoods where intelligence suggested the other prisoners might be held. She was the one who had heard the faint call to prayer of a nearby mosque, which she'd matched acoustically to the voice of the muezzin, narrowing the search area.

Analise looked up from the screen, blinking her tired eyes. She stretched her arms over her head. *It's useless*, she thought. There was no sound. No clues. Nothing clicked and nothing made sense, but then on an impulse she stared again at the video footage. The linguistic serendipity made her pause—thinking that something that didn't make sense might make sense in the particular way that it made no sense. *Gobbledygook*, she thought, *but there's method in the nonsense.* The magician's trick of diverting the audience's eye away from the real action elsewhere—and she looked again at the screen.

She confirmed what she saw from one image to the next, one day to the next—a similarity of repetition. The vehicles changed, times of arrival differed. Routes varied. Decoys were added. But there was always one constant. The driver. It was always the same man who stepped out of the SUV and guided Qassem into the house. It was always Rami's stepfather. She confirmed it, going back through the video. It was always him. His face was visible in several images, though not in all, but she matched his clothing, his size, his tight sport jacket, his baseball cap, and his jaunty step. The obviousness of it was hidden in plain sight. *There is no mystery like the obvious*, she thought.

She pulled up the first days of drone footage and saw him getting out of the SUV. He stood at the driver's door of each of the different SUVs wearing sunglasses and his baseball cap. Sometimes he was alone, sometimes in the company of an armed guard. She studied him for an approach that she could turn into an actionable plan.

He was the proud, confident, diligent driver who wore the importance of his role like an honor. She looked for an inadvertent detail in his manner, advancing through the footage hour by hour, searching for an anomaly or a change that she could exploit.

After several frustrating minutes, it struck her that she was looking for the wrong thing. What stood out wasn't a pattern of change but the persistence of sameness—in every image he wore the same gloves. His clothes changed, on some days he wore a keffiyeh, on other days his baseball cap was worn backward, but in every image he wore gloves cut to reveal the last knuckle of each finger. Gloves like those worn by some professional race-car drivers. The accoutrement of a man who found stature in his official position—driver to a legendary Hezbollah militant.

Analise smiled at his vanity. Everybody had a weakness. Money, alcohol, women. She had found his.

She pondered the discovery. How could she use the driver's predictable behavior to get through the defenses erected around

Qassem? He had to die without others being injured. The driver was expendable, but she couldn't put others at risk.

The answer came to her a few minutes later. She had moved out to the balcony and was looking south toward the incandescent smoke that plumed from the burning oil refinery. She dismissed the thought at first, but once it had taken hold, she was drawn back to its possibilities. The idea surprised her. She considered it, dismissed it for its obvious weakness, but came back to it for its cleverness. It was so simple, so workable, and in the climate of scrutiny in which the CIA now operated, unlikely to be rejected: to make the driver an unwitting accomplice.

Analise had always been painstakingly thorough in her approach to assembling a case, and cautious in her recommendations. But she was also open to serendipity, and when the unlikely presented itself as a flash of inspiration, she turned from a good intelligence officer into a brilliant spy.

She closed the web application and opened a Hotmail account. Malicious software in the hands of Hezbollah had compromised known channels of communication, and her alternate approach was simple. She typed an email message to Aldrich. "Meet tomorrow. I have an idea."

She saved the email in the drafts folder and closed it, but as she did, she was surprised to see that the drafts folder had been incremented to "2." She opened the folder and saw his reply. Somewhere in Beirut he was at his computer. They were separated by location, by place, but in the moment, they shared a virtual space. She smiled. She saw his unsent reply. "Day after tomorrow. AUB. You will recognize the van."

"You're working late."

"Comes with the job."

"No hot dates?"

"Dinner with Hama."

She smiled when he ended the exchange with an emoji, thinking his effort to be stylishly young was hopelessly clumsy.

Analise had signed out of the Hotmail account when her cell phone vibrated. The call number came in as a 0000 prefix, which she knew was the local GSM network's ID for an unknown international number. Aldrich's encrypted phone would show up as a blocked call and she had warned him not to call her Nokia. It was still a workday afternoon in Langley, but no one there would try to call. There was only one rule if you were a NOC in the field. Never reach out to them unless a life was in imminent peril. Hezbollah tracking software had compromised IDF patrols and she knew journalists and UNIFIL officers had been targets. Intercepts were algorithmic, and there were several hours before the acquisition of a phone's location, or readout of a transcription, resulted in physical danger.

Her phone vibrated again. She stared at it, wondering who it might be, and then she cursed. *Fuck. My husband?* She hadn't told him that Paris was off.

"Hello."

"Analise?"

Silence.

"Are you there? It's me, Corbin. I've been trying to reach you."

"Whose phone are you on? The number comes through as an international unknown."

"I'm in Istanbul. Quick trip. My *Times* editor connected me with a source. Did you meet with Hammadi?"

"Why are you calling me?"

"Did you?"

"We had a perfectly unpleasant conversation. Inspector Aboud was there. He asked a lot of questions that had nothing to do with Bauman." She paused. "Did you hear me?"

"What's wrong. You're upset?"

"Did you set him up with questions?"

"We all have questions about him."

"No, you have questions," she said.

"What did Aboud say? What did he ask?"

Analise was annoyed by his persistence. Another night, another day, in a different crisis, or with less on her mind, she would have ended the conversation, or never answered the phone. She listened to his voice and heard an eager reporter on the trail of a story.

"He reports on the war," she said. "They don't like what he reports. They think he's not who he says he is."

"I know the problem," he said, laughing. "I have done some digging on him."

She held the phone at arm's length so he wouldn't hear her audible irritation. "Everyone has a view of him."

"He's Mossad."

A random shot? There was a dismissive ring in her heroic laughter. "Yeah, and I'm CIA. You're groping around in the dark thinking you've found something that's bright and vivid. Well, it doesn't work that way. Not in life and not in journalism."

She was alert but exhausted. She needed to keep straight what she'd told him and what she'd kept to herself. He was an ambitious reporter. Given the choice between betraying a friend or sacrificing a big story, she was certain that he would betray a friend. She listened closely for the blandishments that he might use against her.

Without any conscious effort on her part, she had become a student of the full range of human deceptions; she was an expert in recognizing duplicity—and she heard it in his last comment: "I'm worried about you."

"I don't think of you as the worrying type."

8

Gal's Panel Van

She hadn't seen the Agence France-Presse panel van when she'd looked at the gas station across Avenue de Paris, but it was revealed when a rusting yellow dump truck pulled out in an explosion of black exhaust. Except for a parabolic antenna that nested flat on the roof, there was something deliberately ambiguous about the windowless van's appearance and it might be mistaken for a linen service van or a smuggler's transport. Even the pale blue AFP logo provided cover. Beirut was thick with broadcast networks, print journalists, and the many types of media staff who made a living by satisfying the public's interest in war, so the van's press credential was a natural camouflage.

Analise hop-stepped across two lanes of traffic to approach the van's rear. She ignored the warning painted in red on the twin doors, "*Ce véhicule est sous surveillance*," and knocked twice, as instructed. Whispers inside preceded footsteps on the metal floor.

She glanced at the clock tower on College Hall to confirm that she had arrived at the agreed time.

"So, it is you," Bauman said, glancing behind her.

"Who were you expecting?"

"We thought roadblocks might've delayed you. We're all here."

"What happened?" She indicated a wide bandage on his forearm.

"A man jumped me. His knife went for my neck and I defended myself." He put his arm forward, demonstrating. "He got the worst of it. I didn't see his face."

"It doesn't sound like a robbery."

"All the more reason to finish our work."

She entered the van, her eyes adjusting to the dim interior. Wide-screen monitors and computer equipment were stowed toward the front. Bauman had stepped aside to let her enter. She found Aldrich on a bench, and he retracted his legs to let her move past a narrow bed hinged to the wall.

Gal lay on the thin mattress with his hands clasped together on his chest, quiet, almost meditative. His head rested on a pillow, and when she entered, he opened his eyes. He wore lightweight cotton pajamas and his clothes hung on a hook above the bed. He hadn't shaved in several days and his cheeks had the thin, gray stubble of an old man's beard. She took in the van's several purposes: mobile operations center, safe house, and bedroom.

Gal saw her interest. "This is how I avoid detection. Hotels provide showers but they come with a lot of questions. I did this in Cairo, and the Mukhabarat was blind to a Mossad agent in their midst." He smiled. "Hezbollah will get smart. When they do, I'll find a new trick."

Bauman closed the van's rear door. He wiped his brow with a handkerchief and faced her with the impatience of a restless man wanting to get on with things, his press credential around his neck in a plastic keeper.

When the van lurched forward, Analise grabbed a wall strap, steadying herself. She recognized the smell of street-vendor shawarma and she glanced at the floor, looking for a discarded oily wrapping, believing, in an unconscious association of thoughts, that confirming what Gal ate would help her understand how he lived.

Gal sat up. His slippers settled on the metal floor and he looked at the others. He was a man exhausted by long hours of enforced confinement. He offered mint tea to Aldrich, and the two men sat opposite each other chatting amiably. *Two old spies*, she thought. A Cold Warrior and a Zionist, both in their sixties, with a long habit of lying courteously to each other, which bound them together and kept them at a polite distance—the most intimate of adversaries.

"Good you're here." His weak voice had a solemn tone. "This'll end soon enough. The war. My nomad life. We'll get back to our lives. I have two grandchildren who ask where their zaydee is." Gal arched an eyebrow. "I do this for them. For peace." He smiled kindly at her and nodded at Aldrich. "He says that you have a new plan." His palms opened as an invitation for her to speak. "Please."

Analise opened a portfolio and removed photographs and a printed PowerPoint. She worked as a team with Bauman, but in working together she had discovered they were unalike. She was a young, dark-haired Lebanese-American woman and he was an experienced Israeli spy. He was taller, gruffer, with coarse blond hair, and he seemed to vibrate with restlessness, while her two years in the Middle East targeting terrorists had taught her patience. Analise's Georgetown graduate degree and her father's agency connections had opened the door for her career in the agency, and she had made her way in the Directorate of Operations by pushing herself harder than her male colleagues and by putting up with unwanted advances. She relied on native intelligence and thorough preparation to address challenges, while Bauman made abrupt choices and acted impulsively. Bauman's promotions through Mossad's ranks had come the hard way, in bloody encounters with the PLO in Gaza and later through counterintelligence operations conducted wholly undercover as a war correspondent for APF. His field experience went far beyond the night courses he had taken at Tel Aviv University, and later at Mossad's Negev facility training under Kidon agents who had tracked down and eliminated individuals involved in the 1977 Munich massacre.

Bauman took the PowerPoint. "This is an assassination. Not a graduate school project."

Gal raised his hand at Bauman. "Go ahead. Tell us what you have."

"The driver," she said. "He is the key."

She explained all that she had observed in the surveillance videos—the great care that Hezbollah took to protect Qassem by changing routes, vehicles, the times of his visits, and by using decoys. "For all that effort, one thing remains constant. His driver. He is always driven by this man."

"We're not after the driver," Bauman said.

"Through him we get to Qassem. The vehicles change, the routes vary, but he is always the driver. His name is Ibrahim al-Abub. He's the boy's stepfather and he's a cousin of the boy's dead father. I've found a way to track him. If we track the driver, we'll know their routes and we'll know where to park the Pajero." She turned to Aldrich. "There is no way to avoid killing the driver."

She expected to hear skeptical questions from the three men and she was prepared to address their doubts.

"So," Gal said after a pause, "it's fine to say that we can track the driver, but he travels at the same unpredictable time, on the same unpredictable route, in the same unpredictable vehicle as Qassem. How do you track the unpredictable?"

She held up a small SIM-like card between two fingers. "RFID technology. It's used on limited access highways to identify cars and collect the toll. The wireless tag in the car is identified in a database. This technology can be used to follow a tag on the driver, not the car, and establish a pattern of movement. In a week or ten days we can have enough data to predict a route. We collect the toll when the bomb goes off."

Gal nodded patiently. "How does it work?"

Analise used the presentation to explain the physics: RFID readers propagated wireless signals outward that energized dumb RFID tags and gave them the power to emit a response. Without batteries, the tags could be extremely small.

"Paper thin," she said. "The size of a postage stamp. Easily hidden." She added that a wide array of antennas deployed in a neighborhood would map the travel patterns of the driver's unique tag and send the information to a drone and then to a database. She pointed to the computer. "You can watch the vehicle in real time from this van."

She paused. "I know the neighborhood near Al-Manar TV station. Antennas can be made to look like bricks and placed around the area to capture data from the tag."

"I'm not convinced," Bauman said.

"Why would you be?" she said. "You're the skeptic. If you don't like it, then you come up with a better plan."

"Tomorrow we can send an armed drone against the house."

"That's not going to happen," Aldrich said.

"Act surprised," Bauman said. "Blame it on us. Pretend you didn't know."

"It's not going to happen," Aldrich repeated, irritated. "There are women and children inside."

Aldrich stood. He was Bauman's height and the two men faced each other like boxers entering the ring.

"It's your war," Aldrich said. "You can bomb where you like, but this is a joint operation. I am the officer in charge."

"He's our target."

"And ours." Aldrich's voice lowered and carried a threat.

Gal raised his hand calmly. "Gentlemen." He motioned for Bauman to sit at his side, and when he was seated, Gal patted his hands affectionately. "We need to do this together. Let's be good partners. We will listen to what she has to say."

Gal turned to Analise. "I have a question. Let's assume that you're right and this little tag, as you call it, works. I believe it will work. A solution always appears when the problem is understood. But my question is this: How do you place a tag on the driver?"

"His gloves."

Analise pulled a sequence of black-and-white image captures from the video footage. The images were grainy but the resolution sufficient to make her point. She presented one print, then a sequence of blowups that showed the driver beside Qassem on different days. In each, she pointed out the driver's gloves. Dark leather on the palm, crocheted cotton on the top, and cut-off fingers. Velcro clasps cinched the wrists.

"He wears the same gloves in all the footage. His shoes change, his clothing is different, but his gloves are the same. In his mind, he is a professional driver. A big ego. The gloves appeal to his vanity."

She showed them another video capture image. "This is from the most recent drone footage, two days ago. You can see that the right glove's Velcro strap is torn and he has repaired it with what looks like duct tape. I have found an identical pair of gloves made by Hungant. They are not sold here; I ordered them from Italy. Our colleague in Rome sent a pair through diplomatic pouch."

She pulled the pair from her portfolio. "I opened the stitching and placed a tag inside." She handed one to Gal.

He turned the glove over in his hand, flexing the leather and the cotton, and gave his judgement. "A seamstress too," he said, smiling.

"How do I get him the gloves? That's what you want to know."

He nodded.

"The boy. I evacuated his sister, but the mother thinks she's spending July and August in Aaitat at Halima's summer camp with friends, enjoying her last days as a girl. The boy helped with his sister's escape, but he's worried his mother wants to visit the camp. He asked me to bring photographs of the girl with her classmates. I'll photoshop a group portrait."

Analise knew there was danger in being too candid, but she needed to satisfy their skepticism. She built her case, knowing that consent followed from confidence.

"Rami wants me to tell his mother that his sister is okay, misses her, is having fun, and is looking forward to her marriage. He has a whole script and, of course, he's plotting his own escape to Paris."

She looked from one man to the other, judging their concerns. "It's customary when visiting a family to bring gifts. I have sweets for the mother. And new gloves for Ibrahim."

There was silence in the van, but bumps in the highway jostled each of them, and Gal grabbed the edge of the bed so he wouldn't be tossed to the floor. He looked at Analise. "What makes you think he'll accept the gift?"

"Everyone has a weakness. Ibrahim is vain. The duct tape is a poor reflection on his pride. In a week to ten days you'll know where to park the Pajero."

"No one else will be hurt?" Aldrich said.

"No."

"How do you know?"

"The girl is out of the country. I will have the boy with me."

"And if he's there?" Bauman asked.

"We abort," Aldrich said.

Bauman stood abruptly. "All this and we are exactly where we were last time," he spat. "It's bullshit."

"It's a plan," Gal said. "It may be a good plan. We'll give your plan a chance. If it fails, we have another approach. More people will die." He looked at Aldrich. "Out of respect for the long collaboration between our agencies, we will use your plan. I'll arrange for a driver to park the Pajero. Someone who knows the neighborhood. What do you need from Mossad?"

"RFID antennas from Tel Aviv. Standard technology you can buy in a specialized computer store. We need enough to cover the area, all matched to the tag's frequency."

Gal removed a pocket-size ledger book from his jacket and entered a few words in cramped, precise handwriting using a stubby pencil that he took from the ledger's spine. A brief entry, a reminder to himself, and then he was done and the ledger safely hidden again. They were traveling on a rutted section of the Corniche and Gal knocked on the driver's small window. When the van stopped, Gal stood and the meeting ended. Gal had a pleasant but skeptical smile.

"Let's pray that your plan is successful and only two men die."

Bauman threw open the van's rear doors and bright sunlight entered. "Fresh air," he said. "Fresh thinking." His voice had deepened with skepticism. He looked out at the St. Georges Yacht Club parking lot and the breakfront that protected moored powerboats from the open sea.

"Can this be done before Condoleezza Rice arrives?"

"Get me the antennas."

"I'm not convinced," Bauman said. "I want to meet this boy."

"For what purpose?" Gal asked.

"I want to make my own assessment." He looked at Analise. "The boy is important to your plan. I think it's good that I meet him. We'll make up a story. I'm writing an article on the improbable success of a Lebanese youth team reaching the Paris tournament."

Gal looked at Bauman when the two Americans had left. His face was pensive but his eyes had narrowed. "What do you expect to learn about the boy?"

Bauman stood. "It's her I'm worried about."

9

St. Georges Yacht Club

Gal's van had driven off. Aldrich stood by the marina's outdoor bar and invited Analise to join him for a bite to eat, but she knew very well that he would order a vodka martini and pick at whatever food accompanied the alcohol. The day's heat had subsided and gray clouds brought a hint of weather that lifted her hair and brought briny spray from the choppy sea beyond the breakfront. Helicopters from the HMS *Illustrious* flew low overhead ferrying the last of the stranded English, but with the slowing pace of the evacuation, the port was calm. A solitary Lebanese army jeep guarded the marina's boats.

Analise saw pain when it was in front of her eyes—and she saw it on Aldrich's face.

"This is what we have become," he said. "Nothing good comes from our meetings. The planning of a man's death, even the death of a terrorist, should be done with the knowledge of what it is: murder. They can dress it up, call it what they like, but artful language doesn't change what it is. I can only imagine how many names he's crossed off in his ledger book."

While he took an outdoor table, she excused herself to use the bathroom. When she returned, she saw a bowl of mixed nuts and his vodka martini. He apologized for ordering in her absence, and drained the dregs of what remained, eating the olives. He flagged the waiter for another and invited her to join, but she declined. His face was flushed from the sun, and it was burnished by the alcohol he'd drunk. For no reason other than to confirm that it was early in the day to start drinking, she glanced at her watch. She'd combed her hair and freshened her lipstick so her smile was forgiving.

Analise had seen alcohol sink careers of intelligence officers of Aldrich's generation—men who'd risen in the agency when two-martini lunches and Friday night vespers were deeply engrained rituals. Men who abused the rituals in the act of embracing them saw their careers stall and, in the extreme, destruct. Stalwart drinkers who easily handled their scotch became agency legends about whom notorious stories were told that fed new recruits' need to embrace an agency mythology. Discreet, well-mannered, hard drinkers who remained ably competent after several drinks at lunch. Men who could hold their liquor. Aldrich was one of the agency's old guard who had a bottle of Jack Daniels in his desk that he brought out to end a meeting or to keep up a tolerable buzz as the night grew long. A man seemingly in control of his faculties even when the flush on his cheeks betrayed his abuse.

"You were good in the van," Aldrich said. "I think you convinced Gal. Assertive. Clever. You didn't let them push you around. You've made it."

She wondered what she had made—a mistake, a fan. It didn't matter.

"This is my last posting," he said.

His announcement came out of nowhere and she wondered why he was telling her. He didn't look like a man who was retiring. He was dressed smartly in a linen suit, and his calm, inquiring eyes made his face a marvel of wise concentration. He had none of the slovenliness and weight gain of a man done in by the stress of the game, but he was a vanishing species in a changed world and would soon be extinct. He had used his connections in embassies and stations across the Middle East ruthlessly, but those connections were aging, too, and there were fewer men from whom he could call in a favor, and fewer in the agency who had his back. An old Caesar surrounded by younger intelligence officers letting time do its inevitable work. He had been ubiquitous and charming, always calculating the odds like a gambler, but his dedication to work had cost him his marriage. His wife's infidelities and the whispered gossip that followed had not served him well. Agency mandarins didn't condone the public airing of a man's personal problems. There had once been a favorable comparison to Frank Wisner of the agency's Golden Age, but his wife's adultery and the changing rules quashed it.

Analise looked at him and thought something had changed, a concern in his expression that was unlike him. He was a man who never let his thoughts surface on his face.

"The agency is upset with me," he said. "Living with Hama breaks the rules. They want me back in Awkar, for my safety, and that's part of it, but there comes a time when you know you've stayed in the job too long. Don't worry, I'm not leaving just yet."

Aldrich pointed to the St. Georges Hotel's pink stucco façade. "My first posting to Beirut was in 1962. I had just joined the agency and I was the first Arabic speaker. The hotel was part of the Levantine playboy world of the old Beirut with its nightclubs, gambling, and intrigue. Journalists came here and so did those of us who cultivated them, working the bar and the baccarat tables. I remember coming here one night. Kim Philby was propped up at the bar. He lived not far away in the Christian neighborhood on Rue Kantari. I was told his pet fox had fallen to its death from his fifth-floor balcony. He was disconsolate. His grief seemed odd for a man whose betrayals cost many men their lives.

"We struck up a relationship. I wouldn't call it friendship, but he was interested in how I knew Arabic, and I enjoyed hearing his stories about Angleton in London during the war. Alcohol was always a part of our meetings. I'm ridiculed for remembering an idealized version of him, but that's who he was, a Cambridge-educated Englishman—thin, immaculately dressed in three-piece suits, and his elbow always cocked with a martini glass or a cigarette. He was good at misrepresenting his past and distorting who he was. He opened up about himself, but I learned later that the honest self he showed was the lie he used to obscure the man inside.

"The last time I saw him, we were at the St. Georges bar. He was winkling some truth out of me with his monologues and his gracious laugher. I knew his father spoke Arabic and we had that in common. We were two spies chatting and I recognized a man trying to work his way in. He was good. I was appalled and impressed. I didn't know it then, but I later learned that it was the night before he defected to Moscow. He and I sat at a small table. I remember the slight stutter in his voice, his alcoholism worn like a tailored suit, chatting me up as if he hadn't a care in the world, knowing he was blown, and still casually living out the most audacious lie in the history of espionage."

Aldrich's face was suddenly grim. "The spy business was never a gentleman's game, but by the standards of those days, we've become legally sanctioned hit men."

Aldrich sipped his drink. "Hama tells me that I drink too much. Of course she's right, but I grew up in a time when people enjoyed their martini lunches. At her request, I limit myself to one drink a day." He smiled. "Except today." Aldrich set his long-stemmed glass on its coaster, centering it.

"Don't be taken in by Gal's rabbi act. We have a history. I've intervened against Mossad in the past, but Gal's bosses have cultivated close relationships with the White House and members of Congress. Mossad has gone over my head when I've disagreed. Gal would like to push me aside. God knows what awful thing Bauman would do."

He popped an almond into his mouth. "You need to know the challenge we are up against. When it serves their purpose, we work together, but there are times when our interests diverge. This is one of them. I believe we are being used."

Analise saw the patrician station chief burdened by years of crises struggling with a thought so difficult and intractable that it knit his brow and made him sink in his chair.

"We both want Qassem," he said soberly. "We might disagree on tactics and methods, but it serves our purpose to work together. However, there is something that troubles me. I strain and I stretch every muscle of my imagination as far as I dare into the dark shadows of our long relationship, but for the life of me, I come up short. I put down my pen when I come to the end of a thought, refusing to contemplate the betrayal."

Aldrich paused, aware of the vagueness of his accusation. "I don't have proof, but I see the fingerprints on memos and executive actions. When there are two approaches, one that supports America's interests and one that supports Israel's interests without damaging ours, we take the latter path. Coincidence? Policy? I believe there is a man inside the agency who listens dutifully to a foreign power. I have reason to believe he is aware of my suspicion."

Aldrich sank further into his dark mood. Giving voice to a suspicion was an act of courage and betrayal. Suspicions persisted even if guilt was unproven, and rumors were the end of a good intelligence officer's career. "I don't know if it's true. I have no specific evidence. We worry about a Russian agent in our midst but we're not conditioned to think that our allies spy on us."

He had the vague smile of a sad man telling a funny joke. "I've already said too much. But you are exposed in the field and you should know what I'm up against. We're in a grubby business. We like to believe that our colleagues won't betray us and we're shocked when we discover a traitor." The word *traitor* fell from his lips like a curse.

"Treachery is the ninth circle of hell. It's for men who betray loved ones, friends, and countries. I'm not supposed to know that counterintelligence has opened a file on me."

Analise thought he was rambling.

Aldrich's gaze came off the few sunbathers lounging by the pool, and he looked around to be certain no one was watching. He removed a glassine envelope from his jacket pocket.

"We recovered this from the wreckage of Rafiq Kassir's Mercedes." Aldrich presented a jagged piece of metal the size of a small wrench. "I had it examined by Technical Services. It is from a shell casing of an experimental weapon. The agency technician called it DIME, a dense inert metal explosive. Carbon casing is filled with a mixture of explosive material and very dense micro-shrapnel. In this case tungsten. The weapon is lethal at close range, but the blast loses momentum quickly. The kill radius is small, which limits collateral damage. DIME wounds are hard to treat because powdered tungsten can't be surgically removed. If the victim survives the blast, he dies from untreatable wounds."

Analise examined the shell-casing fragment, turning the jagged edge in her hands.

"Israel is the only country in the Middle East with this weapon. We took this from Kassir's Mercedes, but we also found it in Amir Siniora's Peugeot and in the wreckage of five other bombings. The victims are from different religions and backgrounds, but they have one thing in common. They are members of parliament who have come to support Hezbollah. There may be others. We can't say for certain how many car bombs used this weapon, but we have to assume there are others."

Aldrich took the jagged object. "This complicates things."

He let the thought settle between them and turned to the sunset. The end of the day was a spectacular display of vibrant color—robin's-egg blue filled in behind the scattered clouds and rose above the bright ball of orange fire that settled on the horizon. The dark sea was lost in the extravagant pastels that washed across the little table where the two Americans sat.

"I am doing everything I can to dissuade Secretary Rice from coming." Aldrich leaned forward. "A brokered peace has the chance of a dead man's bluff. Bush is peevishly insisting. He's worried about the midterm elections, so Rice is arriving on a date to be determined at a location to be revealed on a hopeless mission. Our job remains the same. We need to remove Qassem." Aldrich held the glassine envelope, turning it in his fingers. His voice was thick with anger. "Mossad has bigger plans. They are taking out Hezbollah's leadership and sympathetic Lebanese politicians. They want to destabilize the country."

Aldrich finished his martini and ate the two green olives. "Drinking helps me deal with the shit that comes with this job."

"I was questioned by the ISF," Analise said. "They asked about Bauman."

"We need to distance ourselves from Mossad."

Analise's mind was a riot of thoughts. Months of gnomic briefings, weeks of preparation on two continents, hours and days cultivating the boy, and finally a workable plan.

"Who else knows?" She nodded at the glassine envelope.

"Just us. It's my call."

"Perez?" She used the name of the deputy station chief.

Aldrich shook his head. "He keeps the station running in Awkar. He is happy to spend his time on video conference calls updating Langley on the war. Smart but not sophisticated, and he knows that his career advances as mine declines." Aldrich gave a dismissive head shake.

Aldrich, the Ivy-educated Cold Warrior raised as a practicing Catholic, had never warmed to his deputy. They were opposites in background and demeanor. Perez was a graduate of the University of Texas who had joined the agency after two tours in Afghanistan as an Army Ranger.

"What happens next?"

"We go forward until I find a reason to call it off, but we minimize our involvement."

"What does that mean? I am involved. I *am* the plan."

"Plausible deniability."

"What the fuck does that mean? I'm working in a kill zone."

"You are non-official cover. When it's over, you'll get out of Beirut lickety-split. No one can connect us to the killing—or you to the agency. When it's done, you are wiped clean. Gone. Never here."

"And the boy?"

"We get him to Paris. We go forward one step at a time, but you have to be prepared to abort." He looked at her. "The agency will deny you work for it. You're on your own. I will do what I can, but caught, you're a liability."

"Does Gal know?"

"Langley doesn't want to confront the Israelis. Langley knows. Now you know. The invasion, the bombing, and the assassinations are creating unforeseen problems and unwanted attention. Langley is looking at this through the lens of blowback."

She stared at him.

"Corbin is pursuing the story and he is asking questions. Langley is nervous. If we're connected to Qassem's murder, it'll look like we are doing the Israelis' bidding and encouraged the invasion. We will own the humanitarian crisis. Syria and Russia will exploit the situation to their advantage."

He stood and put on his dark glasses, fitting the frames with both hands, and arranged his tired fedora.

Analise watched him move along the marina's boardwalk to his parked SUV and its decoy twin. Before getting in the lead vehicle, he turned and shouted.

"Don't trust him."

Analise put on her Prada sunglasses and wound her head scarf around her head and neck, letting one end hang down, and she stood, distancing herself from the encounter—now loaded with dark preamble. She looked around and saw a European couple who, having heard Aldrich's admonition, stared at Analise. As she passed them, she assumed a brave look and answered their curiosity, "Men!" She briskly moved up the stairs to the Corniche.

10

In the Hills East of Beirut

W hat's wrong?"

Bauman posed the question as they sat on a hill under a gnarled olive tree facing the distant Mediterranean. Cypress and pine trees rose from the field of dry summer grass, and the air was filled with the hum of cicadas. Analise knew he was less interested in her answer than in provoking a response, so she picked up a stone and threw it, avoiding him. She stared into the distance. Normal conversation was a remarkably impaired way for two people to communicate. Words were a fumbling coherence that tested the limits of what she was willing to say and how much he deserved to know.

He watched her pull apart a dry blade of grass. "What's on your mind?"

Analise watched the opposing teams of schoolboys in bright-colored jerseys on the soccer field. Several players cried exuberantly as Rami dribbled the ball toward the goal. Analise massaged her arm to hide the appearance of panic that had come over her without warning, as it had begun to do more often. The heat of the afternoon, her lack of sleep, and the drifting conversation about inconsequential details, and a dizziness of dislocation. It was enough to trigger the image. It was always the same waking dream. She was looking at herself in a white folding chair in front of a shadowy, hooded figure holding a butcher's knife to her throat. Panic breathing in her chest and the cold fear of being kidnapped, tortured, and beheaded.

"You're pale," Bauman said.

She took the water bottle he offered. "The heat," she said, drinking. She could tell he wasn't convinced and she changed the subject. "Corbin thinks you're Mossad."

Bauman shrugged. "He can think what he likes. Ask what he wants. We'll be done soon enough and I'll be gone." He turned to the field, where the ball had changed hands and then changed again as the pace of game play quickened, and then a boy in a yellow jersey dribbled past the last defender.

"Which one is Rami?"

"The one with the ball." She was careful not to be seen pointing. She watched him move quickly down the field with swift, graceful strides. He wore shorts and a jersey that seemed too big for his slight frame, but he was taller than the lone defender and faster. Nimble feet made him a good ball handler and a dangerous attacker. She was entertained by the excitement on the field and felt the sweetness of their youth, free and easy, like yearlings. His long dark hair rose and fell with his leaps and bounds, and his flushed cheeks were radiant with purpose. He was a happy creature in that moment. She was reminded of her brother when he was that age, which brought up thoughts of his death. She pushed back on that part of herself, focusing on the task.

"How old?"

"Thirteen."

"Same as the girl?"

"Twins."

"What does he know?"

"That I work for UNHCR, that I'm a volunteer English teacher, that I'm half-Lebanese."

"Does he suspect?"

"Suspect what?"

"That you're going to kill his grandfather."

It wasn't just the way Bauman put it—his callous coldness—but also that he would even make the stupid comment that annoyed her. "What do you think?"

She turned away from him, irritated. Recruiting Rami had required a different approach than she had used before. She'd spent months in Iraq developing two assets, but in both cases they knew what she wanted and they understood who she worked for. Her goal was to find assets, cultivate them, and pass them along to CIA officers who gathered their information. Rami was a different challenge. As his English tutor at the International College middle school, he confided things to her that no Lebanese boy would share with a stranger, but there was a line they didn't cross, separated by a formality of culture between a boy and an unrelated woman. Trust, she knew, took a long time to build but was lost in a single, careless moment. She had to get his cooperation without alerting him that he was being used.

Her breakthrough came four months into their acquaintance. She was with Rami in the IC cafeteria, talking in the casual way of student and teacher, when she had felt it was safe to step over the line. "Tell me about yourself," she'd asked.

He had looked down shyly, but then opened up. "My sister is going to be married. She says she will kill herself." His eyes had been fierce.

There it is, she had said to herself. The secret. A way in. Every recruit needed a secret to exploit. The moment he had shared his secret was fixed in her mind. She knew that he wouldn't talk unless he believed she could help. Then it started to happen, her questions, his opening up, and then one day, he came to her with a plea to evacuate the sister. The first tentative trust allowed her to ask questions about the family, his stepfather, his mother, and then his grandfather. When she understood the family's complex psychology, she teased out information helpful to the operation. The casual grooming had developed into gratitude when Analise agreed to help Nafeeza escape.

A cry rose from the field. Rami had passed the last defender and faced the goalie, who'd come forward to challenge. Rami kicked the ball across the field to a teammate, who leaped up and headed the ball, scoring.

"He believes me because he wants to believe me. He knows I can help him get to the tournament in Paris." She turned to Bauman. "He wants to play soccer professionally. He doesn't have politics in him. I help him with his dream and he doesn't question why I ask things."

Bauman was skeptical. "Dreams are easy for a boy his age."

"He doesn't like his stepfather. I've found a way to use that." She turned away from the field and looked at Bauman. His tanned face, coarse blond hair, masculine features, and his easy confidence. She was appalled by his attractiveness, but still drawn to him, and thought him a dangerous man to partner with.

"We all have a dream," she said. "What's yours?"

"My dream?" He laughed.

She heard his surprise and understood that unpredictability was his way of exerting control of a conversation. "Most people have a thing they want. A dream. You must."

"My dream?" He looked off at the Mediterranean, then shook his head. "Why are you confident he'll cooperate? It's one thing to help his sister, but it's another for him to join a blood conspiracy against his family."

"I'm not asking him and he doesn't suspect. He's an ordinary thirteen-year-old whose mind is on soccer. He's a normal kid who writes poetry, listens to pop music, and dreams of playing for Juventus. There's only one thing special about him: his grandfather is Lebanon's most wanted terrorist."

Analise paused. "His mother wants him to escape the militia. She got him accepted by IC and pushed him to play soccer. She is a normal mother. She doesn't want her son to put on a suicide vest."

Bauman observed Rami among his teammates—innocent boys exuberant in their moment of triumph. "He has a good kick. I was a good player at his age." His voice softened, lowered, and became vaguely confessional. "Now, I am too old for dreams."

"You have no problem knowing what you want."

"It's not a dream." He pointed to the wispy clouds racing across the pale blue sky. "Clouds are like dreams. Pleasant to contemplate. Out of reach."

She was surprised by his tone of voice. It was the most personal thing he'd said about himself in their months working together. She thought she saw a window open into his mind. "How did you become so cynical?"

"You don't know me."

"I know what you say. I hear your words. I know what you want me to believe about you. Tough guy. Cold son of a bitch. But every good person is a sinner and every evil man has a complicating humanity. I know things about you that you don't know about yourself."

He was amused. "Go ahead. Surprise me."

She touched her ear. "You don't know how to listen."

"Listen for what? Little whispers in my ear. I hear what I need to hear." He looked at her. "You see what I let you see."

She had come to believe that she could never truly know another person, but if she understood what motivated them, she could predict what they would do. In Bauman she saw a driven man, and she knew that driven men were vulnerable to their obsessions. He was a hard case. He, too, had his secret.

She smiled at him. They had fallen into a conversation that had nothing to do with their reason for being on a hillside east of Beirut.

"He is a good kid," she said. "He shouldn't suffer."

Bauman snapped the twig that he held. "There's no room for sentiment in what we do." He raised his bandaged arm. "This is how things get done."

His tone irritated her. "Don't mistake sentiment for softness. There's no place for arrogance either. You insulted Hammadi. You're a person of interest to him. He asked why a reporter for Agence France-Presse with a South African passport also holds an Israeli identification card. He wants to make something of it."

Bauman averted his eyes, and his earlier brusque dismissal faded as he pondered.

"You should avoid the Commodore Hotel. He'll look for you there."

Jubilant cries from the victorious team were a counterpoint to the sullen mood of the losing team, but the players' moods converged when they approached a table laid out with dishes heaped with fried bread, canned tuna, cheese, bags of *kri-kri*, almonds, and pickled turnips. Nearby, a savory smell wafted from a fire pit where Halima's husband held a skillet over hot coals. Aromas of sage, dill, and lamb teased the boys' appetites.

Halima gathered the dozen young girls from school and organized them in a group photograph. Analise arranged the teenage girls into two rows with the tall ones in back and positioned them in the shade of a tree. She took several photographs, keeping shaded faces in the back intentionally dark, and separated one girl so her face could be photoshopped out.

"Eat. Eat," Halima commanded the boys and girls.

Analise joined Halima's husband at the fire pit. He held the skillet in a gloved hand, but his attention shifted to a pickup truck that had stopped near the stone farmhouse at the edge of the orchard. Halima walked briskly to the vehicle, carrying a straw basket, which she showed to the driver. A second man leaned on a large-caliber machine gun mounted on the rear. Halima laughed with the driver, and in a moment, she handed him the food she had brought.

When she returned, she stood at the fire pit. "Hezbollah bastards." She shook her head contemptuously. "I told them to leave. I said that if a drone spotted them, jets would come and drop bombs." She was agitated. "They have no idea what could happen. Pilots see the Hezbollah militia but not the children. I have a school to run. Parents give me their children in the morning and expect me to return them in the afternoon."

Analise heard her restrained fury. "We all have stories that we don't want to share. Untold stories we hold inside that become a kind of poison. We hold on to our silence and it makes us sick. Little things of no consequence—hungry men dropping by to be fed—a stupid act, but there are consequences. The tragedy of unintentional stupidity."

Halima shook her head without finishing the thought.

Her husband gestured toward the departing pickup. "*Zift*," he said. He returned to the skillet. "Do you know *zift*? It's a word we have that means two different things: asphalt and shit. We say in Lebanon everything is *zift* except for the streets."

He savored the smell of the cooking lamb and smiled, sharing the irony. Analise appreciated the many shades of sarcasm that spoken Arabic could convey. "*Zift*," she repeated, laughing, and complimented his cooking.

"This is *awarna*. Mutton cooked with a mixture of salt and melted fat. *Awarna* is a Turkish word that came to us from the Ottoman Empire depositing its coins and its language." He smiled. "Fat was a preservative, and the dish was eaten in winter months before there was refrigeration. Now it is a delicacy all year long. I usually cook it with eggs and *kistik*, a cereal of crushed wheat, but eggs are hard to find now and children don't care, so I am making a simple *awarna*. The lamb was slaughtered yesterday by our caretaker on the occasion of your visit here."

He turned his full attention to the fat sizzling in the pan. "There will always be war in Lebanon. I was born in war, I grew up in war, our eldest son died in war. There will never be peace. A pause in war, yes. A pause, but there will never be peace."

He smelled the cooked lamb's rich aroma. "It's done. Now we will eat."

Halima took a dish and turned to Analise. "I heard Hammadi met with you." She scoffed. "Be careful of him. A big politician with no virtue. *Ustaz*." She raised her hands theatrically. "A man with one mouth and two tongues. Did he tell you that he once offered to marry me? I don't know why he says that. It's not true." She added, "Be careful of him. He tries to charm confessions from his visitors."

⋖⋅⋅⋗

Analise spotted Rami sitting cross-legged against the twisted trunk of an ancient olive tree. He gazed at the coastline that lay beyond the sloping hills of cypress, and further on, the distant sea. He was alone, quiet, contemplating the view. Troubled phantoms had dominion over his thoughts. He ignored the joyful cries that came from boys cavorting in the pleasant summer afternoon among the trees. Girls had joined the boys in excited play, but Rami's attention was turned to a distant vanishing point. He let his eyes drift with the clouds, looking out at nothing in particular, consumed by his thoughts.

Analise sat beside him. Her abaya came over her cargo pants, and her Nokia was shoved in her back pocket. Rami swigged from the water bottle she offered and then set it between his legs.

"Where is Nafeeza now?" he asked.

"Cyprus. The boat arrived three days ago. She is safe."

"How do you know?"

"I was told. She was met by my UN colleagues. This is best for her."

"What do you know about what's best?"

"It's what she wanted. I saw her board the ship. She was nervous but excited. She asked me to tell you that."

His head slumped.

Flushed with concern, she saw herself as a lifeline for his spirits, but she resisted the urge to comfort him. Cultural norms required physical distance. Had he been an American teenager, she would have put her arm around his shoulders. She could feel his worry. He was a boy but he had the burdens of a man. Silence lingered between them.

"What happened?" She pointed to the deep purpling on his wrist. She looked closer, but he abruptly withdrew his arm and covered his wrist with his other hand.

"Let me see."

"It's nothing."

"You don't hide nothing."

He removed his hand and she saw that his little finger was bent at the knuckle and swollen terribly. A spider web of hemorrhaging darkened the side of his hand.

"You should go to the clinic."

"I'm fine."

"What happened?"

"I said nothing."

Rami looked out at the expanse of deep blue sea that stretched before them. Cicadas crackled in the dry heat, and there came a moment when they were both aware that cries from the others had quieted. He took a small stone, threw it down the slope, and watched it roll until it was gone. He presented his bruised wrist, like a shopkeeper holding a damaged fish.

"This is why she had to leave. Ibrahim didn't need an excuse to beat Nafeeza, but he came up with one. She had changed the television channel he'd been watching. When he returned, he slapped her. I stepped between them and said that I had changed the channel. He beat me for protecting Nafeeza and then he beat me for changing the channel. He called me a disgrace. He said that I needed to learn how to treat my sister. He demanded that I beat her. I refused. He beat me again and locked me in the bathroom."

Rami tossed another stone down the slope and then a third. "I had no choice. She's my sister." His eyes lifted to Analise, tearing. "The man she is to marry is old, fat, and smells of tobacco. He looked at her like food in the market. She felt shamed. She refused to marry him. She said she would kill herself first. I didn't tell you that I found her with a razor cutting her wrists. She knew to cut lengthwise, not across."

His head slumped. "My mother." His voice drifted. "She's helpless. Ibrahim brags. He tells grandfather that he is a good husband and a good father." Rami spat.

He turned to Analise. "When do I leave?"

"Your travel is arranged. I'll come to your home with the visa. To calm your mother, I'll bring a photograph of Nafeeza with her friends. The soccer team will go by helicopter to the French frigate and you'll sail to Marseilles and then travel by train to Paris. Nafeeza will join you there."

She saw his face calm with the details of the plan, and the more she talked, the greater his confidence. She spoke in a reassuring voice, and slowly his skepticism dissolved.

"I will bring a gift for your mother and for Ibrahim." She nodded. "You played well."

He shrugged. He took a folded note from his pocket and gave it to her. "A gift," he said. "I wrote it."

Analise recognized a love poem. Alarm bells rang in her head. She tried to sound surprised and pleased, but inside she knew it was a volatile complication. She was not prepared for the consequences of his affection. A part of her floated on a current of time that took her toward a terrible outcome. She could see the danger. She had developed a tolerance for delivering pain to others. But she had never hurt a boy.

"It's very nice," she said, placing the note in her pants pocket.

Rami turned to the grassy field, where Bauman showed off his ball-handling skills for a rapt audience of boys. "Who is he?"

"A journalist. He's writing a story. How a small team from Beirut got to the quarterfinals in Paris."

"*Ibn kalb.*" Rami stared. "He doesn't belong in Lebanon." He watched Bauman bounce the ball on his knees and feet, keeping it in the air, delighting his audience.

Rami lowered his voice. "I saw him look at you. He is a problem for you."

"Why do you think that?"

"Your face. I saw you talking."

"What on my face?"

"He doesn't trust you."

She smiled. "We were talking. He said something I didn't agree with. He's a friend."

"You let him see inside you."

"What should I have done?"

"You could hide your feelings. Lie to him."

She laughed. "He would know. People know when you lie."

"Then you're not a very good liar."

She had looked away but now met his gaze. "I can lie well enough."

Bauman turned the Land Rover's steering wheel hard, taking a sharp switchback on the way back to Beirut. Cars had stopped at a scenic lookout to watch a pair of F-16s make a bombing sortie over the city's southern suburbs.

"Slow down," Analise said, holding the door to avoid sliding across the seat. "What's wrong?"

Bauman ignored her and concentrated on passing a station wagon parked on the wide shoulder, a family leaning out the windows to watch the explosions.

"Did you get what you wanted?" she said, sitting upright. "Are you satisfied with him?"

Analise waited for his answer, but he remained mute, gripping the steering wheel with angry concentration. As hard as she tried, she couldn't understand him. She thought she knew him and then, out of the blue, he confused her, making her think she didn't know him at all. She believed the world was a chaotic surface of impressions that it was her job to make sense of, but sometimes she failed—she felt that failure in the car. She stared at him and couldn't escape the conclusion that she had underestimated how dangerous he was.

"I got a text," Bauman said.

She turned to him.

"The RFID antennas are arriving late—two days." He turned to her. "Nothing is off-the-shelf." Bauman honked at a speeding car that suddenly pulled out in front of the Land Rover.

"Slow down," she said. "You'll get us killed."

"No, you'll get us killed. Stay away from the boy."

"I can't."

He looked at her. His eyes moved back to the road. "The way he looked at you. He will be a problem."

11

Near Rue Kantari

C orbin rolled over in bed and felt a soft arm. He knew it must be
Analise, but for a moment he thought it was the British redhead
he'd picked up the week before in the Commodore Hotel, and then
his fingers found the familiar raised scar on Analise's shoulder. A
wound that she had explained with a story he didn't believe. The
fog of alcohol clouded his mind, but he remembered the details of
the night before. At her suggestion, they'd gone to the Phoenicia
Hotel for a drink, to avoid being spotted in the Commodore by
acquaintances who might make a thing out of seeing them together.
He remembered little of their chitchat except that she seemed
distracted and kept looking to see who entered. He recalled their
long silence in the taxi on the way to her place, thinking something
was wrong.

Corbin opened his eyes into the sun's early light and gazed at
her olive skin with its sheen of dried sweat. She was on her side, her
back to him, and asleep or seemed to sleep. He had been surprised
when they'd arrived at the apartment and she had suggested they

make love. Her offer was at odds with her earlier distant mood. He rolled onto his back and looked up at the ceiling fan, listening to the blades' slow rotations mix with excited voices coming through the open window.

She was quiet now, her breathing steady and her shoulder washed by morning light. Her restlessness had awakened him and kept him from going back to sleep. He gazed at her. Even in sleep he sensed her disquiet and saw on her face a determination so strong that he could feel an unseen adversary in the wild dominion of her dreams.

He thought of the many times he'd lain next to her, surprised that they were still seeing each other. The distance she kept had been understandable when they first met, but with time his impatience had grown. Her invitation to return to her place had come out of the evening's inertia.

Her clothes lay scattered on the floor where she'd dropped them: bra, black panties, a mustard-colored blouse, tan trousers, a belt with gold baubles that matched nothing else. He was drawn to her but was prepared to lose her. It would be no great matter, he thought—Beirut was a prodigal city of uncommon women and he'd had several. Did she know of his interest? Probably. Women were aware of a man's desiring gaze.

He placed his hand on her forehead and whispered something to comfort her. He wished he could provide her with as much solace as her loneliness deserved. He kissed her neck and lay beside her, drawing close.

Morning light woke Analise. She had tried to hold on to the pleasant dream but it slipped away and then it was gone. Her eyes opened to the sight of clothes piled on the floor and she felt his hand on her hip. Part of her wanted to tell him everything about her life, and part of her wanted him out of her life—to keep her distance to protect herself from attachment.

She felt his hand touch hers and his fingers moved until they found hers, touching fingertip to fingertip. Analise rolled over and kissed him on the cheek.

"You talk in your sleep," she said.

"What did I say?"

"Nothing I understood." She withdrew her hand. "I have to leave early." She sat against the headboard and drew the cotton sheet to her chest, covering her breasts. She turned to him. "You look like you have something on your mind."

"Who was the man who waved to you in the bar?"

"A colleague. Are you jealous?"

"Curious, that's all." He nodded at the clothes crumpled on the floor and towels draped over a ladderback chair. "Why don't you have a maid clean the apartment?"

Her mind went down the list of things she didn't want a maid to find. Her Glock. The passports. The miniaturized burst radio transmitter. She smiled. "When a bomb hits, there won't be anything to clean."

He sat up. "The war will end soon enough." He leaned closer and met her eyes. "What's this?"

"This?"

"Between us?"

The pronoun, *this*, implied more than she wanted—a sort of possession. They had taken what they wanted from each other—and she got bits of information that she passed on to the intelligence officer in Awkar.

"It's enough that you're here," she said. Her mind had started to form the thought as "we're here," but she stopped and was careful to say "you're here," knowing that at some point he'd leave and she'd remain. She would choose the moment to end it.

Analise drew her fingernails through his tufted chest hair while she held the sheet over her chest.

"Does this go anywhere?" he asked.

"How can it?"

He frowned. "You're a pessimist."

Analise smiled. "It keeps me from being disappointed."

She thought his green eyes were darker than she remembered, but the sun was behind him and shadowed his face. She smiled affectionately and let the mood linger.

"Love is a privilege," she said. "Real love. What we have isn't real love." Her expression was vaguely serious. "There is also the complication that we're both married."

She knew the mistake women made, the mistake she had seen her mother make—the woman giving more of herself in love, while the man was quick to profess his love—and the deceits that followed: a sudden impulse to use the word *love* to make love, or smooth over an argument, or as a thoughtless aside. She always listened to what a man meant, not what he said. Corbin was a tough case and she thought she'd met her match. They were masters at giving the other a false sense of what was between them, each coy about what went unsaid. Analise sometimes questioned herself, hearing his bullshit, dismissing it, but finding a way to enjoy the game. She was good at maintaining her second skin and she got satisfaction offering one side of herself while holding on to the person inside. She gave him connection and had seen him mistake attention for affection.

She patted his cheek tenderly. "This is enough."

"For you."

"Yes. Enough for me."

They had met several months earlier. Late-season snow had fallen in the Beqaa Valley and she made the drive across Syria to the border, aware of the danger for a woman traveling alone. She was returning to Beirut from Damascus in a UN Land Cruiser. Solitude was a reliable companion in her work but there were few words to adequately describe the day in, day out stress. Every encounter a threat, every casual friendship a possible betrayal. A mistake potentially fatal. She had spent two days in Damascus pleading with Mukhabarat to open the border for Lebanese refugees. Her trip was unplanned, her return unscheduled, and she'd changed routes at the last minute, taking the less-traveled road. No one knew she would be at the Masnaa border crossing on that particular day.

She had passed through the eight-mile no-man's-land and had been cleared back into Lebanon by border control. Just beyond the checkpoint, she saw a disabled bus with its passengers waiting in the meager shade. Corbin was easy to spot. Dark glasses propped on his head like a model at a fashion shoot set him apart from the Syrians and Lebanese huddled on blankets and cooking on propane stoves.

Analise took him in all at once: tall, early thirties, traveling light with a shoulder bag, shouting into his Blackberry. She was confident he was who he appeared to be—a stranded American. A man and woman crossing Beqaa Valley was safer than a woman alone.

She'd honked to get his attention. "Going to Beirut?" she shouted, head out the window, and then said, "Get in."

He finished his call, breaking off the conversation. She heard his Midwestern accent and looked for a wedding band but didn't see one.

"Where in Beirut are you going?"

"Drop me anywhere. I'll make my way."

"You've been there?"

"I live there. Short trip to Damascus. No one tells you how close the cities are. Or how old the buses." He looked at her. "Speak Arabic?"

She wore a hijab and had the facial features and skin tone of a Lebanese, but at that moment, at that time, she thought his presumption revealed a prejudice.

"Muslim," she said to provoke him. Part of her wanted to kick him out of the vehicle, but she needed him.

She glanced at him, thinking he'd be curious, but saw him scrolling through emails on his Blackberry. "Where are you staying in Beirut?"

"Ras Beirut."

"What brought you to Beirut?"

"I work for the *New York Times*."

She laughed.

"What's so funny?"

"You said it like I should be impressed."

Her job was to acquire acquaintances whose brains she could pick for intelligence. Serendipity was not something she planned for or expected, but she knew how to exploit it.

"I didn't ask for the assignment," he said. "My editor wanted to get rid of me. That's it. Very simple." He shrugged. "The editor is a friend. And my wife's lover."

Despite not wanting to smile, she did. "You're married?"

"In a manner of speaking. Happy memories are the hardest. I try to remember only the unhappy ones." He turned to her. "Who do you work for?"

"United Nations High Commissioner for Refugees."

"You're busy."

"Busy with misery." She saw him wait for her to say more. "Last week I wrote 'insufficient evidence' on the case of a young Palestinian family who claimed they had been expelled from Israel without documents. When I scrawled the words, I saw pain on their faces."

"It's not a kind world."

"No one should suffer because of arbitrary rules. I processed them anyway."

Her confession provoked his opinion about the region's hopeless politics and he talked at length in an attempt to impress her, or because there was nothing else to do on the long ride. She listened to him and understood how to play the opportunity. Two strangers thrown together by chance adversity on a car ride that was made longer by roadblocks. She encouraged him to share the thoughts that come easily between strangers who are unlikely to meet again. He opened up about his life and she let him do the talking.

He said that his overseas post was a convenient separation and his marriage was in the process of dissolving, but they were too stubborn to declare defeat. Analise had an urge to mention her own failing marriage, but it was safer to listen. When he became silent, she offered a few innocent details of her marriage as a way to encourage him. She hated the confinement of marriage, she said, but she liked the predictability of the lifestyle. "An insurmountable contradiction." She turned to him. "Why were you in Damascus?"

The intentional vagueness of his answer got her attention and she thought his research might interest the agency.

When he got out of the Land Cruiser on Hamra Street, he proposed they meet again. Her first report on him was sent via scrambled voice recording, and the response that came back from Awkar was succinct: pick his brain.

"Drinks on me," he said, when she called his number.

"A drink won't cover the cost of the gas. Make it dinner."

She saw the expression on his face after two glasses of wine. An expression she'd seen before. The face of a single man in Beirut, lonely, away from home, slightly flirtatious, curious to expand on what they'd talked about on the drive. She didn't flirt with him, but she didn't shut down the idea.

"What's the story you're working on?" she asked.

"Bauman."

She looked up from her plate, startled.

"You know him?"

"I know of him." She listened to Corbin's opinion of Bauman. Agence France-Presse reporter, South African by way of an adopted country. Earned his stripes as a war correspondent somewhere. "It's hard to get that type of job. I was turned down eight times." He sipped his wine. "He was expelled by Syria."

The first time Analise slept with Corbin, they'd been caught unexpectedly in a moment of peril crossing Beirut late at night. Earlier, in a bar, they'd watched a hilarious skit on Beirut's most popular television comedy show, *Bas Mat Watan*, that mercilessly mocked Hezbollah's cleric leader, sending his infuriated followers into the streets. Hezbollah supporters marched toward Martyrs' Square and Druze and Christian neighborhoods, chanting and yelling. She had been driving him to his hotel, but the spontaneous demonstrations made it dangerous to continue, so he stayed at her place on Rue Kantari.

Upon entering the apartment, she made an excuse for the unmade bed, clothes strewn on the floor, dirty dishes in the sink, and bath towels in a heap. Moldy take-out leftovers filled the refrigerator along with a bottle of wine and two boxes of honey-drenched namoura.

She poured wine and they sat together on her fifth-floor balcony, enjoying the view of Al Kantari Palace, listening to the din of protestors. Beirut found its social footing late in the evening, and Corbin suggested they go to a restaurant nearby. She said she wasn't hungry, but if he was, yes, they could go out, but it wasn't her preference to risk the streets. He happily satisfied himself with the sweet semolina cake. Bursts of gunfire in the air seemed to signal the rekindling of long-feared sectarian violence.

They stood on her balcony, safe from the riot, but the evening threw them together and she was aware of the potential for intimacy. She had allowed him to be interested in her as a way to profit from what he knew, and she had inched forward toward a romantic acquaintance. Analise sipped her wine and they joked about Lebanon's politics, crazy to the outside world, and she refilled Corbin's glass. The wine helped. They talked. He had his own stories of the old Beirut. "The Phoenicia Hotel was a film set for all the Euro spy movies shot in the 1960s. Terrible movies," he said. He talked a while more, then, to end his talking, she kissed him. They removed each other's clothing and stumbled toward the unmade bed.

A second evening followed. She knew there was a strict prohibition on romantic entanglements with assets in the field, but she believed it would be over quickly. The conclusion of her tour would end their acquaintance and she would avoid having to inform Aldrich. But her tour was extended, and once she'd crossed the line, her will to resist intimacy and affection weakened. A young woman. Alone. She took what she needed from him. And the agency was grateful for the bits of information that she handed over.

They had opened up about their relationships early in their acquaintance—she about her husband and he about his wife. They repeated that it was poor judgment, that it complicated their marriages, and all the other things that their guilt required them to say. But attraction was the daughter of peril, and they were drawn to danger. She shared private feelings about being a Lebanese-American in Beirut, split between two cultures and two religions, part of neither and both. Things that she hadn't shared with anyone, little details that crossed over into her secret life. It was an odd intimacy, not affection in any normal way, but the closeness that comes from unburdening the secrets of a private life.

For her, casual sex was an escape from the haunting images of the beheading and the daily pressure of watchfulness, always stopping in front of store windows or suddenly turning to see if she was being followed. Her nerves were raw then. Everything a balled-up mass of tension. She ate too much. Gained weight. Sex was an antidote to stress. And why not? She could be dead the next day.

Analise had arranged to meet him at the bar in the Commodore one night. The bar was a loud, boisterous scene among reporters and cameramen who had descended on Beirut, and she moved through the rude, smoking crowd looking for Corbin, but Bauman loomed ahead. Tall, loud, holding court among the new arrivals like an old hand. He waved her over and she put her shoulder into the mass of people and opened a path, drawing attention from the men.

"Finally, a peacekeeper," Bauman boomed, holding apart two arguing colleagues. "Here we have wisdom, mates," he barked in a South African accent. "I want you to meet someone." He tugged her forward, holding a beer in his other hand. "We were just talking about the new network Hezbollah has set up. They've dug trenches for private fiber-optic telephone cables that connect their headquarters in the southern suburbs to military posts along the border. The Israelis won't be able to jam Hezbollah calls. Great guy, knows a lot, asks too many questions. Works for the fucking *New York Times.*"

Bauman pulled her to the bar where he stood negotiating with the bartender. He wore an Oxford shirt and a press badge in a plastic keeper around his neck, which swung as he turned to her with a beer in each hand. Analise's lips parted with an audible gasp when she faced Corbin.

"Do you know each other?" Bauman asked. He looked from one to the other. "Is it possible? Well, I don't have to introduce you." Bauman looked at Analise. "He's close to someone who knows something about their communications, so we've chatted each other up. He wants to know how I've become a celebrity war reporter."

Analise's Nokia rang. She grabbed the phone from the bedside table and swung her feet to the floor, recognizing the four zeros of an unidentified international call.

"I have to take this," she said to Corbin, and walked to the bathroom, closing the door. Her cell phone was pressed to her ear and the door was closed, but still she whispered.

"What?"

"It's me." Bauman's voice was brusque. "Is this a good time?"

"As good as any." She looked at the time on her watch. It was not yet eight A.M. "It's early. Where are you? The number comes in as unknown."

"I'm on someone else's phone. A few reporters have had their phones hacked. It's a precaution. I'm told Rice might not be coming."

She knew it was a random shot from a Mossad agent tracking down a rumor. Everyone connected to the unfolding crisis was a possible source. She massaged her temple. *Think!* "I have no idea."

"I thought we should talk."

"You shouldn't call me on this number."

"We need to meet."

"About what?"

"The antennas arrived. I know you're seeing Corbin. What's going on?"

Going on? The whole difficult history of their working acquaintance was reduced to three words: *What's going on?* With her? With him? With the plan? Bauman's suspicion surprised her. She had to find a way past it, through it, or around it.

Analise happened to glance in the sink's mirror. The bathroom door had drifted open, and through the narrow gap she saw Corbin standing naked at the dresser. His hand was in her purse. She stared and watched, thinking he was looking for a cigarette, but he knew she didn't smoke, and then his hand dug deeper. As his search went on, her surprise deepened. Bauman was still speaking. She cut him off. "I'll call you back."

Her mind went down the possibilities, but she kept coming back to the worst case, that he worked for another intelligence agency. The teeth of reason bit and she resisted the impulse to march into the bedroom and confront him. He'd become cautious if he knew that she suspected something. She flushed the toilet, alerting him she was done.

Corbin looked up. She'd put on a spaghetti tank top and boxer briefs. Her phone dangled in her hand and she placed it in her leather handbag, glancing inside. The snap of her Ferragamo wallet was undone.

"Well?" Corbin said. He sat on the bed with his back against the headboard. She turned to him and was glad he'd pulled the sheet over his waist.

"Bauman," she said.

"Does he know about us?"

"No," she lied.

"What does he want?"

"A few reporters have had their phones hacked."

"He called to tell you that?"

"Someone is peddling a rumor about him."

"Who?"

"He says it's you."

Corbin shifted so he sat on the edge of the bed, and he took out a pack of cigarettes, hitting it on his wrist, popping one. He lit it and drew a sucking breath, releasing a lungful of smoke, slowly, patiently. Thinking.

"Must you?" she said. "The cleaning lady knows that I don't smoke."

"You said you didn't have a cleaning lady."

She crossed her arms, irritated.

"What's bothering you?" he asked.

"Nothing." She stared at him and met his eyes fiercely. "Nothing I want to talk about."

When she had calmed, she considered the question that troubled her, but rejected speaking up, knowing that he would answer with a lie.

"I'm meeting Bauman tomorrow. He says I shouldn't trust you. I don't want him to think that what he tells me, I tell you."

Corbin hopped off the bed and slipped into his trousers, pulling the waist tight over his flat stomach. He pulled his shirt over his head, stuffing the ends into his pants, and put on his boots. He turned to her briskly and pointed at her bag. "I was looking for matches," he said, and then showed her the ones in his hand. "They were in my pocket. I thought I'd lost them."

An uncomfortable silence settled between them.

"He's Mossad, you know."

"You've said that before."

"I don't like him. I don't like him calling you. You might think he's a reporter, but it's not the whole story." He went to leave but turned to her at the apartment's open door. "Ask him what he did in Syria."

From the balcony, she watched him hustle down the street and disappear near Michel Chiha Street. Inside, she took a square of namoura and sat cross-legged on the floor, eating and thinking.

She recorded the incident in the personal journal she had begun when she arrived in Lebanon. Her first entries were anecdotes of the city of her mother's birth; she wrote to understand her affection for Lebanon—her grandmother's farmhouse in the hills east of Beirut, the food, her memory of her first visit to the old souk with her brother. Writing released a stream of associated thoughts and she found herself recording memories of her youth in Georgetown enjoying the daydreams of a normal teenager living a sheltered suburban life, but her parents' divorce and her father's disappearance in Syria, followed a decade later by the loss of her brother on 9/11, tore the fabric of her life. Journal entries about her work started as accounts of her frustrations with the refugee crises, and without any conscious effort, she found herself recording bits of her work as a NOC.

Her entry that morning was succinct. "They don't like each other. It will be a problem."

PART II

12

A Quiet Moment

Analise emerged from the bathroom, toweling her hair dry, and stepped onto her balcony, surprised to see that it had rained during the night. It never rained in Beirut in July. Roses in front of the apartment were folded and droopy, and the sidewalk was slick gray with moisture. The storm and the sea breeze had swept away the acrid smoke that drifted north from the bombed suburbs. Analise reflected on how the overnight rain had cooled the air and soothed her mood, but then her mind returned to the day ahead. Time was running out.

She glanced down at the red Peugeot parked across the street. It hadn't been there when she went to bed, and she didn't know what to make of it—or if she should make nothing of it. Suspicion was a rude companion to her work, and her safety depended on a relentless pursuit of hunches and intuition. At the sink, she splashed cold water on her face and resisted the urge to worry. Then she did what she always did when anxiety took hold. Breathing hard, she did sit-ups. When she finished one set, she did forty more, and then leaned forward, heart pounding. She showered, dressed, made coffee, and ate a pastry.

She unscrewed the gray metal cover of the kitchen electric panel and removed several disabled circuits breakers, revealing a recess in the wall. From the hiding place she took her 9mm Glock and snap-on holster. The magazine was full and she confirmed the gun's action had not suffered in the five months that it had sat idle in the humidity. Agency personnel were not authorized to carry weapons on the street, but Langley was six thousand miles away, so she could do as she pleased. She stood before the mirror and confirmed the gun was covered by her hip-length tunic. It was a double-edged comfort. If she got into a situation where she needed the Glock, her cover was already blown. The gun would be of little use. She held the Glock, thinking about where she was going that day, and then placed it in her chest of drawers, where she could grab it if she needed to. As she closed the drawer, she changed her mind and slipped the holstered Glock on her belt.

Honking outside alerted her. Bauman waved from his Land Rover double-parked across the street. There was a text on her Nokia. *Here.*

You're early, she typed. She packed the small gift box with the driver's gloves in her leather handbag and placed the colorfully wrapped almond pastry on top. She was counting on Ibrahim's vanity to see the beauty of the gloves and not the tiny imperfection of the restitched seam. On her way out, she grabbed a cake slice from the refrigerator. She closed the refrigerator's door but reopened it and took the last piece of namoura, which she ate going downstairs.

As she crossed the street, she made a mental note of the Peugeot's license plate. She threw her handbag into Bauman's old Land Rover and slid in next to him in the front seat.

"What's wrong?"

She nodded at the Peugeot. "It wasn't there last night."

"I wasn't here last night either."

She waved off his glib dismissal. She glanced into the rear seat, where a tan backpack was partly covered by a blanket.

"How many antennas?"

"Thirty. What you requested. Each is matched against the tag's frequency. They have a range of about sixty meters. Enough to cover the neighborhood."

She climbed into the back seat and removed one from the backpack. It was the size of a small paperback, and a gray epoxied surface gave it the appearance of concrete. From a distance it would look like another piece of broken cinder block thrown from a bombed building. She turned it over in her hands—small, gritty surface, and easily placed.

"Remove the tape from the back and place the adhesive strip on a flat surface with a good line of sight."

How dangerous could it be? she thought. A UN worker moving through the neighborhood rummaging in the rubble of bombed buildings looking for artifacts to establish the type of ordnance dropped—no one would notice, but if they did, she had a reasonable story.

"We'll join the press convoy for the Hezbollah tour of last night's bombing. When we get there, you'll take the Land Rover and place the antennae. I'll catch a ride back to the hotel. And the gifts? You'll leave them at the boy's house?"

She nodded.

"Your plan. Let's hope it works."

The best plan, she knew, was the least intuitive, the most outrageous, and the one that no one anticipated. She owned the plan—success or failure.

"What does Corbin suspect?"

"He is so consumed by his suspicions about you that I'm invisible. You're the thorn in his side."

"He's a bored reporter with too much time on his hands. Boredom is the dry powder that ignites curiosity and it leads every reporter to look for a story. He thinks he's found a story in me." Bauman smiled and looked at his watch. "The press tour won't leave on time." He put the Land Rover in gear and did an abrupt U-turn. "There is something I want to show you. A short educational trip to help you understand what goes on in the mind of David Bauman. I don't have a dream, but I have a purpose. Maybe it's a kind of terrible dream. A nightmare."

He gripped the steering wheel and added in a sotto voce, "I saw the boy look at you. This is a complicated country. One day your neighbor greets you; the next day he points a gun. You need to understand my Lebanon."

Beirut's traffic was already congested. Everything was at a standstill in the street, and the throb of car engines mixed with the shouts of drivers cursing motor scooters that whipped through the gaps. The sun had risen and spread its sticky summer warmth over the narrow, clogged street, and cars inched forward. Pedestrians on the sidewalk moved past a one-legged militia veteran with his tin cup out, and in the throng, old ladies in black chadors mixed with young girls in tank tops. A mother held her child's hand. Delivery boys on bicycles slipped easily through the honking cars, drivers throwing casual insults at other drivers, who cursed back.

"I need to get a key to the cemetery gate." Bauman turned the Land Rover into an alley of old shops and deep shadows. "I'll be a minute."

13

The Living and the Dead

Analise stood in front of the display window of an antiquarian bookstore waiting for Bauman to return. He told her he'd be right back, but five minutes had passed, and then ten, and her attention drifted to the books in the window. She texted, *Where are you?*

She glanced at the reflection in the display window, looking for surveillance, but her eyes drifted to the Hebrew, French, and English books arranged in random disorder. Old titles with leather covers mixed with a few newer books. Bookstores had always appealed to her. Standing at the display window, she had a sudden urge to enter. Something in the odd, careless arrangement that wasn't meant to sell the books, but show them, intrigued her, as did the stenciled sign on the door, LIBRAIRIE. She surprised herself thinking that she should enter—that she had time. She remembered what her Lebanese grandmother had told her as a child. There were places you will come to in your life and you'll feel like you've been there before, but you won't remember when. *You must go in and see what there is.* Her grandmother's voice was in her ear, whispering, *Go in. Go in.*

A part of Analise resisted the idea, but the bookstore beckoned. For a moment, she thought she'd stood there before, in that exact spot, as a child. When no answer came from Bauman, she added, *Text me. I'm at the bookshop.*

A voice greeted her when she opened the door. "Come in."

She found herself in a small, darkened store with dim wall sconces and the smell of old, mildewed books. A worn prayer rug lay on the floor and there was an empty umbrella stand set into a nook. All the sensations of the place hit at once—the quiet mustiness of age, dim receding aisles, and the taste of warm humidity. The sharp clang of the closing door's bell startled her.

"*Marhaba.*" Then the man added in English, "What are you looking for?"

The man who spoke sat behind a cluttered desk in one corner by the umbrella stand. His short-sleeved shirt's collar was frayed and he wore a light cotton cloth pulled over his shoulders. He looked over wire-framed reading glasses that had slipped to the tip of his beaked nose and greeted her with a welcoming smile.

"Browsing," she said. "I'm waiting for someone. How long has the store been here?"

He turned his hand over and over, indicating endless time.

"Please," he said. His gnarled hand invited her in.

Analise moved to a dimly lit aisle lined with tall bookshelves. Her eyes scanned the books in the narrow space, gazing at the spines. She took a 1950s French pulp paperback, on the cover a handsome man in a business suit embracing a swooning woman in a bikini. Beside it, an English novel had a one-word title: *Sex*. She removed another book in English. Typed poetry on the right-hand pages resembled handwritten scraps on the left. An editor had transcribed the poet's handwritten scribblings with minor revisions and turned them into neatly typed, punctuated, and properly spaced poems.

The doorbell clanged and she heard the bookseller speak to a customer in Arabic. Analise pressed against the wall and turned to hide, but in doing so she bumped into Bauman. Startled, she stepped back. He pointed to the open page and looked at her with an expression she had never seen—curious, impressed, contemplating her interest.

"It's Marta Werner's transcription of Emily Dickinson's scraps of writing discovered after her death." He nodded. "Rafiq said you were browsing. We can get to the cemetery through the store's rear exit." Bauman pointed to the typed poems. "She's my favorite American poet. I've read all her work—in English, in French, and in Arabic. These are fragments of poems that she never got to finish, but it is an insight into what interested her at the end of her life. Reading these fragments is like having a conversation with a dead poet."

Bauman checked his watch. "We have time for me to show you one more book. Then the cemetery." He moved to a table with old manuscripts stacked at odd angles or standing between bookends. They were in a back corner of the shop. Old leather-bound books lay in no apparent order, Arabic and Hebrew mixed among French works. Bauman found what he was looking for and pulled out a dusty portfolio from a low shelf. He wiped the cover with his sleeve and turned the pages of old maps until he came to a two-page spread of the Middle East from an earlier era.

"This 1914 map shows the origin of Lebanon's tragedy." His finger moved across the facing pages. On the left side, the Ottoman Empire was a vast, undivided pink blush that stretched from the Bosporus to the Arabian Peninsula, and on the facing page, dated 1924, the former empire was divided into pink, black, green, and yellow zones marked with flags from England, France, Russia, and independent Turkey. "New boundaries cut through grazing land, towns, and ancient tribal areas; whole communities that had been indivisible were now carved up with heartless precision. My family held Turkish, French, and Lebanese passports in one generation while living in the same house."

Bauman closed the portfolio and looked at her. "Yes. I am Lebanese. I'll show you my Lebanon."

Bauman paused at the shopkeeper's desk and nodded respectfully to the bookseller. He led Analise toward the rear exit. As they moved to the back of the shop, he said, "My father brought me here as a boy. They were friends. They enjoyed the same poems of Abu al-Alaa al-Maarri, and he had deep affection for Emily Dickinson, which is how I discovered her. He was my father's loyal friend. He visited my mother after my father's abduction and was kind to her when other Lebanese friends shunned us."

He looked at Analise. "For that reason, he is safe." His hand went to Analise's elbow and he hustled through the rear door that led into a narrow alley filled with garbage and cats. "What I want to show you is two blocks away."

They moved along an old Roman wall where age had crumbled the limestone surface and revealed the stone underneath. Upon turning a corner, they came to an opening in the wall secured by a gate, and Bauman took a large iron key, which he used to undo its ancient lock. The heavy iron gate swung open and she followed him into a narrow passageway.

Analise stood at the entrance to an old cemetery of weathered stone crypts. Somber silence filled the quiet place. Time was paused for the dead. He closed the gate and approached an old woman in a black chador who sat on a rickety wood chair in the wall's shade. Her forehead was bronzed and wrinkled. He placed Lebanese pounds in her palm, greeting her respectfully in a dialect that Analise didn't recognize. Bauman knelt at her side and asked after her son, brightening her eyes. After a brief conversation about the small details of the cemetery's upkeep, he stood and put his hand on his heart. *"Allah yeh fazek."* God bless you.

Bauman moved toward the crypts and confided to Analise. "My father hired her to look after the cemetery when I was a boy, and she continues even now. She is from a Shiite clan east of Beirut. I send money every month."

A hot sun beat down on the gravestones, a few of which had toppled. No birds trespassed the inert air. She walked slowly by his side, gazing at the Hebrew inscriptions and from time to time seeing the French translation underneath.

As Analise walked, she was reminded of her junior year in college, when she had lived in Paris one fall and winter in an apartment near the cemetery at Montparnasse. It was a difficult time in her life. Her parents had divorced and she was divided between them—and their religions—and she was deeply depressed. Most mornings Montparnasse was covered with fog and she walked through the cold forest of the dead on her way to class. The path was empty at that hour and she looked at the graves, growing dizzy with thoughts of the lives laid to rest, pausing to contemplate a name, the dates that defined the parentheses of life on earth. Her curiosity came in seductive waves of wonder and sadness. It was quiet in the purling fog, but a quiet of musical serenity, and the walk past the graves always lifted her spirits. Valery's words came to her often as she crossed the cemetery: "The gift of life passed into flowers."

Those words came to her as she followed Bauman through the dry place, but her mind changed the phrase and "flowers" became "dust."

"Most of the Jews in Beirut are here," he said. "It is a miracle, if you are the sort of person who believes in miracles, that so few graves are defaced." His hand swept across the cemetery. "This is the story of the Middle East. Cairo, Tehran, Damascus. The Jews have left. Only the dead remain."

Bauman approached one group of headstones that bore the same name. "My family arrived in Lebanon two hundred years ago. They lived in a small village in the mountains. Seventy years ago, there were five thousand Jews in Lebanon."

He paused and looked. "Jews lived in good relations with their neighbors."

She heard thick irony in his voice.

"Then the violence broke out—the first wave of violence of the 1950s. Many left for France, Canada, Israel, and Argentina. Today, there are fifty-seven Jews in Lebanon."

His eyes moved across the rows of crypts, the names effaced by weather and a few by vandalism, before settling on the grave in front of him. The year of death was 1985, but no day was recorded. He stood quietly for a moment and then leaned forward and touched the name carved in stone.

"My father." His voice lowered. "He was an officer in the Lebanese army and then a prosperous merchant. Many Jews left during the Arab-Israeli war. Some who refused to leave were targeted. My father was a man who thought of himself first as Lebanese and then as a Jew. That was his mistake. He was clever in business, and in other ways, but he was an idealist, which made him naïve."

Bauman's judgment was matter of fact.

"The first to be taken was my father's friend Isaac Sasson. He was kidnapped and then killed by his captors, a Shiite group called the Organization of the Oppressed of the Earth, a Hezbollah splinter group. After that, Jews in Beirut refused to be seen in public or have their photos taken. Everyone was apprehensive, including my parents, but my father believed that good men needed to speak out against the thugs. He refused to be intimidated. He was proud. He believed in Lebanon, but he was incurably idealistic. He made the mistake of believing that if he treated others respectfully, he'd be respected. He was kidnapped, tortured, murdered.

"I was a boy. You can imagine how difficult it was for us—a Jewish widow and her seven-year-old son. We left with two suitcases and whatever cash she could raise by selling jewelry, furniture, heirlooms, and the house. We left our home, my friends, and found our way one night to a trawler in the harbor that took us to her cousin in South Africa. The civil war had come. There was no place for us in Beirut."

Bauman paused. A cloud had passed overhead, blocking the sun and deepening the grim conviction on his face.

"Before we left, my mother changed our name after he was killed, but the threats continued. Our home was marked, his business bankrupted by competitors who took advantage of his death. We didn't understand how this could happen—and so quickly. I was kept home from school. Stones were thrown at our windows. Later, when we talked about it, she admitted that she saw the signs. But she and my father couldn't believe that Beirut—their Beirut—could change so quickly. They'd met in Beirut, married there, and they had Muslim friends. That world vanished. Beirut became a one-way street for Jews. There was no staying. Only the very old and the dead stayed."

"Were they caught?"

"His killers? No."

"Who were they?"

"It took me five years to find the first name. Qassem. Then I found a few others. Khoury. Siniora. Two men who are prosperous merchants, now in parliament. Both took over my father's customers. They have found it convenient to be less violent because the appearance of respectability advances their businesses. Another is in the ISF. One is the port administrator. It was thirty-one years ago. They are now in their fifties. Wiser now, more prosperous, with reputations to protect. They would like to bury the past." Bauman repeated the names slowly, like a prosecutor reading an indictment.

He looked at his father's grave, where the inscription below the name was newer. "In Hebrew it says, 'Blessed be the Righteous.'"

Bauman stared at the grave, his face a mix of sadness, grief, and anger.

"Come. We must go. Now you know."

Analise didn't move. She remained where she stood, head lowered in contemplation.

"What are you doing?"

"Praying."

Bauman said nothing, but touched her elbow to urge her along. "A nice gesture, but prayers won't change the past."

He led the way to the iron gate, and upon passing the Shia woman, he nodded respectfully. *"Allah ma'ik."*

Outside, he glanced at his watch. "We need to join the Hezbollah press tour. Another day, I'll show you my home. It's in Wadi Aba Jamil, the old Jewish quarter, a ten-minute walk from the St. Georges Hotel. A Shiite family lives there. I know their name, but it's their house now."

"Have you visited?"

"What would I say? 'Hello, this was my childhood home before my father was murdered.' There is no point. Nothing would be the same. The rooms, the furnishings, the walls. I was seven when we left. What does a seven-year-old remember? Only fantasies and secrets and the pleasant mist of nostalgia. I prefer to keep it that way. Whatever is there now would disappoint me and I would distress the family if I told them that the house they lived in once belonged to a Jew. They can keep the house and I'll keep my memories."

Bauman passed through the gate but paused at the brass plaque that identified the cemetery for passing tourists in French, Hebrew, and Arabic.

"I grew up speaking Arabic. I spoke Hebrew, but it wasn't the language that I used every day. Arabic was the language of my youth. I spoke Arabic with my friends, and now I live in linguistic exile. English is a practical language, French a pretentious language for the Lebanese elite, Hebrew the language of my work, but Arabic is the language of my youth. I dream in Arabic." Bauman looked at Analise. "I want the same thing as Halima. We both love Lebanon, but we hate what it has become. We both want the old Beirut back." He paused. "Nothing survives except the land." His voice deepened. "The land and the dead."

14

The South

Bauman's words were still with Analise when they arrived at the Commodore Hotel to join the Hezbollah press tour to the southern suburbs. He'd continued to talk, explaining what they would say if militia found the RFID antennae. Analise didn't answer because there was no reason to correct his assessment, and she was still pondering his earlier comment. The idea that land survived was obvious, but less obvious was what he meant when he'd added that the dead survive. At first, she thought he was being ironic, but she had never known him to speak ironically, and so she mulled it over. Death closed the parenthesis of life, passing into eternal sleep, and perhaps that was his meaning, but she couldn't help but think he intended something else.

Analise sat on the Land Rover's passenger side and watched Bauman in the driver's seat talking to a Hezbollah press attaché. Bauman's face was turned away, but she tried to penetrate his mind to understand him. He was a scrupulously cautious intelligence officer, but under stress even the best spy could let slip a compromising comment.

"When do we leave?" Bauman asked the press attaché.

Baalbak Street in front of the hotel was thick with motor scooters and Hezbollah militia moving among the dozen gathered foreign press vehicles. Excited cries and loud orders in English, Arabic, or French urging journalists and photographers to board a vehicle were everywhere.

Analise's eyes shifted from Bauman to the young, bearded press attaché who spoke a crude French. His automatic weapon was slung over his shoulder and he looked into the Land Rover's rear seat at the backpacks with RFID antennae.

"There isn't room," Bauman said politely. "We're full."

"Make room."

Having lost the argument, Bauman leaned back and placed the two backpacks in the rear compartment under a blanket, beside a plastic container with extra gasoline. Analise watched him secure the flaps so the contents didn't spill out, and turned back to the windshield to find herself face-to-face with Corbin.

"Nice to ride with old friends," he said.

She hid her surprise but was less successful in hiding her irritation.

"We'll be good company," Corbin said, making room for his companion. The heavyset photographer slipped in, holding his twin 35mm digital cameras in one hand and his video camera in the other. He heaved himself into an uncomfortable position with little legroom.

"Bloody English engineering," he grunted. "You're American. You wouldn't know."

"What?" she said, looking at Corbin.

"He hates the English."

"I don't hate the English. I have nothing against the colonial bastards. It's a lovely weakened country with a big useless history."

For a moment, Analise thought Corbin's presence was a chance event—but she also knew that it was a mistake to ignore how the magic hand of chance played a role in human affairs. The appearance of coincidence was a clever act—like his hand in her purse.

"You show up where I least expect," she said.

"I think it's the other way around. Is this UN business, or are you enjoying the company?"

"More refugees arrived overnight. This is the safest way to travel to the camps."

Corbin nodded at Bauman. "The Israelis wouldn't bomb a Land Rover driven by a celebrity war reporter."

Bauman turned. "Good to have you with us. To lighten the mood. Let me know when you've got something funny to say." He threw two plastic liter bottles of water into the back seat. "Courtesy of Hezbollah." He looked at the photographer. "Who are you?"

"Simon Bekker. G'day, mate." He turned to Analise. "Nice to see you again, dearie."

Her first impulse was to shove the toothpick in his mouth down his throat. "My name isn't dearie."

"Humble apologies." He smiled crudely. "Looking forward to our little outing into the belly of the beast." He lifted a camera. "My editor wants pictures to excite the sympathies of ladies and gentlemen reading the morning paper."

A circus atmosphere filled the narrow street, but then somewhere a loud cry, an order. "*Suivre le camionette.*" The frenzy resolved into the hasty boarding of vehicles, and the lead press van started forward. A black Mercedes followed, and behind it came the Volkswagen bus crowded with stringers hanging out open windows, and Bauman's Land Rover was last.

A midday sun was bleeding over the tops of buildings on the narrow street, and the convoy burst onto the boulevard and into the day's heat. The vehicles sped along the wide avenue at a high speed to avoid attracting attention from people who cursed Western journalists' depiction of the war.

"Open the windows," Bauman said. "AC is broken." Bauman looked in the rearview mirror at Corbin. "What a coincidence you're riding with us."

Traffic was light on the drive south and evidence of the week's bombing increased as they passed the airport's cratered runways. Twice they diverted around collapsed bridges, moving onto rutted gravel tracks that caused the Land Rover to bounce around. To the south, the smoldering Jiyyeh power station fuel tanks sent acrid smoke into the air, and one by one they closed the windows, adding to the car's stifling heat. Analise, suffering from the heat, opened her window again.

The photographer had stopped talking, but when foul air entered, he made a crude sexual joke. No one laughed.

He lifted a middle finger. "Piss off."

Analise knew the photographer's crack was meant for her. She faced him. "Insult me again and I'll make sure you walk your bloody self back to whatever shithole sewer you climb out of when you wake up in the morning."

They were taking a detour to avoid a damaged overpass. The signs of war were evident in the twisted steel sprouting from shattered concrete slabs that lay around a wide bomb crater. A few cars raced past, heading north. All were packed with families—old women in head scarves, mothers clutching their infants, drivers with grim, desperate expressions. One car had flimsy cardboard boxes lashed to its roof, and the trunk overflowed with suitcases. White flags were attached to its side mirrors. It was followed by a red convertible carrying a young driver and two teenage girls with dyed hair holding pistols in the air.

"Terrorists," Bauman said.

"You don't know that," Corbin said.

"They're all here. PLO, Hezbollah, the Syrians."

Corbin leaned forward and looked at Bauman. "You were in Syria. What were you doing there?"

Bauman turned. "I don't know what you're talking about. Is this the joke you promised?"

Corbin turned to Analise. "Did you ask him why he was in Syria?"

"No."

The photographer spoke up. "Why were you in Syria?"

"Fuck off," Bauman said.

The car was sweltering and Analise had turned away from the argument. Acrid smoke from the refinery darkened one part of the sky and deepened her mood. Wind coming in the window billowed the folds of her head scarf and for a long while she simply gazed at the refugees in passing cars and the roadside bomb damage, thinking about what she had to do and how she would do it. Occasionally, an Israeli jet got her attention, or she heard one of the men in the Land Rover gripe about this or that, but then they stopped talking. She felt calmer, thinking ahead to what she must do. The press of the afternoon's work took her mind off the week ahead, and the year that had passed. She felt an urgency to finish her mission and leave Beirut.

They were coming to a section of road cratered by bombs. Almost lightheadedly, she felt the Land Rover zigzag around the debris. Someone had turned on the radio and the upbeat melody of the Europop music was at odds with the grim landscape. She thought that this was how she would die, listening to silly music when a bomb struck.

"What's that?" the photographer said, pointing.

A family of three sat on the ground in the meager shade of a stalled Mercedes, and beyond it, in a culvert, an exploded van lay on its side, smoke coming off the engine block that had been thrown from the chassis.

"That's a phosphorous bomb," the photographer said, lifting his camera toward the destroyed vehicle. "Banned weapon. It melts steel and incinerates flesh. I need to get a photo of that. Stop the car."

"It's not safe." Bauman pointed at the young man, who had stood. His wife held an infant child, who she shaded from the midday sun and cradled with a mother's deep concern. "It's a trap."

The mother waved a light cloth over the child's flushed face.

"The child is sick," the photographer said.

"Or dead," Bauman said. "This isn't our business. We have to stay with the convoy."

Analise turned away from the argument. She didn't have the will to add her view or the strength to weigh in on the family's plight. Too many scenes of violence had numbed her senses and taken a toll.

"I need you to stop," the photographer said.

"We're not stopping," Bauman said.

"For Christ's sake, they're not terrorists." Analise's outburst startled the men.

Silence lingered in the Land Rover. The driver of the Mercedes had begun to run alongside the slowly moving Land Rover, pleading breathlessly, making a motion for something to drink.

Analise took a water bottle and threw it out the window at the man, who caught it and dropped back, stumbling. Analise saw him stand, palms pressed together in gratitude.

Bauman gripped the steering wheel and drove faster to catch up with the convoy. No one in the Land Rover spoke.

It wasn't until they neared the press rendezvous that Corbin stirred. He rode quietly in the back seat, staring out the window. He pondered what had happened. Once, he glanced at the back of Analise's head. He thought he knew her, or knew her as much as anyone could know another person, but what had happened in the Land Rover made him think that he didn't know her at all. Her outrage at Bauman's indifference and her simple act of kindness had surprised him. He began to see other things she'd done in a different light, unsure what to make of her.

Corbin joined the other journalists walking in the narrow street, looking around at downed electric wires, cut and piled in mounds, and further along at the Coral gas station, where a queue of men with plastic containers waited for rationed gasoline. He thought it looked familiar, matching landmarks to his vague recollections, and then he knew he'd been there before. A different night of bombing. An earlier press tour. He saw a building reduced to a huge mound of concrete, sprouting rebar.

"We were here," Bekker said. "Same neighborhood. Al-Manar TV is over there. I remember the girls at the spigot, nymphs around a fountain."

Corbin saw the Land Rover was gone and turned to Bauman. "Where did Analise go?"

"She left."

Corbin waited for Bauman to say more, but all he saw was a dismissive expression of polite contempt, a man with eyes more dull than wise, a smile that was not a smile. Corbin looked where the Land Rover had been, seeking an answer to Bauman's indifference. He must have looked too long, because Bauman added, "She had work to do."

"She'll get lost."

"She knows what she's doing."

15

Haret Hreik

Analise moved toward the alley, listening for a warning cry from the mix of Syrian, Palestinian, and Lebanese dialects in the narrow street—alert and wary. Young boys played video games at an outdoor arcade under a tangle of overhead electric wires, and old men chatted amiably in a barbershop window, watching her. A huge faded poster of Yassir Arafat looked down from a billboard onto passing motor scooters that sputtered black exhaust.

Her handbag was inside the backpack slung over her shoulder. The last RFID antenna had been placed on an electric substation so the brick-like object could be mistaken for a piece of concrete. Two Hezbollah guards slouched casually midway up the block, sharing a cigarette and chatting with the relaxed concentration of bored sentries. AK-47s slung over their shoulders, they took an interest in a shouting match between a deliveryman and the irate driver of a motor scooter.

Fifty meters away, two SUVs were parked in front of Rami's home. That day it was a Jeep and an old Toyota. She remembered them from the drone footage. The drone's two-dimensional black-and-white world was replaced by a vivid three-dimensional streetscape. Everything in front of her was alive with color and motion and danger. From memory, she recovered the details that she needed to confirm: the guards, the SUVs, the sight line for the spotter, and the bright green wood door that sat innocuously among other doors along the street. The attached three-story house stood in the middle of the short street with little to distinguish it from its neighbors. Other houses on the street, reflecting the decent lives within, had windows open with washing hung out to dry.

Positioning the antennae had gone as expected and the Land Rover gave her the freedom to return to West Beirut when convenient. Her blue beret was in her bag and she wore a loose cotton jacket to cover her bare arms. She fixed her head scarf, drawing the cloth down on her forehead, and settled her nerves.

Analise approached the bright green door with her bag of wrapped gifts. She was aware of the inquisitive men who sat in the barbershop and she saw one boy in the arcade take interest. She assumed that they knew what went on in the house and the appearance of a stranger excited their curiosity. Gray metal louvers covered the first-floor windows and kept out the afternoon sun, but the double doors on the second-floor balcony were thrown open for the breeze. She took in the details, recorded them, and kept them in the back of her mind for the unforeseen future when her life might depend on what she knew.

Her hand was raised to knock when the door opened. The woman who stood before Analise was the same height, younger, and dressed in white slacks and a tightly wrapped turquoise hijab that gave prominence to her brown eyes, olive skin, and aquiline nose. She saw a similarity to Rami's narrow face and intense expression. *A woman not yet thirty with two teenage children*, she thought.

"You are Rami's teacher," the woman said with a welcoming smile. "I am Fatima." She offered her hand. *"Marhaba."*

"Analise." She nodded politely.

"I know your name."

Fatima leaned forward and exchanged three kisses, alternating cheeks, surprising Analise. "Come in. We are expecting you. Rami told us you would be coming. He said you had news about my daughter. Is she well?"

Analise heard concern in her voice. It wasn't ordinary concern, but the worry of a mother for a much-loved daughter soon to be married off. "She is in the hills with friends enjoying the cool weather." A detail of truth helped put the mother at ease.

"Come in."

Light seeped through the closed louvers, dimly illuminating a small dark vestibule. Fatima led her to an interior door, which she opened. Lamps on side tables combined with an overhead chandelier of colorful glass gave the room a warm, lived-in feeling. Worn carpets covered the floor, and an ensemble of low chairs was arranged around a mosaic coffee table. Pale green walls were bare. A large television with rabbit ears dominated one side of the room, and on the other side was a plush sofa with a small table. A Koran was prominently displayed and its ivory cloth bag sat beside it. The Koran's black cover was ornately etched in gold and its leather frayed from age and use. Silence in the room was punctuated by sounds on the street and a male voice somewhere deeper in the house.

Fatima had left but now returned with a tray that held four demitasse cups, sugar, a long-handled pot, and a plate of delicate biscuits. Cinnamon mixed with the aroma of coffee.

"Sit."

Analise took a chair and opened the backpack at her feet. "I have gifts for you."

She handed the square box wrapped in patterned gift paper to Fatima, who carefully removed the wrapping.

"*Ghazel el banet*," Analise said. "It's from my favorite pastry shop in Hamra."

Fatima admired the individually wrapped cotton-candy sweets topped with pistachios, and offered one, but Analise declined.

"This is for your husband." She produced a flat rectangular box wrapped in tissue paper.

"He will be here shortly." She set it aside and poured coffee, handing Analise a cup. "How is my daughter?"

"Happy. Enjoying the holidays and her friends. She wishes you to know she is preparing herself." Analise saw anxiety in the mother's eyes. She could not imagine the burden Fatima carried, a defiant daughter looking to her mother for comfort.

Analise produced the photoshopped photograph showing Nafeeza's face shadowed in the back row among the eleven girls standing by the wood table. A distant shot. The girls were small and the late afternoon light reduced the photograph's resolution.

"This was a few days ago. See how happy she is. The hills are cool and the war is distant."

Fatima looked intently, turning the photograph to catch the light from the lamp. Analise pointed to Nafeeza in the back row.

"Why is she the only one with a head scarf?"

"She is a good Muslim girl."

Fatima studied the picture, drawing it closer, then she handed it back and looked directly at Analise. "She isn't happy." She looked at Analise, evaluating her, judging her.

A man entered the room suddenly, bringing Fatima to her feet. Analise stood as well. She recognized Ibrahim, the driver, and saw deep apprehension on Fatima's face. He'd entered through another door, which he shut when he saw Analise, but in the moment it was open she spotted three bearded men sitting in front of laptops at a long table.

Ibrahim was thick-chested, heavy, and gruff, and he glanced at Analise with deep suspicion. Fatima presented the gift and whispered rapidly in Arabic. It was not until he took the gift that he acknowledged Analise.

He tore the tissue wrapping, handing it to his wife. He examined the leather gloves without any reaction. His eyes were dull and unappreciative. A burly man with fat fingers and a wine-colored Polo shirt that didn't quite cover his belly. He put his right hand in the glove, pulling it onto his fingers, working the new leather over his thick hand, and then he tried on the other. He attached the Velcro over each wrist, tightening the fit. He worked the gloves between his fingers and presented his hands to his wife, satisfied.

A perfect fit, Analise thought. She waited for him to discover the restitched leather seam on the right glove, but he was too pleased with the gift to notice the imperfection.

Ibrahim crossed the room and stood in front of Analise. Fatima spoke quickly in Arabic, explaining that she was Rami's teacher.

"I know who she is," he said, dismissing his wife. Ibrahim let his eyes drift over Analise. She felt the creepy sensation that he was mentally undressing her.

"Thank you," he said.

She averted her eyes. "*Shukran tasharraa fna.*" I am honored to meet you.

"*Bitikalami Araby.*"

She nodded and saw his suspicion.

"Your family name? How do you spell it?"

Analise had been asked that before and the question was never innocent. "Asad" and "Assad" were common transliterated spellings of the Muslim name, but different versions obscured clan and religious associations.

"A-S-S-A-D," she said. "Like Basher."

"You are from Lebanon?"

"My father."

"Where was he born? What village?"

She knew the danger. Outside of Beirut, in mountain villages, blood feuds passed from one generation to the next, neighbor against neighbor, and the hatred persisted long after the original insult was forgotten. Grudges against killers were handed down from father to son, and often no one knew how the feud began, or how to end it. Lebanese were difficult people to understand—green sorrow and great endurance for revenge. She gave the name of a village in the south, cleared by agency analysts who'd created her legend.

"Have you been there?"

"As a child. It's not safe now. My grandmother had a farm but she died."

"May Allah bless her memory." He looked at her. "I want to meet your father."

"He left in the civil war." She added a few details about the village and the farmhouse, using the word *mahjour*, which she knew meant abandoned, forsaken, lonely, a place that had gone through difficult times.

Ibrahim raised his hand in an exaggerated gesture of great lament. "We all suffered then." He looked at her. "Rami speaks well of you." He shouted Rami's name. "He is difficult. Boys his age need discipline."

Rami entered the room, glancing at Analise, and approached his stepfather. Ibrahim cuffed him with his palm and Rami's hand rose to protect himself from a second blow, but it didn't come, only a playful threat.

"Why didn't you tell me your teacher was bringing a gift?" Ibrahim ruffled Rami's hair affectionately, then pushed him away.

Rami retreated to the television, where he stood quietly, his face sullen, his eyes dark. He looked intently at the floor.

"Now he's angry at me," Ibrahim said. "So be it. He has a sister. Disobedient like him. You've met her. Soon she will bring honor to the family. A big wedding is planned. I have paid a fortune. There will be many guests. Lambs will be slaughtered." He smiled.

Ibrahim presented his gloves. "How did you know my glove size?"

"One size fits all."

He laughed. "A clever answer."

"Rami said you have strong hands, so I bought the large size."

"*Shukran.*" He presented his two hands with the fine leather gloves snugly fitted. "I am a professional driver. I know Beirut and Damascus better than any other driver. I have driven in Cairo, Aman, Yemen." His chest rose boastfully. "I drove Anthony Quinn. He was in Beirut making a movie about the Prophet Mohammad, and I was a young man who knew English, so I drove him. My first celebrity. I also drove the Prince of Wales. He didn't know a word of Arabic. He was with a friend and they asked me to take them to the ruins. I misunderstood them. He meant the Roman ruins, but I took him to the ruins of the bombed American embassy."

Ibrahim touched Analise's elbow, indicating she should sit.

"I must go," she said, apologizing. She suddenly remembered a surprise that wasn't a surprise. "I brought this award that Rami earned." From the backpack, she removed a small plaque. A brass plate on the wood base was engraved with Rami's name.

"This is the school's writing award," she said. "It is given to the student athlete whose writing has feeling, vivid images, wordplay, and comes from the heart. It is a high honor. The award comes with a travel stipend to join the school's team to compete in the Paris regional soccer tournament. We are delighted for him. I have arranged his departure."

Ibrahim took the award and tossed it back at her. "Poetry?" His words were mocking. "He has no need for this. He won't travel to Paris."

Rami, who had been standing sullenly by the wall, ran from the room, disappearing through the door from which Ibrahim had entered, and in his abrupt escape he left the door wide open. Behind it, another open door led to an interior room. Bearded men inside looked up, startled to be visible through the open door. Wary tension stirred among them when they saw Analise watching them. Fatima went to follow Rami, but Ibrahim restrained her.

"Leave him. He needs to understand disappointment."

A grandfatherly man appeared in the second doorway, affectionately comforting Rami with an arm around his shoulders. He was of medium height with a close-cropped beard and graying hair combed back on his head. He wore a lightweight, loose-fitting sport jacket over a white shirt, and cloth slippers.

Analise instantly recognized Qassem. In person, he was kinder-looking than in his file photographs. His dark eyes flashed with irritation when he saw Analise. He judged her clothing, her skin color, her gender, and her foreignness. A man who didn't want to be seen or photographed was being looked at, and he disliked the unexpected attention. He patted Rami on the shoulder and sent him on his way to the street before he shut both doors.

Perspiration dampened Analise's neck, and the palpable fear of being in Qassem's presence made the muscles on the back of her neck constrict. Her visit over, she put the award in her backpack and moved toward the door. Behind her, she overheard angry whispers as Fatima confronted Ibrahim. Analise knew not to intervene. It wasn't up to her to understand the family's unique unhappiness.

Analise was at the front door when she heard her name. She turned and found Fatima, who apologized for her husband's rudeness and politely expressed gratitude for Analise's help. Fatima's trusting face made Analise feel uncomfortable and she averted her eyes. "Your daughter is safe. I will look after her."

16

In the Box

You've met my family," Rami said. He was leaning against the parked Land Rover and looked up when Analise approached. She had parked the vehicle a five-minute walk from the house and had walked back slowly to avoid attracting attention. He had been throwing stones at a pigeon standing on a nearby ledge. He threw another stone and the pigeon stepped aside, puffing its feathers, taunting his lackadaisical effort.

She saw a Disney-branded tote bag on the ground at his feet. She heard his comment as a judgment. "Your mother loves you."

His hand dismissed her remark. "What she thinks doesn't matter. I'm coming with you." He threw one more stone, sending the pigeon into the air, and picked up his bag. He tried the passenger door.

"It's locked."

Rami held up a long metal sleeve used to break into cars. "It was locked." He sat in the passenger seat, placing his tote bag at his feet.

"You have to go home."

"Home? To what? I'm coming with you."

There was no point arguing with him. She considered the complication. Analise got behind the wheel and placed her hijab on the seat. "Fine," she said in a low voice.

She inserted the key in the ignition. Plans change. Adjust to the circumstance. *Fuck*. Part of her wished that everything was over—the lies, the deception, the killing. "Seat belt." She added, "Stay down. You shouldn't be seen riding with me."

Analise knew the route and avoided streets that she had walked earlier while deploying the antennae. Analise organized what she remembered of the scene in the house, rehearsing how she would describe it. There was no intelligence that indicated the house had a large interior room. Laptops, servers, cables dropped from the ceiling, and the cool air of an air-conditioned facility. Her mind went over her time in the house minute by minute, separating each chaotic impression into a logic grid. Her mind's eye looked past the distraction of Qassem's appearance to the activity in the room behind him. Papers spread on the table, multiple computer screens, and the appearance of an operations center. She'd heard a voice speaking urgently through a computer speaker. A different dialect that she had not recognized. Her memory of the room was clear but the mystery of what they were doing tugged at her.

She glanced at Rami. They were traveling north through a bombed section of the refugee camp. He sat low in the seat, staring out the window. "Who were the men in the room?"

He stared at her for a long moment and then looked back out the window. "I don't know."

A lie, she thought. Analise considered calling Aldrich on her Nokia, but her phone wasn't encrypted. The risk of blowing her cover was more critical than the urgency of her discovery.

Cell-phone intercepts in the neighborhood would pick up a trace, and even if the call wasn't recorded, it might be flagged. An alert Hezbollah technician could triangulate the call's origin from cell towers and match the number against a target list of suspected cell numbers. Qassem knew he was being observed by drones and he would ask who the foreign woman was. It would only be a matter of time before the call was associated with her presence.

"Why so many computers?"

"It's not your business."

She steered the Land Rover through the light traffic.

"You're quiet," she said.

"When do I leave for Paris? What is the plan for me?"

There had never been a real plan to get him to Paris. The assassination was meant to have happened and she was meant to be away by now—gone, vanished, disappeared. She had groomed the boy and now she was responsible for the consequences of his trust.

"What are you thinking?" he asked.

"Stay down. No one should see you."

They were passing through a section of the camp that was being cleared of rubble from the week's bombing. Analise gently pushed him further down into the well of the front seat. Months of work were at risk because a thirteen-year-old boy suddenly decided to run away. His disappearance from home would go unchallenged for a day, maybe two, if a good excuse could be invented, but his mother would ask around. Analise could send him back but that would anger him and he would likely reveal his sister's evacuation. From there, the whole elaborate fabric of subterfuge would begin to unravel. She had no choice. She had to go along with what he expected of her. It was the only way to buy time to finish gathering information on Qassem's route. She had always known that Rami was the plan's single point of failure.

"Stay down."

Having turned north along a wide street, she came upon a recently bombed mosque. A convoy of refugees in old cars had been caught in the attack, and a small group of people—men, women in Western dress, and children—were talking and crying all at once. A tall man in a green T-shirt walked along the edge of a bomb crater. He appeared to be in shock, walking back and forth, trembling and shouting; several men tried to calm him down. He was soaked in sweat. His pregnant wife was wounded, having been in the lead car, and now was sitting on the sidewalk in the company of a young woman. Behind them, the bombed mosque was a ruin.

The man approached Analise in the Land Rover, eyes wide with anger. He shouted, "You were there yesterday with the others. I talked to you. And now they bomb us."

Analise didn't recognize the man but remembered visiting a shelter. She saw a three-banded cross tattoo on his neck and knew he was a Maronite Christian. The group had been traveling north, away from the Shia-held suburbs.

Analise got out of the car and went over to the woman. Her face was flushed, one hand on her swollen belly, and the young woman at her side dabbed her forehead with a wet cloth. Shrapnel had ripped her blouse, exposing a bloody shoulder wound that was crudely dressed with torn cloth from her companion's blouse. She looked up at Analise with eyes wide with fear and pain. *No more than twenty or twenty-five years old*, Analise thought.

"Have you called an ambulance?"

The husband confronted Analise fiercely. "There are no ambulances for us in this neighborhood."

Analise took out her Nokia, but there was no signal. She looked back at the Land Rover, where Rami's head poked above the dashboard, and then turned to the pregnant woman. She briefly thought that this was not her problem, but then she felt the terrible pull of the woman's desperation.

"She can come with me." Analise pointed to the Land Rover. "Put her in the back seat. I'll take her to the hospital. Only the two women."

"What's happening?" Rami asked when Analise opened the rear door.

"Nothing to do with you."

Analise sat behind the steering wheel and looked into the back, where the pregnant woman was being attended to by her companion. She handed them a bottle of water.

"It's fifteen minutes. Not far."

The Land Rover emerged from a narrow alley into an intersection crowded with men. Some were laborers covered in fine gray dust, others carried guns, but all crossed the street indifferent to the stop sign. Analise waited for the crowd to move on, and she felt the drumbeat of impatience loudly in the silence.

One man happened to glance into the Land Rover's windshield and stared at Analise.

His eyes flashed a particular type of anger. She recognized the look of rage and depravity that a deeply conservative Shia Muslim felt toward a foreign woman with uncovered hair. She had not seen it in Beirut, but she had seen it in Iraq, and she saw it on that man's face. She averted her eyes and grabbed her scarf to cover her head, but in turning away she saw the whole of him: wispy beard, dark angry eyes, keffiyeh, and a long, sheathed knife at his waist.

"Cover yourselves," she said in Arabic to the women in the back.

Analise stared past him into the distance and gripped the steering wheel, waiting for the light to change. A UNESCO billboard across the street advertised the benefits of milk. There was a modern image of a woman holding a glass of milk for a child.

Someone had defaced the sign, ripping off the shaming image of the woman's eyes and mouth.

Her fingers tapped out the seconds until she could drive.

The man remained in front of the Land Rover while his companions crossed the street. He moved closer, peering through the windshield, and he smirked. He planted himself and pumped his arms and hips, simulating a sex act. He grinned rudely and yelled at her to get out of the Land Rover.

She knew not to engage him and she avoided his eyes, waiting for him to tire of his crude antics. He spat on the windshield. When Analise did nothing, he pounded on the hood and shouted an obscenity. Analise looked in the rearview mirror and saw that a pickup truck had pulled up behind her, blocking her retreat.

"What's happening?" Rami asked.

"Stay down." She saw confusion on the faces of the women in the back. "Stay quiet."

The man's lewd behavior drew the attention of workmen clearing debris from a nearby building. They dropped their shovels and approached. Two called out and were joined by others, who gathered from different places to surround the Land Rover. A big woman with two children stopped and stared at the back seat.

One bearded man stepped out of the crowd and pushed his face against the driver's side window. His nose was flattened against the glass, and his mouth had opened to show tobacco-stained teeth. Another crossed in front and pressed close to the passenger window. He tried the door handle, jerking harder the second time, and then his palm slapped the glass. Voices outside called out, summoning more people.

"Stay down," she said, trying to be calm.

How did she not see this coming? She had to get off the box. It had happened once in Iraq. People died doing nothing. Fight, flight, or freeze. The worst place to be was at the site of an IED attack. Crowds were drawn to the spot, increasing the danger, and the momentum of the crowd fueled the fury. Her hand moved to her holstered Glock.

Fists pounded on the Land Rover's windows, and then the encircling men began to rock the vehicle, pushing and tugging. Analise's world got very small and very dark. She calibrated her thinking to control her fear and tried not to look in their eyes. Angry men shouting terrible things. She looked around, counting, and remembered to breathe.

She pressed the accelerator, loudly revving the engine, startling the men in front. Caution was alive on their faces, and several pulled back. The bearded man unsheathed his knife and stepped forward as others withdrew. Loud cries drew attention, and several men with AK-47s hurried along the street to join the crowd. Somewhere outside, she heard a voice raise the alarm of an Israeli spy. *I am not going to die here.*

Her hand shifted the gear and she took her foot off the clutch. The Land Rover lurched forward. The bearded man jumped back, and she repeated the motion, foot releasing the clutch while her hand worked the emergency brake. The Land Rover lurched forward again and again, pushing the man back. He saw her game and stood his ground directly in the vehicle's path. Analise pressed on the gas and struck him, sending him flying several feet.

She had reached the point of no return. Men gathered around the fallen man, helping him to his feet. He threw off their assistance and approached the car with his long, curved knife, his fiery eyes looking for blood.

Analise pointed the Glock, sending the men back a few steps. A small gap opened in the crowd and she accelerated through it. The rear tires spun and sent a cloud of dust into the crowd. She drove straight through the narrow opening, making people jump out of the way. She gripped the steering wheel and felt the adrenaline rush of fear, waiting for a bullet to shatter the rear windshield or pierce a tire. She drove straight ahead toward Damascus Street and the safety beyond.

Rami raised his head. The pregnant woman moaned and her companion screamed in Arabic. *"Alaynā al'isrā'a."* We must hurry.

Analise pressed the accelerator to the floor, causing a man crossing the street to jump back onto the sidewalk, cursing. In the rearview mirror, Analise confirmed there were no pickup trucks in pursuit. Her knuckles on the steering wheel had gone white and she was trembling.

17

The Panel Van

W hat happened to the woman?" Gal asked.
  "The baby was saved."

"You compromised the mission," Bauman said. "It's not your job to be an ambulance driver."

"I work for the UN," she said. "I help refugees. Did you forget?"

Gal raised a hand to intervene. "Where is the boy now?"

Analise sat across from Bauman and Gal in the rear of the Agence France-Presse van parked in the shaded cul-de-sac of a quiet street on the campus of the American University of Beirut. Aldrich was behind her, looking at the computer monitor, but his attention shifted to her.

"He's safe. Nearby." She returned to the red dots on the computer screen that were arrayed with information recieved from the antennae. "What have you collected?"

"First, the boy," Gal said. "Where did it happen?"

She pointed to a spot on the monitor's map. "Here."

"Why did you wait to tell us?"

"It was four days ago. What was I supposed to do, pick up the phone and say, 'Oh, by the way, I had a problem and now the boy is with me'?"

"Yes," Bauman said.

Analise stared at Bauman and glanced at Aldrich, but no one said anything for a moment. Gal raised his hand slowly, his face patient. "It is done. We won't waste time on what might have been. I always say there are only two reliable disappointments, bad luck and the lottery." He smiled. "You had bad luck. Did anyone recognize you?"

"As what? A woman?"

Gal put a hand on her shoulder. "I can only imagine how it must have felt. We move forward. The boy is a risk. He must be moved to Paris. We have good data, but not good enough yet."

"Does the boy suspect anything?" Bauman asked.

"How can she answer that?" Aldrich asked. "How would she know? If she has been compromised, I have no choice. She has no diplomatic immunity. NOCs are on their own." He looked at Gal. "I would have to pull her out."

"Of course." Gal smiled. "I would do the same. But she is confident, so we move forward. Nothing has changed. We wait for more data." He turned to Analise. "Where is the boy staying?"

"With Halima. He told his mother he is with his sister in the hills."

"He is safe, then," Gal said. "No children will die."

She nodded at the computer monitor. "What have you collected?"

Bauman hunched forward at the monitor and pulled up a screen that displayed the data collected from drones. "This is where we think the Pajero should be parked."

Bauman pointed to a location on the screen's map where red lines converged on one spot in Haret Hreik. The lines began on the periphery and made a spider web of routes in the maze of streets, but in almost all cases the lines met in one place, which was a knotted red ganglion. Bauman put his finger on the spot.

"The data point here. That's where we park the Pajero. A few more days of data will confirm it."

Bauman leaned back to allow the others to view the map. "Qassem varies his route and changes vehicles. There is a decoy. But your little idea has delivered a plan. The driver takes a turn past the barbershop here." Bauman stood and stretched. "It's obvious now that we have the data, but it's not intuitive. There are other approaches the driver takes, but this route emerges from a narrow alley and the driver can see in several directions."

Bauman had their attention. "The data is clear, but we can only speculate as to why he takes this route. I suspect he is sloppy. He takes all these precautions, but when he is close, he gets confident. He is a man of habit."

Gal smiled at Analise. "You called him vain. He drives by the barbershop, where he is known, and they are impressed when they see his bigwig passenger." He looked at the others and pointed to the knotted ganglion. "The needle's eye."

Bauman leaned against the van's wall and nodded at Analise. "We park the Pajero in front of the barbershop in the morning. I will have more data, but let's assume it confirms this spot. The noon call to prayer will give us a small window. His vehicle arrives when there are fewer people on the street.

"Qassem's car will pass within ten feet of the Pajero. Semtex has been shaped inside the Pajero's door to direct the explosion outward. Steel balls are packed around the explosive and will strike the vehicle's passenger door, shredding it and killing him. The wireless detonator is on an electrical loop powered by the Pajero's battery that closes with a cell-phone trigger. That's it. Bingo."

He turned to Analise. "We've applied UN decals, so it looks official, and it's similar to other UN SUVs that regularly move through the refugee camps. Our driver will empty air from one tire and leave a sign in the window that road service has been called."

Gal looked at the others and folded his hands in his lap. "We had a plan that didn't work. Now we have a better plan."

Aldrich stood and moved away from the others, which drew their attention. He carried himself with a heavy weight and his expression was somber. He turned and faced them. He took an envelope from his jacket and presented a piece of carbon tungsten shrapnel.

"This was found in the wreckage of Khoury's car. Inspector Aboud showed it to me. Have you ever seen anything like it?"

"Why did he show it to you?"

"We have a long relationship."

Aldrich placed the shrapnel in Gal's hand and he turned it over, studying it. There was a long silence while he pondered the jagged metal. Gal offered it to Bauman, who returned it to Aldrich without looking at it.

"So what."

Analise saw contempt in Aldrich's eyes. She knew the meeting was veering into a bad place and wouldn't end well.

"It's a dense inert explosive," he said. "I have had our OTS technicians confirm it. We have these weapons. We've supplied them to Israel. No other country in the Middle East has them."

"You've been drinking," Gal said.

Aldrich took the remark with the patience of a man not easily offended. "Sometimes it's necessary to stomach what goes along with my job. Sometimes it's not. How many of these have you placed?"

"We're not here to discuss that," Bauman said.

Aldrich held up the shrapnel. "This has complicated things." He loomed over Gal and Analise to stand eye to eye with Bauman, agitated. His voice deepened. "The ISF knows about this. They've connected the shrapnel fragments to a handful of bombings. They showed this to me and I've shown it to Langley, which makes us complicit in the murders. We will be connected to Qassem's assassination. I can't let that happen."

He looked at Gal. "You don't need our consent to use this war as a cover to take out Lebanese politicians, but you've left a trail that connects us to the murders."

Aldrich let the implications sink in. "I can't stop you from targeting Lebanese, but I can withdraw our support for killing Qassem."

"It's too late for that," Gal said.

"The Pajero belongs to the CIA. It can't be traced to us, but it belongs to us." He looked at Analise. "And she works for us."

"This is your decision?" Gal asked.

"I have the authority."

"And Madam Secretary Rice?"

"I've told the State Department to abort. We can't guarantee her safety." He looked at Gal and Bauman. "We don't know what the men in that room are planning."

Bauman and Aldrich were the same height, and had the same commitment to their work—and the same contempt for each other. "So that's it. We're done? It's over. You want us to believe that your scruples control this operation? Is that it?" Bauman's voice vibrated with incredulity.

Gal raised his palm. "May I speak with Rick alone?"

Analise joined Bauman outside the van. They moved into the shade of an old gnarled cypress tree bent from ancient winds. It was a bright sunny day and the eerie peace of the landscaped spot mocked their grim mood. The meager shade did little to relieve July's heat.

She felt time slow down waiting for whatever was being discussed in the van to conclude. She heard Bauman mumble that they were wasting valuable time—irrevocable time. They stood in the cul-de-sac's natural beauty, surrounded by sparrows eating ripe cherries on a nearby tree—waiting out the judgment of a terrorist's killing.

"I don't know what's on his mind," she said.

Bauman picked the petals from a blossoming cyclamen and tossed them one by one onto the cypress's gnarled roots.

"This is going to happen," he said quietly. "Too much work has gone into it. Too much is at stake for an alcoholic has-been to suddenly find his scruples. He's not going to pull the plug."

Ten minutes later, Aldrich emerged from the van visibly upset—more upset than when he had arrived, and angrier. Analise had heard raised voices, but she couldn't make out what was said.

He walked past Analise and made his way to the second of the two SUVs parked at the bottom of the hill. She ran after him and called his name. Helen held open the passenger door for Aldrich and cautioned Analise as she approached.

"What happened?" Analise asked.

Aldrich was stepping into the SUV when he turned to her. "Now is not the time."

"You owe me an explanation. Is it happening?"

Aldrich waved off Helen's command to get into the vehicle. "I've got to see the ambassador. Things are complicated. Gal sees only inept Lebanese leadership." His voice deepened with sarcasm. He turned to step inside but hesitated. "I'll know more after I speak to him. Come to the house. Arrange it with Helen. We have a day while the data is collected."

18

Halima Monsour's Dinner Party

One day became two, and waiting for word to proceed was a torturous experience. Patience was an unreliable companion, and at the end of a long operation it was hard to find and difficult to keep. Long early morning jogs helped Analise manage the stress, and on that particular morning she rose at dawn and jogged through deserted streets to Ras Beirut, where she found a big beach party of young people that was just breaking up. They had spent the night drinking and watching the evening fireworks display: Israeli jets bombing the southern suburbs. Life in wartime Beirut was becoming surreal.

When she got home, the morning television was full of war news. There were terrible images of children lying next to each other as if peacefully sleeping. A distraught mother standing over her dead child described to the camera how bunker-busting bombs had hit their underground shelter.

It was a relief when Analise got a call from Halima inviting her to a small dinner party. "To lift our spirits."

That night, Analise stood alone on Halima's balcony and looked at the orange sun sinking into the dark horizon—a glowing ball of fire quenched by the sea. Golden light danced on the red tile roofs of the older homes in Ras Beirut, and the tall cypress on AUB's sloping hills lost their shape in the encroaching darkness. Streaking light warmed the clock tower on College Hall and she listened as it marked the hour, as it had done for decades. She wondered if the clock was tolling for a dying city. Thick plumes of black smoke rose from barricades of burning tires that had been erected further south.

Earlier she had passed Philby's fifth-floor apartment on Rue Kantari. The wraparound balcony was intact, but the building was a neglected structure still in disrepair from the civil war. It had been a different time and different weather, but she could imagine the pressure on Philby the night he vanished. A winter storm had raged when he excused himself from joining his wife at a dinner party given by the British consul. Instead he made his way by taxi to a Russian trawler docked in the harbor. She imagined his ghost walking in the street, and experienced the pressure he must have felt, the pressure every agent in the field lives with. Her mind was alive with the terror of his last days as he scrambled to escape the net falling on him.

"What are you thinking?"

Analise turned. Corbin had opened the balcony's sliding glass door and was watching her. He held two phosphorescent drinks sprouting tiny Lebanese flags.

"You scared the shit out of me."

He handed her a drink. "Lost in thought. Better than lost in Haret Hreik." He raised his glass. "To the little things that get us through the day. I heard you had a problem after you left the press tour."

"A misunderstanding."

"Misunderstandings can kill you."

"I survived. Who told you?"

"Hammadi. He drove me tonight and he shared what he had heard, and he has his own views of Bauman. Everyone has a view."

Analise had turned away and was gazing at the brightly lit French and English naval vessels moored outside the dark harbor. She considered his comment and what he expected her to say. Later, she found it odd that he had raised the topic of Bauman out of the blue. She sipped her drink. "You don't like him, do you?"

"I look for the good in everyone, but he is a hard case. You should stay away from him." He nodded into the apartment. "I brought a gift for Halima."

Abundant cut flowers filled a glass vase that sat in the center of a table heaped with overflowing savory dishes. A box of chocolate had been pilfered by Halima's two children, who sat with Rami in front of a video game screen.

"Who is the boy?"

"A student. He is going to Paris to play in a tournament."

"If only we could all get away from the war." He nodded at the Corniche, where a road crew filled in a bomb crater. "What are the chances we'll be hit by a stray rocket?"

She heard a note of sarcasm in his querulous tone.

He pointed to a building nearby where an errant rocket had punched a hole in an upper floor. Fire had darkened the façade. "Who wants to be the person whose epitaph reads, 'Wrong place, wrong time.'"

Analise looked at him. "You're a cynic. The curse of your job. Do you believe in anything?" She didn't expect an answer and she didn't get one. She leaned on the railing and felt cold. It was warm out, but she felt a chill in her hands.

"Don't judge me too harshly," he said, then pointed at the street. "That's Bauman's Land Rover. Is he coming?"

"He wasn't invited."

"Hammadi asked about him on the way over. He seems to know him."

Analise didn't offer a view.

"He's looking for a pattern in the car bombs. He thinks that Lebanese politicians are being targeted. He thinks it's Bauman."

"Are you working with Hammadi?"

He laughed. "Have you forgotten? My job is with the *Times*."

"Your only job?"

Corbin laughed and sipped his drink without answering.

"He's a journalist like you," she said.

"Not like me. He's becoming the story."

"*Your* story," she said flatly.

"Are you protecting him?"

"Don't make me part of your crummy little conspiracy."

"My editor wants a second source. You know Bauman. He seems to trust you."

"If he's Mossad, would he trust me? That defies logic."

"Someone tapped my phone." He removed the SIM card from his cell phone and replaced it with another, but he didn't remove the battery. "Let them wonder why I'm here talking with you. It might excite their fevered imaginations."

"You're out of your mind."

"He's killing people."

"You don't know that."

"Are you helping him?"

Analise took his arm and put her hand on his cheek, letting it linger. She brought him closer, startling him. They stood close but apart and she looked into his eyes, seeking a hint of their old intimacy, but saw only his skeptical expression.

"You lied to me," he said. "You were in Haret Hreik. You were there twice. The first time when you denied you were there and then on the press tour. *Are* you helping him?"

She pulled away. "You don't know the danger that you're putting yourself in."

"Tell me."

She saw in him the vanity of a reckless person pushing for an answer. She looked off at the view of the Mediterranean but turned back and saw an appalling determination in his eyes.

"I'm not part of his story." She put a finger on his lips, silencing him, and did what was needed to distract him. She kissed him.

The balcony's glass door opened. Rami stood in the dim light, surprised to come upon them in an intimate moment. She saw his startled expression and went to take the long-stemmed red rose that he offered, but he dropped it.

"Who is he?" He looked hostilely at Corbin.

"A reporter. An old friend."

"The food is ready. I was told to bring you." Rami looked at Corbin with brooding jealousy.

Analise picked up the rose. "Thank you."

Dinner was presented on a long table covered in a white linen cloth. Abundant dishes with fragrant smells and colorful presentations were assembled into a feast. Guests took plates from a nearby credenza and stood in line to serve themselves. All the urgent conversation about politics, the war, and corruption in the port vanished into a pleasant discussion of the various dishes that had been prepared.

Outside, a loud pulsing siren sounded. Startled guests looked up. In the following silence they heard the shrill whistle of an incoming rocket. A bright flash a few blocks away lit up the window, and the percussive shock wave rattled stemware and the guests' nerves.

Halima addressed her guests and said there was nothing to worry about. Dinner would go on—one random rocket wouldn't spoil the event. But the wisdom of experience told her to prepare for the worst, so, even as she encouraged others to eat, she began to place her family's passports, cash, and precious photographs in cloth bags. It was a precaution, she said, against the possibility that the evening would end badly. She reassured her guests that they were safe, and if there was danger, she would lead them down the staircase into the garage shelter. Guests added food to their plates without great enthusiasm as she bustled about, filling the go-bag.

"Eat. Eat. The lamb will get cold."

Another explosion shook the apartment building, and a wineglass fell from a shelf, shattering. At the window, Analise saw an Apache helicopter hovering near the clock tower. A third rocket shot from underneath the aircraft and exploded in a nearby construction site; a tall crane slowly toppled, but the clock tower was not damaged.

"They've mistaken it for a Katyusha rocket facility," Hammadi said with grim humor. He stood at her side, holding a bottle of French burgundy, and filled her empty glass.

"It's time to move to the shelter," he announced. "They are drunk hunters. We don't want to be their evening's sport."

Car alarms had begun to go off on the street and secondary explosions could be heard. Analise calmly issued instructions and took Corbin's arm. He had moved to the balcony, dictating his observations into a small tape recorder. "You don't want to die for this story," she said.

Communal fear came gradually and without panic. Halima's two children, a teenage boy and his younger sister, rushed to their bedrooms to collect keepsakes. They had done this before and were excited by the drama. "There won't be school tomorrow," the boy said.

Halima guided her guests from the apartment door to the stairwell for the trek to the garage. Then the electricity went out. Unanswered telephones could be heard ringing stridently in empty apartments. A flashlight appeared from somewhere and guided the group down the dark stairs.

Corbin had the presence of mind to bring utensils and covered dishes of *shish taouk* and *baba ghanouj*, which he set out on a car's hood when they decamped in the garage. The building's emergency generator came on and a guest who had brought a standing lamp plugged it in, illuminating the group. Corbin served the food, declaring that inconvenience was the mother of invention.

"It might be a long night," Hammadi said. He poured wine into paper cups that had mysteriously appeared. He made generous pours for Analise and Halima. "To my friends." He lifted his glass and then waved over a young man. "You've met Fares, my brother's oldest son. He has graduated from the law faculty at Beirut Arab University."

An hour passed. Excitement turned to boredom, and patience was a casualty of the long wait for the all-clear klaxon to sound. Gossip was a wildfire of speculation that the rockets were the start of the invasion of Beirut. Eyes lifted to the lights that flickered each time there was an explosion. There came a time when silence outside lengthened and the group became hopeful.

Hammadi's pleasant manner and endless stories entertained guests. He was polite even if immodest, and he carried on conversation in English, French, and Arabic, choosing the language that best suited whomever he spoke to—French with the Lebanese, English with Corbin, and Arabic to his nephew. He spoke to Analise first in Arabic and then in English, assuming a philosophical tone when the conversation turned to the war. "I look for uncommon sense in things, which is often hidden in common nonsense, and in that way, I make sense of things."

"I can't help you with that," she said.

Hammadi was the first to notice the long silence. "It's over," he said. He sent his nephew to the street to confirm that his Mercedes had not been damaged. "It's late and now we go home to celebrate passing his exams."

Electricity returned, brightening the dim garage, and the group made its way back to the apartment. The party picked up where it had left off. Rami played video games with Halima's son. Analise saw two boys who were giddy, happy, and unafraid. Two boys of different backgrounds sharing the innocent exuberance of youth. She couldn't imagine the horror that would soon visit his life, but that wasn't her worry. Hearing joy in his voice was meager comfort. She wasn't responsible for bringing him into the world or looking after his future. She had excised empathy from her heart to do her job, but it wasn't easy and it wasn't without pain.

Analise was in the kitchen thinking about Rami when she heard the explosion. There had not been the shrill whistle of an incoming rocket.

She turned to face Corbin, who had opened a beer.

"In the street. A car bomb."

She threw off his restraining hand, thinking his concern misplaced.

From the balcony, she saw the chaotic scene on the street in front of the apartment building. The tableau of a car bomb was uncomfortably familiar, but steaming vapor from a damaged fire hydrant gushing onto the hot pavement softened the violence. A black Mercedes had been lifted by the force of the blast and lay on its roof. Radiating from the mangled car were seat cushions, a debris field of shattered glass, and the contents of a briefcase. A man's arm hung out the sprung driver's door and lay on the pavement.

A crowd formed a semicircle around the car, reluctant to get close in case a second bomb had been timed to follow the first. Several men yelled into cell phones, and others waved excitedly to passersby, who pointed in the direction of an approaching siren.

"It's Hammadi's car," Analise said.

Corbin was quiet. They were drawn together by the uncomfortable fraternity of witnesses to death. Neither spoke because there was nothing either could say in the face of the devastation. Gushing water washed the explosive residue from the street, moving in rivulets to the gutter.

Halima joined them on the balcony with a glass of anise-flavored Arak. She shook her head. "Humor helps on a night like this. When the bombs end, we laugh. We laugh because we can."

She looked down to the street, where a weeping Hammadi helped ambulance workers pull his nephew's body from the crumpled Mercedes. "Poor man." She shook her head. "It is the second attempt on his life. One day he won't be so lucky."

Her right hand, adorned with silver rings, trembled with her glass. Her sad eyes were wide and confessional as she turned to Analise.

"I lived through the civil war and I still live here. We refused to move. Many friends left Beirut but we stayed because we had lost our eldest son and we couldn't bring ourselves to become refugees. Staying was the right choice. Why go to London to be miserable when we can be miserable in our country." She laughed grimly. "All our friends who left want to return. They send their children to our school so they can learn Arabic. A mother came to me embarrassed that her Lebanese daughter only speaks English."

Halima sipped her drink and looked off into the night. "I stood here one morning during the civil war after a night of violence—a night like tonight. I saw a shiny new car driven by a prosperous Saudi sheik stalled on the street. Over there." She pointed. "By the Corniche. No matter what the sheik did, the car wouldn't start. He wore a long white robe and *ghutrah* and was frustrated by his broken-down Mercedes. A young man offered his help, which the sheik accepted, and the man fiddled under the hood for a minute. The young man gathered passersby to push the car while he sat in the driver's seat to jump start it. He got a hotel concierge, a policeman, and an Englishman. Well, I don't know if he was English, but he carried an umbrella open against the sun, so I assumed he was. The group gave a big push, sending the Mercedes rolling along. Sure enough, it started and everyone clapped. The sheik was ecstatic. His joy turned to outrage, though, when he saw the Mercedes speed off."

Analise had heard the old stories. Reselling stolen cars to their rightful owners had been a brisk business during the civil war. The horrors of that war were now reduced to anecdotes.

Halima was philosophical. "It isn't that bad yet. It's a different type of cruelty." She looked south, where smoke plumed and fires lit the darkness. "I hate Israel and I hate Hezbollah. I hate both. But Israel's attacks make the enemies of my enemies my friends. I hate Hezbollah but I support them."

She paused. "Israel wants to punish the Lebanese elite for putting up with Hezbollah. Do I think it will work? No. They are stupid. Stupid with power."

Halima pointed to the flames illuminating the sky. Then she pointed to a building at the nearby grammar school that had been hit by a rocket. She spoke with savage irony. "A Hezbollah rocket factory. They defend themselves by saying that our twelve-year-old sons launch Katyusha rockets from their classrooms. And why? To justify their targeting errors."

Her voice was impatient with rage. "They say the only deterrent to terror is to kill terrorists. It's the same argument that dictators have made to murder opponents throughout history. Say it whatever way you want—whether it comes from the mouth of a dictator or as an excuse to repress people of different political views—it's the same old serpent."

Halima swept her hand across the evening. "All this violence. The idea that killing people solves problems. War is all they know, and they are good at it, so they kill people thinking that war will bring peace. It never brings peace. There is only a pause in the war."

She was quiet for a moment, struggling with her indignation. "They are not a kind people. Some are kind, some are wise, but not the politicians. The opposite of kindness is not cruelty. It is indifference. All this"—she looked across the bombed city—"is indifference. Our suffering isn't about who we are. It is about who they are. Airplanes and tanks give them the power to be indifferent."

She sipped her drink, and her voice lowered and softened. "Israel's prime ministers—Sharon, Olmert, Netanyahu—believe they can solve these problems with toughness, but things have changed. The Islamic faith has spread. For better or worse." Her hand went to her heart. When she spoke again, her soprano voice was strident. "How will they frighten jihadists who love martyrdom?" She shook her head. "God forbid."

"You're wrong," Analise said. "Not all Israelis are that way."

"*Je le croirai, guard je le verrai.*" She paused. "Let them show it." She waved dismissively. "Beirut survived the Romans, the Ottomans, the French. The land and the people endure. That land has defeated stronger enemies than Israel. Israel is an idea. Ideas come and go. Land endures."

She lowered her head and looked out at the darkened city. Her words came in quiet lament. "The scourge of this land is the curse of revenge."

19

Café l'Étoile

Hammadi rose and called out to Analise. She had looked for him where he said he would be seated, but not finding him, she had started to leave. When she approached him, he stood.

"*Marhaba.*" He kissed her on one cheek, then the other, three times in the Lebanese style, and touched her elbow, inviting her to sit. She saw a black armband on his white linen suit.

"His funeral was this morning. The car bomb was intended for me. We buried my nephew next to his father."

Analise's face paled with sympathy, which he waved off. "He should not have been the one to die. He was young with a bright future." Shallow breaths unmasked his tender grief. "We all suffer. I am not alone." He pointed to a French woman. "She is a sad case. Do you know her? I saw you looking at her."

"Why does she sit alone?"

"Her son was kidnapped by militia who demanded a ransom. She begged for time. The boy's ear showed up in a shoebox outside her hotel room. It is like the civil war. Militias have different strategies for raising money to buy guns. Everyone in Beirut is arming."

Hammadi had ordered ice cream. The bowl in front of him had three scoops: strawberry, chocolate, and vanilla. "The best ice cream in Beirut. I know this will sound strange, but eating helps when I am like this. Would you like some?"

"No, thank you. Why did you want to see me?"

"You don't mind if I eat?"

"Please."

He lifted a spoonful of chocolate and enjoyed the flavor. "I wanted to speak with you at Halima's party, but there were too many people, too many ears in the room. And then the explosion. The men who planted the bomb were experts."

"Who did it?"

"What interests me is not who planted the bomb, but who paid for the bomb." He looked up. "Coffee perhaps?"

She was curious now. "Please."

He motioned for the waiter, who recognized the hand signal and disappeared inside. Hammadi nodded toward the French woman. "It was this way in the civil war. It has always been this way. Political exiles came here from Cairo and Tehran because we were the Paris of the Middle East." He laughed. "The French deposited their language and took our dignity. Our streets are still named after generals who invaded the country."

He savored a spoonful of vanilla and the irony. "The West sent us their spies, who drank at the bar at the St. Georges Hotel. Did you know Kim Philby's father is buried here in the Muslim cemetery? Yes, he converted to Islam, and who knows what the young Philby made of that. Berlin had more spies, but we were the exotic center of Cold War espionage. Now what are we?" He looked at her. "What does a young Lebanese-American woman working for the United Nations make of all this?"

Analise's coffee arrived. She lifted the cup and looked at him, wondering what he really thought of her and where he was going with his comments.

"My favorite," he said, tasting the strawberry. He added, "Murder has become a methodology of suppression in Beirut. My nephew's death is the latest. I showed you the twelve photographs in my office. There have been no arrests. There are never arrests in Beirut. Only murders. It is a bitter city. Ancient and young. Tough and cruel. The sea breeze cools the air, and the fragrance of jasmine sweetens the stench of murder. It was once a Republic of Letters. People lived together. Muslims, Christians, Jews, Druze. Now, everyone has a bodyguard."

He shook his head sadly. He put down his spoon and leaned forward, looking directly at her. "Why does the West hate us?"

Analise didn't answer. She had no answer.

"This is what I think. The West is attached to Israel over the PLO. It infuriates us. Being Arab, we have a different view. But we are weak. Our voice isn't heard and we suffer a feeling of helplessness. That is who we have become. Ignored. Powerless. Bombs fall on our homes."

Hammadi placed three spoonfuls of sugar in his demitasse cup of coffee and stirred slowly. He lifted the cup to his lips and drank it all at once.

"Inspector Aboud has questions about Bauman," he said.

Analise knew they had come to the purpose of the meeting. "I answered his questions."

"I heard your answers."

"What are your questions?"

Hammadi's thick eyebrows arched. He shrugged. "I have the same questions Corbin has. Do you know why I asked you here?"

"Everyone seems to think I know something privileged."

"Do you?"

"I wouldn't tell you if I did."

Hammadi laughed. He leaned forward. "You were in Haret Hreik several days ago."

"United Nations business. I work with displaced refugees."

"What is the UN's interest in the boy? The grandson of Imam Najib Qassem?"

"He is my student. I teach English."

"Have you met Qassem?"

"What is this about?"

"What is your interest in Qassem's driver?"

"What makes you think I have an interest in him?"

"You brought them gifts."

"He's the boy's stepfather. It's polite to bring gifts when visiting a home."

"There are no secrets in Beirut."

"The boy, Rami, wants to play soccer in the Paris tournament. Every child should have a dream. The stepfather doesn't approve. I'm helping him live his dream."

Hammadi weighed his response like a butcher watching his scale. "*Connaissez vous* Rick Aldrich?"

"*Un peu.*"

"*Vous aussi.*"

"You may use *toi* with me," she said. "There is no need for formality. We both want what is right for the boy."

"*D'accord.* What happened in Haret Hreik?"

"I offended a man. I was not wearing a head scarf."

"Your Land Rover?"

"Bauman's. I took it when he stayed with the press tour."

"Rick Aldrich lives with a Lebanese woman. All the American diplomats stick to the compound in Awkar. What does he do?"

"You should ask him."

"You know him well?"

"I'm American. He's American. It's a small community. He likes to drink and I sometimes drink with him."

"He's very polite. He has a remarkable way of speaking at length and never quite answering my questions. Tell him I want to talk about Bauman."

"What's your interest?"

"I am a Muslim and an Arab, but I am Lebanese first. I knew Bauman's father, but of course his name wasn't Bauman. Did you know that? No, why would you? His father was a good man, but like so many families, the father's qualities didn't pass to the child.

"For me and for his father, speaking Arabic was the exception. We spoke French and we went to the lycée. I was told by my mother, God rest her soul, that I spoke French before I spoke Arabic. I have Christian in-laws, we have a few Sunni-Shia marriages, but not many. The only sin in my family was to marry into poverty. We looked to France, learned French, and now we are obliged to speak English."

He laughed. "You are American. You don't have to pretend. You look Lebanese, but I see an American." Hammadi nodded at the distraught blond French woman sitting alone. "No one should negotiate with the life of a child." He looked at Analise. "I understand the boy is in your care."

"He is spending the rest of the summer in Aaitat with his sister."

"He should go to Paris. He is our future."

Hammadi left several Lebanese pounds on the table and stood, bowing slightly. He had taken several steps toward the sidewalk when he turned.

"Bauman is a clever journalist and a dangerous man. I think you know that."

20

Rue Gouraud

Analise moved along the narrow street, passing old stone steps that rose to a garden higher on the slope, and stopped at a store's display window. She looked at the glass's reflection of the few people on the street behind her and glanced at the balcony, where she saw Aldrich.

Analise crossed the street and opened the front door of the Ottoman-era home. She had been there before and the lush jasmine hanging from the balcony identified the door among similar-looking homes on the street.

Her eyes adjusted to the dim light in the vestibule, and she felt its soothing coolness. Hectic sounds from the street were muted by the heavy wood door. Out of an excess of caution, she placed her ear to the door and listened for the sound of hurrying feet or the urgent cry of thwarted surveillance. She knew that one moment of quiet on the street could erupt into chaos if gunmen jumped from passing cars. Vigilance came naturally to her after two tours in Middle East war zones.

She quietly ascended the stone stairs and entered the second-floor parlor. Aldrich turned to greet her. He had heard the click of the closing door and invited her in with a brisk wave.

"I thought I heard someone downstairs." He nodded at the Ferragamo shopping bag she held. "So, Hama found you." The brush pass in the street had happened in an instant. Two women moving along the sidewalk with identical shopping bags, one carrying socks and the other an envelope with a key. The moment of contact passed unnoticed by shoppers in the street.

Analise placed the house key on the small lacquered table. "She looked upset."

"I've been ordered back to Awkar. There have been threats."

He moved away from the balcony's double doors and went to the bar, where he finished the dregs of one martini and refilled his glass from the sweating stainless-steel shaker. He held up a stemmed glass, inviting her to join.

"Drinking was de rigueur when I started at the agency, but times change, habits differ, and us old guys hang on to our liquor cabinets."

Two martinis, she thought. Analise had committed the room to memory on her first visit, but in the moment of her heightened awareness, she now saw details she had missed. General Henri Gouraud's framed photograph hung where she remembered it, but she didn't recollect the photo of a smiling older couple illuminated by light passing through gauzy curtains. She remembered the pattern of the Persian rug, but now she saw the worn spots. Also new to her were several old photographs of a lost Beirut.

"Hama's parents," Aldrich said, seeing her notice the photograph. "Her father was an important merchant. He traveled between Damascus and Beirut, shipping art and furniture to Europe, exporting Orientalism, and imported Swiss clocks, radios, and men's suits to satisfy the Lebanese obsession with the West. He made money and facilitated cultural exchange. He built this house with the profits. He was killed in the civil war and his wife moved to Paris, where she died. Hama spent what was left of his wealth on repairing the damage caused by the fighting."

Aldrich lifted his martini glass, sipping the chilled vodka. "Philby was a promiscuous drinker: scotch, vodka, gin. Whatever was offered. In the end he was a sad drunk living on a pension in Moscow. We learn to lie to the world, but we don't recognize the lies we tell ourselves. He saw what he wanted to see in the world. That's going on in Langley right now."

He raised the shaker. "Are you sure?"

"No thanks."

He poured what remained into his glass. He moved to the balcony and motioned for Analise to join him. He pulled the curtain aside enough to open a view onto the street, where Hama stood at a display window. "She doesn't know what I do. Does she suspect something? Maybe. I lied about why I am moving out. She got upset when I told her."

"Are you happy with her?"

The question startled Aldrich. Layers of subterfuge separated officers in the field; the introduction of a personal question was unexpected. He smiled. "We're not here to talk about happiness—mine or yours. Ours isn't the type of job where we judge ourselves by happiness or salary. If we're lucky, we're content to believe we prevented war or saved a few lives." He dropped the curtain. "If we're unlucky, we become a black star on the Memorial Wall."

He motioned for her to sit on the sofa. "I've gotten death threats in the past, but they are more credible now. We are being blamed for this fiasco of a war. I have worked hard for an independent Lebanon—to free it from Hezbollah, Syria, and Israel. Qassem is a problem, but so are Assad and Netanyahu." Unprompted, he said a few personal things about life in Lebanon, acknowledging her concern for his well-being, but then he abruptly stopped.

Aldrich handed her a document marked "Top Secret." "The ambassador shared the State Department's assessment of the war with me. It won't surprise you. Take a look."

Analise glanced at the three-page report written in the bland bureaucratese that emerged from the writing mill of agency analysts who stripped stylistic color from their prose. Nuclear threat assessments and holiday invitations were written in the same tone. Most of the grim war statistics in the report she knew already, but the repetition had a numbing effect: fifteen thousand combat sorties, ten thousand artillery shells, thousands of homes destroyed, a million displaced Lebanese.

She set it down. "Why are you showing me this?"

"It's the disproportionate response. Two IDF soldiers kidnapped and a furious response. It doesn't make sense unless you see it as a subterfuge. What I can't explain, and neither could the ambassador, is how ineffective the IDF has been. Five Hezbollah soldiers killed. Not five thousand, not five hundred. Five," he repeated with a kind of bewilderment.

Aldrich crossed his legs and sank into the ponderous contemplation of an old Buddha. "The war is a public relations disaster for Israel. The IDF is too smart to fail, too good at war to come up short—unless they had no intention of winning. Unless it was a cover."

He produced the glassine envelope with the shrapnel fragments. "Twelve Lebanese politicians who support Hezbollah have been assassinated. All the refugees. The evacuation. The air raids. It's the old magician's trick. One hand holds the audience's attention while the real action is elsewhere."

Aldrich stood, but then thought better, sat down again, and rubbed his hands together like a man coming in from the cold. "Some of the killings are Lebanese power struggles, but most are not. I believe Mossad is taking out a generation of Lebanon's best politicians. They want to turn the country away from Hezbollah. They want to sow chaos to create an unstable situation that gives them cover to annex Lebanon."

Analise stared. "You're speculating."

"That's what we do. We gather intelligence, make an assessment, and share an unpopular opinion with agency mandarins whose job it is to share bad news with POTUS." He paused. "Everything points to that conclusion. Nothing points away."

Aldrich sat back in his chair, his expression grim. "We are the heralds, the Mercuries, the good shepherds. Whatever name you want. Our job is to speak truth to power."

Analise wished she had taken the drink he'd offered. She didn't know whether to believe him or to conclude, as Bauman had, that Aldrich was a tired, cynical intelligence officer elbowing his way forward with dangerous speculation, knowing that his storied career permitted him heretical views.

"Sometimes you have to call it as you see it," he said. "Bauman wants to make me out to be a drunk because that makes me sound unstable." He lifted the report. "Facts don't lie. Statistics speak for themselves. But this," he said, waving the report, "doesn't tell you what's on Gal's mind."

Aldrich paused. "The ambassador doesn't want to hear this either. Langley is caught up in a flatulent debate about the Middle East, and the endless requests for information are an excuse to avoid making a decision. Mossad spies on us, on me. They mislead us, and now they want us to take the fall for this crisis they've created. This isn't a story about two kidnapped soldiers. This is the manipulation of Washington."

Aldrich clapped his hands together slowly three times. Performing. "Thank you for your candid assessment, Mr. Aldrich. We will take it into consideration.

"*Take it into consideration*," Aldrich mocked. "Endless words from bureaucrats who won't risk their careers with an unpopular opinion." He smiled and shook his head. "The ambassador called me back to his office to complain. Israel's allies on Capitol Hill whisper against me. The ambassador is furious. He didn't have to caution me, but he did. We're bogged down in Afghanistan. We've lost credibility in Iraq. No one wants a Middle East catastrophe that Russia can exploit. The White House wants to airbrush the tits off this hooker."

Aldrich smiled. "That's the ambassador's very colorful way of describing it." Aldrich looked at her with somber eyes. "What would you do?"

"About?"

"Qassem."

"Go forward. He's still our target. He killed Buckley."

"We're being played."

"It's your decision."

"I haven't made up my mind. I told Gal it was off. I did that to see how upset he would get. I watched his implacable calm crack. I respect his intelligence. I admire his doggedness. I appreciate his wisdom. But I detest his fucking with me."

Aldrich stood and moved to the balcony view, where he opened the curtain and stared at the bustling street. He stood there for a long moment, lost in thought.

"I don't know what I'm going to do," he said, turning back. "I'm angry, as you can see, but I'm also fully aware that I shouldn't let anger interfere with my judgment."

Aldrich slowly set down his glass and raised his eyes to her. "There is something that I haven't told you that complicates my work. Against my urgent appeal, Secretary Rice is coming. They've advanced the date. God knows what crap the White House is getting from political flacks on the National Security Council. She'll land at the embassy helipad, drive to meet with the prime minister in Parliament, and then go to Speaker Berri's West Beirut home. They think that an unannounced, lightning-fast visit makes it safe, but they don't know the danger. Narrow streets. Parked cars. They won't see the bomb. It's my nightmare."

Aldrich stood, inviting Analise to leave, then added. "I'm seeing the ambassador in the chancellery in an hour. Rice's stunt is dangerously stupid headline diplomacy that puts our job at risk. The press on her plane won't know she's flying to Beirut, but logistics require that Speaker Berri know, and if he knows, it's certain Hezbollah knows."

"What will you tell the ambassador?"

"I'll make up my mind on the drive." Aldrich moved to the door, hands behind his back. He turned, his voice grave. "I've discovered a new problem, and knowing that it is there happens to be more important than finding a solution to the problem that we're already faced with. It's the old question. *Cui bono?* Who benefits from her death?"

He handed her the Ferragamo shopping bag. "Hama is down the street. Her bag will have a new SIM card for your phone that I can call. Let yourself out. I will follow shortly."

21

Death Comes Forward

Analise moved a few steps from Hama's front door, away from the secluded cover of the narrow alley that climbed up the slope to a small garden. Fragrance from the hanging jasmine freshened the air. She peeked around the corner and studied the street. It had been an odd conversation with Aldrich. She couldn't tell how much of his fierce complaint against Gal was a personal gripe about a rival and how much was the justified suspicions of a good intelligence officer. Perhaps it was both.

Analise saw Helen further down the street by the lead SUV, nervously glancing at shoppers and motorbikes weaving between the slower-moving cars. The scene froze in her mind, a snapshot that she would remember. A woman in blue jeans and a green blouse talked on her cell phone while two children quarreled. The street suddenly began to empty. The mother of the two children grabbed them and hustled them along the street to a doorway. A garbage truck moved slowly down the street, driven by an old man, who shouted at the motor scooter passing in a cloud of black exhaust. The distinctive chime of an ice-cream truck rose above the din.

Analise stepped back from the edge of the house, retreating into the alley, to answer her vibrating phone. Sounds of the street dimmed when she cupped one ear.

"Hello." The activity in the street receded in the confinement of the narrow alley, but then the sound of honking seemed to grow louder. There were shouts and a cry.

"Hello," she repeated, pressing the phone to her ear.

"It's me." Bauman's voice was garbled.

"You shouldn't be calling me. It's not safe." She heard background noise on the phone, a cry of surprise, and the ice-cream truck's musical chime.

"Where are you?"

"What's up?"

"Stay where you are." Silence. "Meet me tomorrow. I will get you the Pajero's keys. Same place."

His number had come up as an international unknown again. She stared at the phone, which had gone dead, wondering about his tone of voice.

The explosion came as a sudden flash of intense light. She was thrown to the ground. There was a moment of unconsciousness from which she slowly emerged, finding herself on her hands and knees covered in dust. Her world was soundless. She became aware that she was crawling and that a bomb had gone off. Her phone had fallen to the ground and she picked it up thinking that she had to answer it, but there was no one on the line.

She searched for her dark glasses on the ground, feeling for them in the debris. When she found them, she saw that her hands were covered in gray dust and so were the glasses and her shirt; there was no point in trying to clean them. Analise sat on the bottom step of a narrow staircase. For a moment, she had no memory of how she had gotten there. She felt for blood on her face.

When she stood, she was dizzy. She steadied herself before she moved to the street. She saw people with their mouths open, screaming, but she heard only ringing in her ears. She shook her head to awaken her hearing, and the knobs in her head that controlled sound turned up. The world around her filled with chaotic noise: cries, moans, and shrill commands.

"Are you okay?"

Helen stood in front of her, eyes wide with concern. Analise nodded.

"Hurry," Helen said. "They time a second bomb to follow the first. Come with me."

Analise allowed herself to be led past the garbage truck's shattered rear, which spewed its smelly contents onto the street. A policeman with a bloody face stood nearby waving energetically to get stumbling pedestrians out of harm's way. A motor scooter was tipped on its side covered in dust. Its driver was crumpled in a ball, facedown, ten feet away—motionless. Fabric and bits of paper drifted in the air and floated down onto the body like confetti.

The concussive blast had set off alarms, but there was little sense of urgency in what she saw of the bomb's aftermath. Moans of the wounded were soft and pleading, and there was a serene placidity to the scene of destruction.

The decoy SUV had been lifted off the street by the blast and lay on its side. The windows were blown out and the roof was peeled back like an opened can of sardines. Intense fire consumed the interior, and black smoke poured from shattered windows. The wheels had burst. The SUV was a gutted shell of mangled steel lying in a sea of glass shards darkened by the flames. Overturned food carts formed a perimeter around the blast zone. Farther along, a man sat in the street, holding a torn and bleeding arm.

Analise stared at the grim tableau unfolding before her in slow motion. The face of terror was always the same. Body parts were scattered like detritus left by a receding tide—a severed arm with a gold wristwatch. A leg with a shoe. A teacher with a gash on her forehead leading students away from the horror. One child stared at the severed leg.

Bright sunlight bathed the scene in pastel watercolors, softening the violence. Crimson blood became pink as it mixed with the street's dust.

Analise moved toward the decoy SUV, but Helen took her arm and restrained her, directing her to the lead vehicle. Its rear window had blown out and its white exterior was streaked black, but it was beyond the concentrated blast and largely undamaged.

"Don't," Helen said, directing Analise away from the two burned and mangled bodies that spilled from the upside-down decoy SUV. "We need to get out of here."

Cries for help from the injured became louder as the neighborhood awakened to the explosion, and residents emerged from homes and side streets. The cautious crowd kept its distance, but seeing the carnage, many covered their mouths with their hands.

Analise looked but allowed herself to be led to the lead vehicle and shoved into the front seat. Helen jumped into the rear and hit the driver's head rest. "Drive. Now. Get out of here."

Analise turned to the back seat and saw Aldrich's double. She had a brief moment of confusion. Her unconscious mind wondered why it wasn't Aldrich. She didn't breathe for a moment when the realization struck. She turned to look back at the decoy SUV and the two bodies.

Analise grabbed her door to open it, but Helen restrained her, voice fierce.

"You're in danger. We need to get the hell out of here now."

22

Journey Home

Rick Aldrich's remains lay in a metal transport case that was rolled on a stainless-steel dolly toward the Chinook helicopter waiting by the pier. What was left of him was packed inside a black body bag covered in ice for the journey to the mortuary processing center at Dover Air Force Base in Delaware.

A small group from the embassy stood at attention as marines lifted the container. Rotor wash from the helicopter swept the ground, and the ambassador held on to his hat. Analise watched from the back seat of Bauman's Land Rover parked across the street. Helen had discouraged her from attending the brief ceremony, but no amount of institutional caution was enough to chill her desire to see him off. She had stayed away from the UNHCR office and avoided being seen on Helen's instructions. Waiting made her restless. She wanted to know who was responsible for the murder and she wanted to know what would happen to Aldrich. The details, as grim as they were, were comforting. Mystery was unsettling. She preferred to know, and she had asked to be there when his remains were transferred, but she was cautioned against joining the informal group. Helen told her that one killing on her watch was all that her career could handle.

Analise wore dark glasses and watched quietly. The sun was bright but her mood was gray. She'd hardly known him, but she grieved deeply.

No bugles played Taps. There was no rifle volley to mark the loss of a CIA station chief. A man whose presence in Lebanon had gone unannounced, whose identity had been a closely held secret, was leaving the country in the same manner that he had arrived—quietly, privately, without ceremony.

The improvised helipad was crowded with the ongoing evacuation operation, and making space among the living for Aldrich's transfer case had required the ambassador's intervention. Two marines in battle fatigues lifted the container off the dolly and into the Chinook's open bay, where two airmen accepted the transfer case and slid it inside.

Analise had seen too many of these sad farewells. She had stood on the tarmac at Qadisiyah Airbase in Baghdad when fallen colleagues were sent home. Saying goodbye to the dead never got easier or became routine. Each death was alive with grief. Bugles playing Taps worked itself into the fabric of loss and evoked a profound melancholy. The gravity of honor and sacrifice in the conduct of secret work tugged at her pride. Nothing seemed so real, so true, so hurtful. Seeing a fallen colleague leaving in a transport container, knowing that body parts were packed in ice, left a hole in her heart. There had been honor guards at the small ceremonies on the tarmac at Qadisiyah, but it was meager recompense for a life ended early. She had come to resent the wars in the Middle East—police actions with vague goals and wasteful death no longer connected to the attack on the World Trade Center. Wars without heroes.

She watched as the transport case was pushed along the freight-ready rollers, disappearing inside. She saw herself leaving that way. The thought left her cold. Aldrich summed up so many qualities she admired, qualities that had drawn her to the agency. Qualities that Americans admired in themselves. He was dedicated to his agency service, but she also knew that he was a man who had no illusions about his work. His reckless drinking was his way of dealing with a changed world where he was out of step—but he believed certain principles survived across time and across conflicts. He was undeterred in his crusade to find a way to redeem the irredeemable—putting a good face on a policy he knew was a lost cause. He had confessed his view that peace in the Middle East was doomed. And now he was a casualty of the war he didn't believe in.

Analise had no tears to wipe. She watched the small group that stood near the helicopter lifting off. The American ambassador was there with Helen and several others from Beirut station. The non-ceremony was over quickly and the crowd dispersed toward parked vehicles.

Hama wasn't there, which did not surprise Analise. She was not officially in his life and he had never confided who he worked for. Analise thought of their last conversation—the word *happiness*. He'd dismissed it, but thinking about what he'd said—his visit to Hama's farm in the Beqaa Valley, the peace he'd found sitting in the sun enjoying her cooking—he had seemed content.

She wondered how much she could believe of what Aldrich had told her. His claims, his allegations, his suspicions about competing factions in the agency, the old concern that outside influences contorted the truth the agency was to deliver to the Oval Office. Of the many problems that he carried, none challenged his rigorous discernment, or his faith, as much as the specious advice offered by colleagues with corrupted loyalties. Loyal to themselves, their careers, or to a foreign master. Was he trying to warn her? She recorded his concerns in her journal that night.

Analise had delivered the news to Hama. She'd felt it was the decent thing to confirm his death, even without offering an explanation. Hama would have to make her own judgment. Confusion in the street—one SUV safe and the other destroyed. Analise had been mistaken about which vehicle he had been in, and Hama would have doubts. He had switched cars unexpectedly. He usually took the lead car, but for some reason that day he'd chosen to ride in the decoy. A small change in routine.

Analise had presented herself at Hama's door. Hama had been several blocks away at the time of the explosion and there had been no official announcement of Aldrich's death. She only knew that the man who shared her house hadn't returned. When the door opened, Analise saw that Hama had been crying. Her news was cruel comfort. Grief, too, can be fierce. Analise said that Americans would arrive later to ask questions and she should cooperate.

Analise watched the helicopter fly off. She knew what would come next. The Chinook would land in Cyprus and the transfer case would be lifted onto a Falcon 20 chartered to fly to Dover Air Force Base. Upon arrival, the aluminum case would be moved to an explosive ordnance disposal room, where the body would be screened for embedded bomblets or ammunition—none would be found, but it was standard procedure for the victim of an IED in a war zone. The body would be taken to an examining room, where it would be removed from the body bag. What was left of Aldrich would be lifted onto a metal table. His remains would be photographed, tagged, and archived. His body and the severed parts in the transfer case would be coded so none were misplaced. In a day or two, his remains would be released. Analise didn't know who would collect Aldrich. A divorced wife with a new husband, or two estranged grown children to whom he'd never fully revealed what he did? All the ghosts in his life made their appearance at his death.

"He was a good man."

Analise turned to Gal, who sat beside her in the Land Rover as the whump of the helicopter's rotors grew faint as it flew out to sea. Two old adversaries. Men alike in many ways, but they had come to violently disagree. She didn't doubt Gal's sincerity; the moment required him to be gracious. She had no idea what insult or betrayal had disturbed their acquaintance.

Gal took her hand, comforting her. "There will be an investigation. Answers will be sought. Those responsible will be tracked down and punished. Hezbollah hasn't claimed responsibility, and until they do, or someone else does, we can only speculate. But I believe it was Qassem. I can't prove it, but having been in this business a long time, I have learned to trust my nose. If it smells like Qassem, it will turn out to be him. He killed one station chief, now another. They knew which SUV he was in."

Gal paused. "The woman, Hama. She is gone. We went to visit her. The neighbor said she left that afternoon. We can't find her."

"He trusted her."

"And for that he forfeited his life." Gal wheezed in shallow breaths. "He was a difficult man, but a good spy. In our work it is better to avenge the dead than mourn them."

Gal was quiet and then turned to her. "We're going forward."

"He wouldn't agree."

"If we'd acted last time, he would still be alive. A wolf hunts until it's put down."

Analise considered the pathetic irony of his observation.

"And you," Gal asked. "You have a role to play."

Her eyes came off the Chinook, now a speck on the pale sky.

"This was a rehearsal for an attack on Madam Secretary Rice." Gal looked out at the distant helicopter. "It would be better if she postponed her visit, but there is greater danger if she doesn't come."

Gal sat quietly but then stirred. "She arrives in three days, so we must strike in two days. Her security has arranged a convoy of SUVs and they will do a big show of zigzagging in the streets, thinking they are safe, but when they visit Berri in West Beirut, their precautions won't help. We must act before she arrives. We don't live in a perfect world, but the data we have is good enough. We move the day after tomorrow."

He faced her. "There is something we need from you."

"I'm done."

"Our driver was due on one date, but now we have a new date, and he can't be here."

"No." She shook her head violently. "I did my part."

"Madam Secretary's life is at risk. You are familiar with the neighborhood. Trusted. It will be a simple job. Park the vehicle and leave." Gal leaned forward and patted Bauman's shoulder. "He will protect you. He has my blessing."

She faced him. Gal's breathing was shallow and his voice soft. His lips were pallid, his face pale, but the intensity of his patient conviction startled her. She thought him a man who had fought vindictive forces like no other man she'd met, who carried a deep faith in the redemptive power of retribution.

"You know," he said, smiling, "the moment Rick told me that there was a young woman on the team, I knew that we would see this through to a successful conclusion."

She ignored the easy compliment of his calculating mind.

"You must be invisible for two days. Then we move."

23

Going Dark

A nalise was awakened by the morning call to prayer from the nearby mosque. Exhaustion was the unwelcome companion of stress. It had been with her when she left Gal, at her side when she'd walked home, and it had accompanied her to bed. The muezzin's singsong voice entered her consciousness and then she fell back to sleep.

Loud voices outside woke her for a second time. She dropped her bare feet to the floor and sat on the edge of her bed, head in her hands. The heat of the day had already made the room feel warm and she felt the unpleasant stickiness of last night's damp sweat in her loose T-shirt. She blinked into the sunlight streaming through the window. In a moment, she recognized another sound, a knocking on her door. She padded across the bedroom, taking her 9mm Glock from the drawer. She stood just to one side of the locked door.

"Who is it?"

"Helen."

Analise quickly brought her inside, looking both ways in the hallway. Helen moved to the balcony and closed the curtains to keep herself from being seen from a neighboring building. Her blousy shirt hid a Kevlar vest, and a vaguely friendly smile covered her urgent expression.

"You might have been spotted," she said, looking at Analise in a T-shirt and underwear. "We picked up chatter after the bombing. Whatever you're doing in Beirut has put you at risk. You can't stay here."

Analise moved to the kitchen to heat water. She carefully spooned grounds into a paper filter, ignoring Helen. "Then nothing has changed," she said. She looked up. "Coffee?"

"You don't understand. You have to leave this apartment."

Analise pointed toward a small backpack that sat beside clothing laid out on a credenza. "I'm aware of that."

"You have to leave now."

"You don't know what's going on." She faced Helen. "I can take care of myself."

They had trained together in counterintelligence and their bond had been forged on the anvil of covert operations. They were schooled in the techniques of clandestine work and they understood the danger of knowing what they shouldn't know. In their world, it was enough to be alert to danger.

"This apartment is no longer safe." She nodded at the sink of dirty dishes and the clothes on the floor. "How do you live like this?"

"How much time do I have?"

"No time." Helen unzipped a small backpack and produced a manila envelope from which she removed documents. "Your new passport."

Analise took the black passport. She looked at the name.

"This gives you diplomatic cover. It will give you some protection if you're caught." Helen opened a tiny gap between her finger and thumb. "Better than nothing. New name, a new legend. Memorize it."

She handed Analise a clunky cell phone. "Incoming and outgoing calls are encrypted. It's ugly, but it's safe."

"Anyone who sees this will conclude it's encrypted, and they'll say, 'Oh, look, a woman who doesn't want her calls intercepted.'" Analise tossed it back. "I could wear a big red badge that says, 'CIA.'"

Helen studied Analise. "My job is to make sure you don't leave like Aldrich. I'm good at my job, but I need you to cooperate."

"I'm not finished with my work in Beirut."

"How long?"

"Two days. A week. I'm not a train. I don't have a schedule."

Helen looked around the apartment. "You can't stay here. Hotels are out of the question." She pulled a key from her bag and handed it to Analise. "Aldrich kept a safe house nearby."

Helen motioned for Analise to move with her toward the balcony. She pulled the curtain back and pointed two blocks away. "There. The shuttered building on the corner that looks like a ship's bow with a wraparound balcony. Fifth floor. It was damaged in the civil war and it has remained locked and vacant. Aldrich arranged for access and a caretaker to look after it. No one lives there. He used it to meet assets. Safer than Awkar."

Helen dropped the curtain. "He chose it because the balcony has a view of all the street approaches. It was Kim Philby's place. Aldrich detested Philby, but he admired his tradecraft. The man went undetected for almost two decades. It's bare, but there's a bed. A bath. It's safe for a few days. How long before you leave?"

"A week. Two? I don't know."

She looked at Analise. "You won't see the bullet that kills you."

"Helpful advice," she said sarcastically. "What do I do with it?"

The two women faced each other at the door. Analise had the urge to embrace Helen, but she was conditioned to keep her feelings to herself. And then, despite her reluctance, she did. Then she kissed Helen on the cheek.

"This isn't a training mission."

Analise handed her an envelope. "In case anything happens to me."

Analise stood at the balcony and watched Helen disappear around the block. She was superstitious and had procrastinated in naming a designated beneficiary on her agency insurance policy, but after Aldrich's death, she gave in. If she died, her mother would get a check and maybe finally understand what her daughter had been doing in the Middle East.

She left her apartment as it was: bed unmade, towels on the floor, handwashed underwear hanging in the bathroom, a box of pastries in the refrigerator. Analise stuffed two pairs of socks and two pairs of boxers in a small backpack and pulled a second pair of trousers and a blouse over what she was wearing so she'd have a change of clothes. Anyone on the street watching her would observe a young woman going to work and think she would return that night. Nothing was predictable except the speed with which the unforeseen could turn a familiar world into a frightening labyrinth.

Outside, she double locked her door. She plucked a strand of hair and placed it high across the gap between door and jamb, attaching it with egg white. No one would see it covering the crack. There was nothing in the apartment that she cared about, or would miss, but if the strand of hair was gone, she would know someone had entered. Survival depended on continuous vigilance and a vast capacity for suspicion.

24

Safe House

Analise pushed open the door of the fifth-floor apartment and listened for telltale sounds inside. Aldrich's safe house was a few blocks from her apartment, but it was separated by the lost era of the Cold War. She had watched the lobby for two hours before she was confident no one would see her enter the boarded-up entrance.

She stepped inside the empty apartment. Hazy sunlight warmed the living room. Plaster blistered at the base of the walls from moisture that had seeped in from the cracked windows, and old wall paint had peeled in sheets and lay on the floor. She was surprised when the light bulb dangling from the ceiling fixture turned on. Copper electric wire was pilfered from new buildings, but no one had bothered with an old ruin. She found a bottle of vodka sitting in the middle of the empty room. It was half-full. She set it down again and imagined the apartment's ghosts.

A large porcelain tub in the bathroom was covered in debris and the toilet had no seat. The basin was bone dry. She tried the handle but no water came out. A safe house, she thought. Safe from use.

The kitchen was bare except for a refrigerator and Formica cabinets with doors thrown open to reveal empty shelves. A small red table had a single chair. Pale slatted light came through the blinds. She stood in the center of the room and listened to the distant sounds of the city. She crossed the kitchen and opened the refrigerator and was met with a rotting stench. A mousetrap with its catch was under the sink. Trash piled in a corner.

In the bedroom, she found a single bed with a thin mattress. Sheets and a wool blanket were neatly folded on top of a pillow. An old wardrobe door was askew and looked as if there had been a previous houseguest. A clean towel was folded on a shelf. A small wood table sat by a window with its pane intact, and sitting on top of it was an open laptop. An ethernet cable exited the rear of the laptop and connected to a wall outlet.

She knew it must be Aldrich's computer. Agency laptops weren't allowed outside Beirut Station, but he needed a way to communicate. She typed in a few obvious choices of passwords to unlock the screen: personal things easily remembered that didn't have to be stored and coded. Her fourth choice worked. His address. She saw the Hotmail account they'd shared, and his search history included the antiquities website that covered for an agency drop box.

She opened the account to a map of Haret Hreik that had been created for her. She had committed its broad outlines to memory, but she studied the detours and pathways by which the house could be approached. Beirut's southern suburbs had grown up in a chaotic disorder of unregulated sprawl as old orchards were developed to serve waves of people drawn to the city. Street signs were often missing, or never placed, so she memorized landmarks on the route she would take. Images from the drone footage came to mind. When she was confident about her route, she closed the computer.

Analise moved to the balcony. Her Nokia buzzed and she saw a text from Corbin.

At your apartment. Where are you?

She wondered about him. His usual pattern was to show up late at night with alcohol on his breath. She looked at her apartment building two blocks away and saw him emerge onto the sidewalk from the lobby. She stepped back under the overhang into the shadow of the midday sun and watched him walk toward the port. She understood why Philby had chosen this apartment. Four streets converged in front of the building, and Philby would have been able to spot his KGB handler approach from any direction.

Her eyes turned away when Corbin was out of sight. She turned off her phone without answering his text. She needed to avoid him until it was over.

The civil war had not been kind to the neighborhood. Ottoman-era family palaces that showed the scars of past fighting sat beside modern apartment buildings. As she looked down, she had the eerie sensation that she was Aldrich looking down, like Philby had looked down—inhabiting the mind of a man inhabiting another man's mind. *What drew Aldrich to Philby?* she wondered. A spy curious about another spy's betrayal, wandering inside the labyrinth of a traitor's mind looking for an answer to the unknowable mystery of his life. *Aldrich, too, was a tough case*, she thought. So careful and yet so careless. It was as if he had an unconscious desire to leave the world behind.

Their last conversation in Hama's parlor stuck with her. He had confided that he'd sent a private note to the DCI praising Gal for a backchannel effort to recruit Moscow's Beirut rezident. Aldrich had said, "It will sound alarms in Langley. Mossad has played us all along. The idea that Gal has been fooling the CIA will create a tremendous flutter in Langley's seventh-floor dovecote." He had added his view of the new DCI, a political appointee, and he had ended the conversation on an ominous note. "There is a penetration agent in the CIA. He's a man whose Israeli sympathies advance his career and make him useful to his handler. There is a war inside the agency between those who share my view—who believe we've been compromised—and those who denounce it, who work against me. This will not end well."

She considered Aldrich's endless game of thinking, unthinking, and rethinking. He understood the function of trivia and disconnected information, and in understanding it he could pluck the important bit from a torrent of data and turn it into a Rosetta stone that gave coherence to the noise. Aldrich rose in the agency as a field officer, but he had a sharp mind for analysis. She pondered the message on his computer. *It's not who they think it is.*

Bauman had parked the Pajero within sight of her old apartment. El Murr Tower was visible ahead, and Al Kantari Palace was close by on Michel Chiha Street. Beyond that, at the intersection, she could see the Red Cross building. Cars, vans, and motor scooters moved through the pleasant streets. Trees cut down in the civil war had been replanted and rose where the sun wasn't blocked by newer apartment buildings. Pedestrians walked in the shadows of the buildings, moving alone or in pairs. Teenagers taunted each other for a smoke, and modern Lebanese women in short skirts moved past women in head scarfs and chadors. Everywhere, subdued Beirutis took advantage of the day's peace to run urgent errands. It had been just over three weeks since the bombing had commenced, and the city looked forlorn and bruised. A red Mustang convertible drove by packed with young men yelling chaotically, honking at nothing. War was madness; it made people crazy.

The Pajero was three blocks away between two smaller cars. She had stepped out of the overhang's shade and was craning her head slightly to look at the streets converging into Rue Kantari. The Pajero was innocuous except for the large pale blue UN written on the roof to protect it from Israeli bombs.

It was a duplicate of the vehicles she drove for the UNHCR. Bauman had gone over the vehicle. Extraordinary effort had been made to make the Pajero look old and used—cracked leather seats, a broken side mirror, the patina of its white paint aged with sophisticated heat lamps and weathered by sandstorms in the confined warehouse in North Carolina where it had been put together. Semtex had been molded into the door and shaped with diligent care by expert technicians working thousands of miles away from where the killing would take place.

She held the Pajero's key in her hand. She had not confirmed that it would open the door. It was a silly worry. After all the careful preparations, endless days of surveillance, and all the stress, the idea that he'd given her the wrong key nagged at her. It was silly paranoia, but overlooked details undermined the best plans, and she would sleep better if she knew it worked.

Analise stood just inside the dark lobby of Philby's building, hesitating. She heaved her courage into her heart and stepped through the barricaded door into the bright sunshine. No bullet struck. No car squealed to a stop. She relaxed into the ordinary moment and quieted her fear. Key in hand, she approached the Pajero. She walked casually among people on the sidewalk, alert to a young man in a café and two women with quarreling children chatting. The appearance of normal life in a city where everyone was caught up in their own personal worlds. Caution came instinctively to her, and with caution came the quiet voice of sanity. Fear's demons confused her judgment, but she'd learned to quash fear with the soothing comfort of observed details.

She clicked the key and the lights flashed. She continued to walk past the Pajero, feeling a little victory. Clear-headedness had always been a North Star. It was too early to return to the apartment's suffocating confinement, so she kept walking. Walking gave her time to think and to again rehearse the route she would take through the maze of streets.

The day's heat, rising in undulating waves from the pavement, was a blanket on the neighborhood. Older men sat shirtless in lounge chairs on balconies and observed the street below, grateful for the tepid sea breeze. They fanned themselves, indifferent to crying children and barking dogs.

Analise passed the Pajero a second time from the opposite direction and confirmed that it was parked legally. It wouldn't be towed and car thieves wouldn't be interested given its weathered condition.

She saw the man by Banque Libano-Française in the reflection of the pharmacy's plate-glass window. His eyes were on her from across the street. He was thuggish, resembling a fire hydrant, self-conscious with his newspaper, and when she moved away from the window, he followed. He struggled to keep up with his short legs. She'd seen him from the lobby looking at young girls. His tight shirt stretched over a gut, and his blue jeans were a stiff girdle that gave him a duck-like walk.

The man following her was an amateur who she had spotted at once. He might be a pickpocket looking to snatch her handbag or a pervert excited by an attractive woman walking alone without her headscarf.

Her Glock gave her confidence, but the real danger was the attention she would get if she drew the weapon.

Analise turned and approached the man, looking straight ahead as she passed, avoiding his eyes but in her peripheral vision seeing the whole of him. Pudgy face, narrow eyes behind black glasses, and a chin that disappeared into a thick neck. She walked past him and stopped suddenly, looking at her watch. To no one in particular she said, "I'm late. How could this happen? Damn it."

She crossed the street in a run, avoiding a taxi, and went in the direction of Martyrs' Square. Surveillance teams operated in pairs, and sometimes several teams coordinated around a target so if one watcher was spotted they could be replaced by another, the new team picking up the target without being observed. The squat man kept up behind her, but it was his partner that Analise looked for.

The second man showed himself as she moved toward the square. He moved quickly to keep up with her, darting across the street when she ran through traffic, giving her a lucky break. He was the physical opposite of the squat man—tall, thin, gaunt face, wispy beard, and short arms that were out of proportion to his height. His jeans ended high on his ankles, he floated in a billowy pullover shirt, and his red baseball cap was facing backward.

Luck helped if she knew how to use it, but she couldn't rely on luck. She had done the hard part in discovering she was being followed. Her mind mapped her location and considered how to lose them. She was near Clemenceau Street heading toward Bab Idriss. In her mind's eye, she saw the streets she had memorized and came up with a route. Her advantage was time. She had no immediate deadline that day, no urgency, nowhere she had to be by a particular hour. The hard work for the tail was the persistent attention needed to watch for sudden evasive movements, all the while trying to remain unseen.

Analise found her chance farther on. Mohammad Al-Amin's blue domes were described by the four minarets that rose from the corners of the mosque's stone walls, bleached by the timeless sun. She joined a small group of pilgrims who moved to the mosque's steps. Men went to one entrance and she joined the women, who approached a different entrance, wrapping her head with her scarf and tying the loose ends around her neck.

Analise looked back and saw the two men in the square moving from one tall woman to another, stopping each and moving to the next. She removed her boots and placed them in a small cubby beside the other women's shoes. The water was warm when she splashed her face and washed her hands, reciting the gratitude. She moved through a narrow doorway, fixing her scarf tighter on her face. Her father had taken her to Islamic services as a young girl, so she knew the rituals. She was a devout Muslim when she entered the domed space, which rose to a breathless, exhilarating height. Hollow quiet filled the open space, but the silence made its vastness feel intimate. She padded across the sweeping carpet and joined a group of kneeling women.

Head lowered, she heard shouts and running footsteps, and she glanced toward the main entrance. She saw the squat man enter, stop, and look toward the kneeling women. *Hezbollah*, she thought. Syrians would be more cautious in a public setting.

Analise's head was still lowered as the man drew near; her scarf hid her face. The man's rude approach irritated an older woman, who shamed him. He moved away but continued to look. He fretted impatiently, giving away his interest. His eyes kept coming back to the kneeling women until his persistent, annoying gaze came to the attention of a mullah, who confronted him. A heated discussion ensued, ending when the squat man was escorted from the mosque.

Analise left with a woman who went to a different exit. She found a stranger's sandals that fit and put them on, placing a few Lebanese pounds in the cubby. To avoid the front of the mosque, Analise approached an old retaining wall. She dropped six feet into the Roman ruin that lay between the mosque and the adjacent Saint George Maronite Cathedral.

It was midafternoon and sweltering heat and carnivorous mosquitos landed on her neck as she moved among the overturned marble columns and weathered stone blocks. Prickly weeds tore at her trousers as she stepped around the huge stones. She stayed in the shadow of the retaining wall, hugging it to remain invisible from above. She heard voices beyond the lip of the wall, yelling. Four men now, she thought. They had the urgent, desperate tone of men consumed by the prospect of failure.

Analise flattened herself to the wall when she heard men's voices just overhead. They swore in a dialect she didn't recognize. Hissed, angry commands were made, and then excited cries came from elsewhere, and footsteps running away. Her breathing came quick and loud, her pulse was fast, and for a moment she feared a heart attack. She repeated the prayer that her father had taught her.

When she was certain the men on the parapet were gone, she climbed the embankment using gaps in the stones for handholds. She faced the bell tower that rose from the neoclassical cathedral and a neatly manicured rose garden. She entered the cathedral through a side entrance, which caught the attention of an old priest. It was dark inside except for dim light entering the high stained-glass windows. The nave's reaching height made the few visitors in the front pew look humble and small, sitting quietly, gazing at the bloody Christ on the cross. A young priest entered from a hidden door in the transept, and the brushed hiss of his rustling robe moved across the stone floor.

She walked to the cathedral's main entrance, putting on her dark glasses against the sun's harsh light. Few people stood in front of the cathedral's stone steps, but she remained in the shadows as she confirmed the men were gone. Cautious, she stayed just inside the huge wood double doors and surveyed the scene. A garbage truck moved slowly across the square and interrupted several boys playing soccer. Two cars were parked at the taxi rank.

25

A Misunderstanding

What happened next startled Analise, and later, when she reconstructed the incident, she realized how her eagerness had been the enemy of caution. She hopped into the back seat of the first taxi and settled into the car's blessed air conditioning, feeling the excited blush of escape.

"Rue Kantari," she said.

Her cell phone vibrated just then and she saw Corbin's number pop up, but the car's rapid acceleration threw her back, knocking the phone from her hand. She pulled herself forward, groping for the phone under the seat, but the call had ended. Angry, she turned to the driver, who was indifferent to his passenger. The taxi had already gone halfway around the square and was traveling at a high rate of speed.

"Excuse me," she said, not seeing a taxi meter. "How much is the ride?"

A man in the front passenger seat popped up, looking at Analise, and an audible gasp slipped from her lips. The pudgy-faced surveillant wore a satisfied expression. She tried one door and then the other. Both were locked.

"Sit back," he said.

"Who are you?" she demanded.

Both men had impassive faces with the same dull expression, but that was where the resemblance ended. The driver had a coarse beard, deep-set eyes, and his attention was focused on the clogged streets that he navigated with sharp turns. His thuggish companion had a boxer's misshapen nose, a square jawline, and he stared straight ahead with an implacable expression. She glanced behind for a second car, considered the speed at which they traveled, and the risk.

"Where are you taking me?" Her hand went to her holstered Glock. "I am an American diplomat. I demand to be taken to Awkar." She pointed the pistol at the driver's head. "Do as I say."

The car slowed as it turned onto Place de l'Étoile, coming to an abrupt halt in front of Parliament. The back door opened to reveal Inspector Aboud, who smiled and offered his hand.

"You won't need that," he said, seeing the Glock.

"What's going on?" she asked. "Who are they?"

Inspector Aboud lowered his head and spoke to the driver in rapid Arabic. He turned to Analise with an apologetic expression. "They were ordered to bring you here. He said that you ran when they approached. A regrettable misunderstanding," he said. "After Aldrich's death, we are concerned for the safety of Americans in Beirut."

She was flush with anger. "Another minute and I would have shot him."

"They don't speak English."

"I spoke Arabic to him."

"What is important is that you are here. That you are safe. Please follow me. I want to continue our conversation."

Analise knew very well that he wasn't interested in a casual exchange of opinions, and the absurd abduction portended an uncomfortable meeting. She was led through an arched corridor, past pink marble colonnades, and then up a wide stone staircase toward a large office at the end of the hall.

General Adham Hammadi welcomed her, bowing slightly. His hand on her elbow ushered her in.

"Thank you for coming."

"I didn't have a choice. I almost shot your man."

"It's not permitted for foreigners to have guns, but perhaps the United Nations thinks you need protection from our desperate refugees."

Analise didn't rise to the bait of his sarcasm. "Why am I here?"

"Please sit."

Analise sat in the bergère chair that she had occupied during her first visit. She didn't recognize the young adjunct who took orders for coffee and sweets. She was about to decline as she had in the first meeting, but to avoid creating a pattern, she asked for coffee. She turned to Hammadi. "What's this all about?"

Hammadi pointed to Inspector Aboud on the sofa, who sat exactly where he'd been in the first meeting. She had a disagreeable moment of déjà vu and felt an urge to walk out when, in shifting her position, she saw Aldrich's photograph had been added to the gallery of assassinated politicians.

"A tragic loss," Inspector Aboud said. "He believed in Lebanon." He lifted a document from the coffee table and handed it to Analise, like an offering. "This is what Hammadi wanted to show you last time, but I objected."

The one-page document was in Arabic and she handed it back. "Another report on Bauman. You brought me here for this?"

"Think of this as one of our regular meetings. Have you seen him?"

"He's around. Try the Commodore Hotel bar."

"We did. His neighbor hasn't seen him and he's not registered at any hotels."

"Why are you asking me?"

"You were intimate. Has he come to you?"

Analise scoffed at the suggestion and considered the technique of his interrogation, using a false claim to excite her. "We were on the press tour together. He drove and I was in the front seat. Intimate, perhaps, but not by American standards." She looked at him. "You're acting like he's a fugitive."

"He behaves like one."

"He's a journalist following a story."

"We want to question him."

"About that?" She indicated the document she had rejected. "Someone has a gripe against him."

"Not just someone. The Syrian Intelligence Service. Bauman was arrested by Mukhabarat for spying and delivered to Israel in a prisoner exchange." Inspector Aboud leaned back. "I've been rude." He lifted the plate of sweets the adjunct had left. "Please. The almond crescent rolls are from my favorite pastry shop in Hamra."

Analise picked up the cookie, taking her time to consider what she would say to the questions that would follow and how far she could go with her false ignorance.

"Syria's interest in Bauman interests me. But I have another question for him. I want to ask him about the murder of Rick Aldrich. I understand you were there when the bomb went off."

She nodded.

"Visiting Hama."

"Visiting Aldrich at her home," she corrected.

"I don't understand how he was allowed to live with her while other Americans are confined to Awkar. Did you think that odd?"

"He did what he wanted. It was his choice."

"You knew him well enough to know that it was his choice? Did you know he was CIA station chief?"

Analise held on to her silence without any expression whatsoever. She knew that it was dangerous to underestimate what Inspector Aboud knew and equally dangerous to inadvertently acknowledge a fact he was trying to establish.

"When I needed to process refugees, he provided travel documents to America. A man with his authority might be CIA. Aren't all Americans suspect?"

"Are you?"

She laughed. "If that is what you'd like to think, then please, enjoy the speculation."

He looked at Analise. "We are a small country. It's my job to know things I'm not supposed to know. Rick Aldrich was a great friend of Lebanon. A good friend of mine. This is a difficult time in Beirut. The war. Corruption. But back to Bauman. You haven't seen him?"

"He was on the press tour."

"When was that?"

"A week ago."

"Before Aldrich was killed?" He leaned forward. "You were with Bauman at the port when Aldrich's body was taken to the helicopter."

"We were there and so were a dozen others. I was paying my respects. It's hard to watch a man leave the country that way."

"Where is he now?"

"Who?"

"We were talking about Bauman."

"Ask Agence France-Presse. He works for them."

"They don't know. Or so they say. Journalists get nervous when the police ask questions."

"What do you expect?"

Inspector Aboud poured coffee into a demitasse cup. He added four sugars, stirring briskly. He set the silver spoon on the tray and raised the cup to his lips, sipping. He set the cup down, centering it on the tray, and lifted his eyes.

"Men in Aldrich's line of work make enemies." He pointed at the photographs. "Crime doesn't end when war starts, and neither does my job. War makes my job more difficult, but the war will end and the dead will still be dead. They all died in car bombs, and there are other links between the assassinated Lebanese politicians, but Rick Aldrich's murder is different, at least that's what I assume. The CIA station chief would be an enemy of Hezbollah, or even the Syrians, or perhaps Russia."

Analise knew she was being closely watched by Hammadi while Inspector Aboud spoke, judging her response, testing her.

Inspector Aboud stood and approached Hammadi's gallery of immortals and drew a large red X through Aldrich's photograph. He spoke with the brisk efficiency of a diligent investigator in possession of enough evidence to make an indictment.

"You were there. You left the scene with an American woman. You were a witness, but you didn't come forward. We sent two men to find you, and you avoided them, acting like a fugitive. Should I detain you as a witness? Perhaps a week in jail would facilitate our conversations and your cooperation."

Hammadi hadn't spoken, but he leaned forward in his chair and planted his elbows on his desk. His voice was grimly matter-of-fact. "What are you hiding?"

Analise looked from one man to the other. She felt the indifferent arrogance of police authority. No single explanation would undo their suspicions. A dark cloud of hesitation came over her, and she bent to retie her loose shoe laces, taking a moment to think.

"There is one thing," she said when she looked up. Her forehead knitted in a serious expression and she was politely contrite. Only one kind of lie had the chance to be effective—one that in no way deserved to be called a deception—but sprang to life as reasonable truth in the listener's lively imagination.

"I don't know where Bauman is, but I know who might. There is a Shia woman in the Jewish cemetery. He sends her money."

26

Outside the Commodore Hotel

C orbin was talking on his Blackberry in the midst of a heated conversation with his editor in New York. He was trying to convey that the war was not something picturesque, like an illustrated panorama of Teddy Roosevelt's charge up San Juan hill. Or the calm picture of allied troops parachuting over French pastures. Shelters with children were being bombed and Beirut was overwhelmed with desperate refugees. Aldrich was dead, assassinated. Corbin's mind was focused on the arguments he needed to make to justify his latest dispatch to the *Times*'s newsroom, and in the mental tangle of his thoughts as he turned off Baalbek Street into the Commodore Hotel, he didn't see Inspector Aboud before bumping into him.

"I've been waiting for you."

Corbin lowered his cell phone and stared. "Waiting for me? What for?"

"There's been a development."

Corbin recognized the grim expression on Inspector Aboud's face. Without forethought, he glanced along the street and noticed several military vehicles parked near the intersection, including Inspector Aboud's unmarked police sedan. His driver was by the open door.

"What's going on?"

"I need to speak with you."

"About what?"

"Sit with me in my car. It's better that we speak privately."

Corbin lifted his Blackberry. "I'll call back." He hung up.

Inspector Aboud nodded at the long queue of taxis waiting for a fare to come out of the hotel. "The war will end but tourists won't return quickly. Their families are suffering. Every Beiruti home is crowded with refugees who have fled the fighting. UN centers hold displaced people, but most go unaccounted because they are with relatives."

He reached his sedan, and the driver held the door open as he slipped into the back seat. He turned to Corbin, who had joined him. "So much has happened, but we know so little. All we have are rumors. Rumors and war. Rumors of more war."

Corbin felt the heat of the day contained by the car and he opened his window.

"I met with your friend."

"My friend? Who is that?"

"The young woman who works for the UN. Analise Assad. I'm told you're friendly. Have you seen her?"

Corbin had looked off but turned back and met Inspector Aboud's gaze. *So polite and so determined*, he thought. "She's avoiding me."

"She was also a friend of the American, Aldrich."

"If you say so. I don't keep track of the friends of my friends."

"But you know David Bauman."

"We all know him."

"They were acquainted."

"Who?"

"Aldrich and the young woman, Analise."

"Acquainted. Like us."

Inspector Aboud waved off the suggestion. "Not like us. I hardly know you. What I know is that you ask many questions."

"That makes us alike," Corbin said sarcastically. "It's hot in this car."

Inspector Aboud said something in Arabic and the driver started the engine, turning on the air conditioning. "We both ask questions, but what I do with the answers and what you do with them are different."

"As far as I know, neither of us has gotten good answers, but if you have, please share them. You have a dozen murders and no suspects."

"Eleven. Aldrich adds one to my list. His death is also of interest to you, I think."

"I never met him."

"Never? I would have thought—"

"What? He's an American and we all know each other? We're not penguins. We don't all look alike and live together in rookeries."

Inspector Aboud vaguely smiled. "Penguins. Press. Plastique."

Corbin turned to Inspector Aboud. "It's not plastique as far as I know. A newer explosive that accomplishes the same thing."

"How well do you know Analise Assad?"

"We're friendly. She likes champagne. I prefer scotch. Anything else? If she returns my call, I'll let her know you've asked about her. She doesn't like attention and you shouldn't believe everything that she tells you."

"Would she say the same about you?"

"Then you've spoken to her."

"We had a not very cordial conversation."

He laughed. "Did she insult you?"

"She was hostile. I asked about Bauman, who she knows, and she got upset. Do you know why she might be offended by my questions?"

Corbin looked off. He started to speak but felt sarcasm rise up with his words. "I don't know."

"Is she protecting him?"

"From what?"

"From me. She gave me the name of a Shia woman at the Jewish cemetery who she said would know how to contact Bauman. But I couldn't find such a woman. So I assume she lied. We are putting together a case to arrest her for obstruction of an official proceeding, providing false information to an ISF officer, and collaborating with a foreign agent."

Inspector Aboud looked at Corbin across the back seat. His voice lowered and his expression darkened. "If you have feelings for her, you should inform her of my actions."

Corbin went to open his door, but he felt a restraining hand on his arm.

"Aldrich's murder. I have something that might interest you. You're a journalist with a return ticket so you can afford to be courageous."

Corbin listened to Inspector Aboud, thinking all the while that he'd rather be a reporter than a policeman because the standard of proof was less, and then, before stepping out of the sedan, he took the glassine envelope that Aboud offered.

"This was found in the wreckage of Aldrich's SUV."

Corbin handed it back. "What would I do with it?"

Aboud waved off Corbin's offer. "I have more. You're good at asking questions."

Corbin placed the object in his pocket and stepped out of the car into the bright sun. He entered the Commodore Hotel lobby and found a quiet corner. He dialed Analise's phone number but got voice mail. *Fuck.* "Call me when you get this. It's important."

Corbin looked at the bar and then at his watch. It was early even for him. As he passed the front desk on his way to the elevator, he was greeted by the slightly built hotel clerk waving him over.

"This came for you." He presented a letter, holding it forward with two hands.

Corbin saw the American postage stamp and recognized his wife's loopy, cursive handwriting. He knew it would bear bad news. He stood in the lobby and suddenly felt uncomfortable among the guests who moved past him to the street or laughed brightly on their way to the pool. He felt the loud silence of the news inside.

He entered the bar and picked a spot where he could be alone, dropping the letter on the table. He was reluctant to open it but also eager to know what she had written, those opposing feelings acting like a pendulum between anxiety and acceptance.

The bar was quiet, except for a few Englishmen who had already gone one round with warm beer. Corbin looked up at the familiar waiter, who greeted him as he always did, with his usual order. "Almaza?"

Corbin considered ordering the new cocktail the bartender had promoted the night before, but didn't feel like he could handle a new drink and the surprise of the unexpected letter. "Yes, please."

He picked up the letter, then put it down again. It lay on the table like a verdict waiting to be read. He opened it. When he finished reading, he refolded the stationery and slipped it back into the envelope, where it belonged. His beer had arrived and he sipped it slowly, patiently, looking at the envelope. When he set the glass down, he saw his reflection in the large bar mirror behind the colorful display of liquor bottles. He looked a little stunned, a little relieved, but there was no pain on his face and no sadness in his expression. He put a few Lebanese pounds on the table and returned to the lobby elevator.

His room on the sixth floor was warm, so he opened the window for the light breeze. Inspector Aboud's sedan was gone but the military vehicles still guarded the end of the street, and the taxi drivers stood lazily by their cars. Nothing was different, but everything had changed.

He sat at the small hotel desk and opened his laptop to draft a response. He read the letter again. The paper still had the faint smell of her perfume and he imagined she had written it after an evening at the theater or a late-night dinner at a restaurant. She found her courage after an evening cocktail. It was handwritten on personalized stationery and he knew that she preferred letters to email for important news. It was a short letter. She'd addressed him as "Charles." She used "Charles" and not "Charlie" when she wanted his attention, or was upset with him, or wanted to put a distance between them. It was five sentences, but he stopped after the second. Everything that she wanted to say came in that sentence, and what followed were guilt-driven afterthoughts and vague claims that this was best for both of them, which irritated him because she had no right to assert what was best for him. Anger welled up, but he calmed himself.

He chose to respond with an email. The cold and impersonal nature of an electronic answer served his state of mind. His fingers hovered over the keyboard as he considered how to make her feel the consequences of her decision—of her adultery.

In the second draft, he found the words to express the tone of politeness and disgust that he intended.

Dear Laura. Your letter arrived today and I am not surprised by the choice you've made. As you say, it's best for both of us, which may be true, but you got to be the one to say it, which I resent. I'm not returning to New York for a few months, which you probably already know from Thomas, but what you don't know is that I have met someone here in Beirut. She works for the United Nations, helping refugees get through the crisis. Beirut has been dangerous for some time and I've discovered that physical danger is a kind of aphrodisiac, making it easier to escape from the stress of the war. Our life in New York was too stable, our dreams too ordinary, and I think that we were victims of not having enough excitement in our lives. We were living small. I think you know what I mean, even if my words might not express the thought perfectly.

I could end this email on a sad note, but what would be the point of that? It's not right to pretend what we don't feel, nor is it honest. We started off our relationship by telling each other the truth and it only seems fitting that we end it with the truth. I have found a way to forget the happy times we had together. Sticking with bad memories makes it easier to move forward.

The woman I've met is half-Lebanese and fluent in three languages. I'm not comparing you to her, which wouldn't be fair, but it's a way of saying that she is smart and very clever, and she has her own independent professional life. We'll never be victims of a dull day in Beirut. I don't expect the relationship to last. She'll leave Beirut, find a lovely man, marry him, and have a family. It's silly of me to tell you this, but we always did have a way of sharing our thoughts, talking about other people. We were always better suited to be friends than lovers. I think you would agree.

I'm writing this in my hotel room. Evening here is beautiful when the bombs stop and the sea breeze blows away the chemical smell. Good luck with Thomas. Tell him I'm working on the big story that I pitched.

Corbin reread the note. He wasn't happy with it, but it expressed his feelings in the moment, and it was better to say what he felt than to try to draft a note that was precisely right. Emotions were clumsy. No amount of editing would make the note better reflect their failed marriage. No amount of fiddling would make it read better or be truer to his complicated feelings.

He pressed the Send button and closed his computer. In a moment, he went to the balcony and looked out over Ras Beirut, wondering where Analise was.

27

Moving Forward

The bottle of gin sat in front of Analise on the living-room floor of Aldrich's safe house. She had bought it at a nearby shop and then returned to buy olives, but the store had none, so she'd made do with a lemon. She sat crossed-legged on the floor and held up the small glass with its twist. Gin wasn't Aldrich's drink, but she knew that he was a promiscuous drinker, so it was one that he might have enjoyed. She wondered if Aldrich had ever sat alone in the living room communing with Philby's ghost over a fierce martini.

"Cheers, Rick," she said, lifting her glass. "Bloody fucking cheers. To you. To Buckley. To leaving Beirut alive."

Alcohol and men had never been reliable allies in her battle against the loneliness of covert work. She set the glass down and moved to the wood desk.

From memory, she drew the street map of Haret Hreik that she would navigate in the morning. She marked the barbershop, the video game parlor, Rami's home, and the spot where she would park the Pajero. On United Nations stationery, she wrote an Arabic sign for the dashboard. The trip south would take forty-five minutes in traffic. She would park the Pajero, and Qassem would arrive during midday prayer. The bomb would be triggered by Bauman from a vantage point—somewhere on a rooftop. Or by Gal, looking at the scene on his computer through the eyes of an overhead drone. Her job was simple: park the SUV and get the hell away.

Analise opened Aldrich's laptop and went through his unencrypted files. Memos he'd written to the file and several after-action reports. She wasn't looking for anything in particular, but delving into his work focused her mind and gave her something to do. The Hotmail account they'd shared had their last unsent email exchange in the drafts folder, and his final note to her, which she'd never seen. She pondered the words: "Remind me to tell you about my new problem. We think we're solving one problem, but it's a shiny distraction, and the real threat is in plain sight. Who gains from the chaos? I have passed my suspicions on to the right person."

Analise pondered what the "new problem" was, and his reference to "my suspicion" and the "real threat" were equally ambiguous. There was the assassination of Qassem and there was Aldrich's threat to call it off. Was it Gal's meddling in Washington, or was it his concern that America would own the humanitarian crisis? She had no way of knowing, and in the absence of certainty, the protocol was to move forward. At the sink she splashed bottled water on her face.

She moved to the balcony. Night had fallen and there was a thin ribbon of moonlit sea visible. Cars' headlights carved arteries in the streets among the darkened buildings and were a reminder of the city's spirit. She held the Pajero's key in her hand. Pressing the yellow hatch-release button would trigger the bomb. She had that responsibility if the spotter didn't act.

The evening's sea breeze cooled her face. She was unsettled but strangely calm. A dreamy moment—a quiet peace before a violent battle. Her shadow world was closing in around her. It was getting harder to tell which part of her was genuinely her and which the acquired identity she inhabited. Her real self was somewhere underneath—locked in a dark chamber of her mind, and slowly it seemed that person was becoming distant and remote. There were two of her, and the one she had been stood across the room, judging her. She had not been alert to the change and she hadn't been aware of the ways in which she was losing track of her real self.

She gazed out at the starless night. Closing her eyes, she rid her mind of all that would follow in the days and weeks after the assassination. She focused on the next hour and the next morning.

Analise went to the computer again, opening her Starbucks account as she did every night before sleeping. She had given Rami a Starbucks reward card as part of a simple way to communicate confidentially with him. The account number had no identifying personal information that tied her to the account. If he wanted to meet, he bought a latte at the Starbucks on Hamra Street with the card. If she saw that the account had been decremented by one latte, she knew that he wanted to meet the next day at noon at school. If the account was decremented two lattes, it meant that it was urgent that they meet as soon as possible. She was to go to the Starbucks store and wait until he showed up. The account was unchanged.

She moved to the bedroom, where she stuffed the feather pillow into its case and made the bed. After aligning her boots on the floor, she lay fully clothed on top of the fitted sheet. Her hand rested on the Glock at her side. At some point she drifted off to sleep.

28

The Kill

Bright sunlight streaming through the window woke her. Her sleepy mind tried to hold on to the pleasant dream, but it slipped away and then was gone. She opened her eyes and for a brief moment she didn't know where she was or even which part of her life she was in. Her hand went for her Glock, but it wasn't at her side. In the middle of the night it had fallen to the floor.

She sat up, slipping her feet into her boots, and slowly laced them. Her mind began to engage with the day. Familiar sounds from the street came through the open window. She recognized the vibrato voice of the ice-cream peddler moving his bicycle up the street, calling for customers and to cheery children marching to school. From the balcony, she confirmed that the Pajero was still parked on the street. In her dream, it had been stolen.

She splashed her face several times with bottled water and toweled herself dry with the bed sheet. Her Kevlar vest fit snugly over her T-shirt and it disappeared inside her blousy tunic. In front of the mirror, she confirmed the armor wasn't visible. There was little left to do—drive the Pajero, park it at the designated spot, place the sign on the dashboard, and walk away, disappearing into the neighborhood. After the bomb went off, she'd be on her way out of Beirut.

Her first surprise came when she checked the Starbucks account and saw that the balance had been decremented by the price of two lattes. The sale had been made half an hour earlier.

Analise called Halima's apartment. "It's me. Where's Rami?"

"I called your apartment. Where are you?"

"There was a problem. Is Rami with you?"

"No. He was upset when you missed class yesterday."

"Upset about what?"

"I don't know. He left class. When I came home, he was playing video games."

"Where is he?"

"I don't know. He was gone this morning. My son didn't see him go."

"His boat leaves tonight."

"His mother called last night," Halima said. "They had an argument. I was in the other room but I could hear his anger. When the called ended, he went back to his video game. What's happening?"

Analise pressed the cell phone to her ear, thinking. "How did she get your number?"

"I don't know."

Analise pulled the Pajero into an empty parking spot a block away from Starbucks. She had driven past the store once, hoping to spot Rami, but it was on her second pass that she saw him at an outside patio table. She honked once and watched him approach in the rearview mirror, dodging cars as he ran through traffic. Her eyes moved back to the patio to confirm that he was alone. When he made it to the car, she reached over to unlock the passenger door, and she saw his face was drawn and pale. He faced her but then sank into the seat, sullen and quiet.

"What's wrong?" When no answer came, she turned the ignition.

"You were late. I waved when you drove by. I thought you didn't see me."

"I was parking." She glanced in the rearview mirror.

"I'm alone."

It was the tone in his voice that surprised her—brusque assurance about a concern she hadn't expressed. "We can talk in the car."

She pulled the Pajero into Beirut's morning traffic. Taxis filled with passengers nudged their way through the chaotic intersection, honking their way forward. A pickup truck with a mounted machine gun in the rear bed moved among the cars, the gunner waving his red baseball cap. An occasional weapon was fired into the air without drawing any interest from the Lebanese patrol that stood beside an armored personnel carrier. The soldiers were indifferent to the celebration.

"There will be a cease-fire," Rami said. "It was in the news this morning."

"We'll see," she said. Every day brought the promise of peace, every night the disappointment of war. Analise guided the Pajero through an opening in the slow-moving traffic and entered a broad avenue lined with barricades for the route set aside for Secretary Rice's quick trip. Further along, helpers on a flatbed truck lowered steel barriers to create a fast lane for Rice's convoy of black SUVs.

She turned to Rami. "What is so urgent?"

"Where did you get this car?"

"My vehicle is being repaired."

"You didn't come to class yesterday."

"We're meeting now."

"Who is Bauman?"

"You met him," she said, turning to see Rami's face, seeking to know what was on his mind. "He was at Halima's farm. He's a journalist. How did you get his name?"

"You told me."

She knew that she had not. Their moment on the field in the hills was fixed in her mind. It would have been reckless to use Bauman's name. She gripped the steering wheel and pondered whether to confront him.

"How did you meet him?"

"Why are you asking?" Not getting an answer, she glanced at him. Quiet. Subdued. Still a boy. "What's so urgent?"

"I don't have my passport."

"Where is it?"

"I put it in my backpack at home. When I looked again, it was gone. I called my mother and she said she found it and removed it."

Analise remembered Halima's report of the conversation. "You called her?"

"I called her when I didn't find the passport. I can't leave without it."

"You called her?"

A car swerved in front and Analise braked quickly to avoid a collision.

"Watch the road," he said. "You'll kill us."

Analise considered Rami's lie, but Halima might have been mistaken about the call. She turned to Rami, pondering his expression, and then continued along Damascus Street, uncertain about what to think but certain she had to drive the Pajero and park it.

"Where is my sister?"

"Cyprus. I spoke to her last night. She wants to know when she will see you." It was the way that he had asked the question, forcefully, like a command. It was a tone of voice she hadn't heard from him. "Why are you asking?"

"I need my passport."

"We'll get it." She looked at him. She could abort the mission. No one in the agency would begrudge her the decision to turn the Pajero around and drive to Awkar with the boy. She had that excuse. No one wanted to put the boy at risk, but that choice didn't feel right. Too many hours, too much effort, too little to show for months of diligent work. She turned to Rami and saw a young boy upset by circumstances he had helped set in motion that were now playing out in unexpected ways. She would keep him close to keep him safe. She would park two blocks from his home and invite him into the video game parlor. He would be at her side, engrossed in his game, when the bomb exploded.

"We'll go there now. You'll get to the boat on time."

They had been driving south along Damascus Street, leaving West Beirut and entering the suburbs. Tall apartment buildings were left behind as they entered an area heavily damaged by bombing. Piles of rubble had closed some streets, and backhoes worked to clear the area.

Analise felt her cell phone vibrate. She saw a text from Gal. *Turn left at the cemetery.*

She was a moving dot on a computer screen inside the panel van. Without telling her, Bauman had placed an RFID tag in the Pajero. Gal was following her progress—the errand girl delivering death—making sure she didn't get lost.

"Who was it?" Rami asked. "The man I saw you kissing?"

"He's just a friend. I told you that." She saw the jealous expression on his face. "An old friend, that's all."

"Does he write poetry?"

"I doubt it."

"Israeli?" He spat the word.

A boy too young to know better had been taught to hate. "American. Works for a big newspaper." Analise turned on the radio to distract from the conversation and give herself time to consider what lay ahead. Traffic thinned out as they moved south out of central Beirut, but dust had risen from the unpaved streets in the wind. Head scarfs flapped, and pedestrians walked close to buildings to avoid the worst of it. The Pajero entered Haret Hreik and moved past the Coral gas station, where drivers lined up in their cars to buy a meager gasoline ration. Young mothers with children in tow carried large plastic containers of water on their heads. Electric wires were a tangled overhead web, and as she turned into the neighborhood, the two-way streets became narrow alleys.

Analise's cell phone vibrated again. *Do you see him?*

Who, she texted, tilting the phone so Rami didn't see.

Bauman. Three blocks away. Park. Walk away.

Analise placed the cell phone facedown on her lap and looked out the window and up at the roofs of the buildings. She turned to Rami when he asked what was going on. "Nothing," she said. "I thought I heard an airplane."

She saw the barbershop on the next block and looked again to the rooftops for Bauman's signal or his half-hidden form. He would need a clear line of sight to the Pajero. Not seeing him above, she studied the people on the sidewalk. He was taller than most Lebanese, and though he would dress to blend in, disguised as just another man on an errand, his height would betray him.

"What are you looking for?"

She was stopped at an intersection where a three-wheeled tuk tuk carrying construction debris was stalled. The driver twisted his hand at the ignition but the engine didn't turn over and the rickety vehicle remained motionless, blocking the way. The driver cursed the old vehicle but no matter how frequently or firmly he moved his hand, making a great show of frustration, the engine refused to start. He pumped his hand at Analise, asking for patience, and she saw that he wasn't holding a key. *This is no accident*, she thought.

Analise turned to Rami, who had slid away from her, and she glanced in the side mirror. The street behind had begun to empty of cars. The amplified call to prayer from the nearby mosque had not cleared the street and she saw two men moving on the sidewalk, staying close to the buildings.

Something was not right. A sudden tremor in her hand. She honked loudly at the tuk tuk driver, who raised both hands in helplessness. He gestured at the old vehicle and pressed his foot on the gas, but the stalled vehicle didn't move.

Analise reached for Rami to reassure him, but he threw off her hand. His eyes were wide and tearing and there was fear on his face.

"You lied to me. You lied about my sister. You aren't who you say you are."

A shot rang out. Shouts in the street, behind and in front. The three-wheeled tuk tuk lurched forward and loose debris fell from the rear onto the street. Analise saw a drone ahead, hovering roof-height two blocks away. The muted whining of its rotors drew the attention of the driver and people who were leaning out second-floor windows to witness the commotion of the stalled tuk tuk. The drone advanced slowly, dropping in altitude, a gnat-like remote-controlled machine. It hovered in the middle of the street, shifting slightly from side to side. Two more shots came in rapid succession and the drone fell straight to the street, where it lay tipped on its side like a broken toy.

The man who had fired was behind the Pajero. He stood beside a companion, and both men held their AK-47s over their heads in victory, pumping the weapons up and down, enjoying the attention of the people on their balconies. The shooter did a little jig.

He lowered his weapon and pointed it at the Pajero, advancing slowly with a jihadist's grim expression. Analise worked the clutch and gear shift to drive the Pajero through the cleared intersection. More shots were fired. The Pajero's rear window shattered and then she felt the rear tires decompress.

Men in the barbershop stood at the large display window and looked on. Boys in the video game parlor pressed their faces to the glass. The street was clear but eyes were everywhere.

Analise swung around, looking from one side of the Pajero and then the other. The way forward was open but the Pajero's tires were flat. The militia man stood behind with his AK-47. He was a big man with a thick beard and broad shoulders, gloating in the praise of men at his side, but then an arm pushed him away.

Ibrahim was there. His eyes were fierce and he stepped forward with the confident swagger of a humorless prize fighter. As he walked, he held up his leather driving gloves like a war prize. He waved them over his head for the crowd to see. A voice called out and Ibrahim moved aside to make room.

Qassem emerged from the back of the gathering crowd, and the two men stood side by side. Qassem was the holy jihadist—dignified, utterly implacable, and unmoved by the drone's downing. He was stoic among the restless men and women who emerged from their doors and joined the militia.

Qassem's Western-style sport coat fit loosely over a crew-neck shirt and billowed in the wind coming up the street. Grit was in the air. His eyes were dark and steady, his face expressionless, and he had the look of a man who knew exactly what he intended.

He raised one hand slowly and invited the armed militia to move toward the Pajero.

Rami tore his arm away from Analise's grip and bolted out the door. He ran toward his grandfather, who embraced him and held him at his side.

Danger came to her in synesthetic waves of saturated red and purple. *Think.* She turned away from the men approaching the rear of the Pajero and looked for an escape. She gunned the engine and released the clutch, but the rear wheels flapped and the vehicle lurched without gaining speed. Everywhere, faces stared. How many times had she dreamt this nightmare?

Her cell phone vibrated. *You're not moving. What's happening? Trap.*

Get out of the vehicle.

Her mind grasped for the errors of judgment that had brought her to this reckoning. She craned her head out the window, looking at the rooftops, and scanned between the tangled web of overhead wires. Bauman was there. Somewhere. Looking down. Then she knew. She was never meant to survive.

Her world got very small and very dark. In the rearview mirror, she saw Qassem pat Rami's head and then gesture to Ibrahim, who advanced toward the Pajero with the AK-47 he'd taken from a militia man.

Women on the balconies looked down through the web of wires. Somewhere a woman began a high-pitched trill, and others joined. A growing chorus of long quavering trills resounded in the narrow street and filled the air, drawing more people to witness the killing.

Analise heard her death sentence. The end of her life approached on a different plane, a timeless drumbeat recorded in the universe that on that precise day, at that exact hour, on that dusty street, she would meet her ghost.

She stepped out of the Pajero, hands raised high and to the side in helpless surrender. She backed away from the Pajero, but she kept her eyes fixed on Ibrahim. He pushed Rami forward, slapping the boy on the back of his head, a violent gesture that sent Rami stumbling forward.

"He is only a boy," Ibrahim shouted. "You used him."

Analise took a step backward, and then another. Her eyes fixed on Ibrahim's weapon, and she thought about the holstered Glock under her tunic. Her chances were terrible.

Ibrahim pushed Rami forward again, but he moved too slowly and his eyes looked down at the ground. Ibrahim scolded Rami, slapping him again, badgering him.

"Look at your little boyfriend," he shouted.

She heard another drone, but she kept her eyes on the approaching men. Gal would be at his monitor observing everything from the drone's camera—the tag in the leather gloves, the stationary Pajero, a visual of the SUV. Analise stepped back again and estimated the blast radius of the explosion.

"He knows your lies," Ibrahim said. He dropped the gloves and crushed them with his heel. *Thirty yards away*, she thought, watching him move toward the Pajero, Rami at Ibrahim's side. Ibrahim hit Rami on the back of the head.

Qassem intervened. He gently moved his driver to one side and exchanged a few words that were lost in the women's shrill chorus. Qassem took the AK-47. He opened the action and confirmed that a live round was chambered. He presented the weapon to Rami, placing a comforting hand on his grandson's shoulder. He spoke softly to the boy and pointed toward Analise, gently encouraging him to fire the weapon.

Rami held the heavy AK-47 with both hands, steadying the stock on his hip, and aimed.

"You took advantage of him," Ibrahim called out.

Voices in the crowd chanted for mercy, others were aghast and astonished, and several urged for blood to be spilt. A woman in a hijab dashed from a doorway toward Rami, tears in her eyes, but two men intervened and held her back. Analise recognized Fatima. Distraught, screaming at her husband.

Analise met Rami's eyes. He was moving past the Pajero, looking at her with anger and fear. One hand held the front of the automatic weapon and his other was on the pistol grip, finger on the trigger. He pointed the muzzle across the thirty yards that separated them. He might be lucky with one shot, but he wouldn't need luck if he fired on automatic. She saw that it held a twenty-round magazine and knew it was lethal in bursts. It fired six hundred rounds per minute on full automatic. She had trained to calibrate the scope of danger, to control it, to understand it, and to open up a calm place in her mind. She didn't know all that passed through her thoughts in that moment—fear, contrition, regret, anger. She held the Pajero's key in her right hand, arms raised in surrender.

She looked for clues in Rami's eyes and she saw his anger, his hurt, and the shame of betrayal. He was a boy confronted by a test of manhood—the ritual killing that would make the militant's grandson a jihadist. Without any conscious effort, she said a prayer for herself, for him. Her lips moved silently and her hand trembled. *You don't plead with a child wearing a suicide vest. You kill him.*

Analise's thumb felt for the hatch-release trigger button.

Fatima broke free of the men restraining her and stepped in front of Rami. She pushed the muzzle to one side and angrily beseeched him, taking him in her arms and rocking back and forth. Other women came forward and surrounded them to protect them. Yelling erupted from the armed men, who stepped forward. A raucous scene broke out in the street. The sympathetic support of a few people was met with craven insults from others, and in that moment, the violent Hezbollah militia and their indignant opposite formed a tarnished throng that was a version of the divided Lebanon.

Analise stood absolutely still, the key in her raised hand. Ibrahim picked up the discarded AK-47 from the ground, where Fatima had tossed it. He was furious and his anger diminished his marksmanship. His first short burst was high and wide, shattering the barbershop's plate-glass window. He took long determined strides toward her, closing the distance to improve his aim.

Analise dropped to one knee and took the Glock from its holster, the key falling from her hand. She held the weapon in a two-handed grip and sighted with one eye, firing twice. Her first shot struck Ibrahim in the thigh, throwing him forward, and the second shot struck his forehead, sending him backward onto the street, where he lay faceup in a slowly widening pool of crimson blood.

The gunshots agitated the crowd, and people dispersed into doorways or behind parked cars. Those on balconies retreated into the safety of their homes. Hushed quiet lingered in the aftermath of the killing. The high-pitched trilling had stopped and there came indignant shouts from the militia men who ran crouching toward the fallen man.

Qassem joined the two militia men standing over Ibrahim's body, pausing a moment to consider his dead relative.

It had been part of her professional training to target wanted terrorists, watching assassinations from a distance, but unexpected threats had required her to kill in self-defense once before. She had not liked doing it, but she knew what to do, and had done it. The driver was her second kill. There was something mesmerizing in the moment a human's life bled out and was no longer anything. The driver had been someone and now he was no one. Fear was human and so was survival.

She saw the muzzle flash at the same time that she heard the gunshot. Qassem had fired the weapon he'd picked up. The bullet entered her right shoulder just beyond the Kevlar vest. It struck her with the force of a sledgehammer, and the aching pain radiated to her elbow and her hand. The Glock fell to the ground. Blood flowed down her side, and her hand came off her tunic covered in sticky wetness. She wanted to sit down, and for a brief moment she felt gratitude that the bullet hadn't struck her in the neck or head. She stumbled forward and dropped to one knee.

Qassem stepped away from the driver's body. He had been smoking, but now he threw his cigarette to the ground. Quiet and gentle in his demeanor, he unsheathed a long, curved knife from his belt and walked forward, his eyes dark with vengeance. As he passed the Pajero, his free hand made a cutting gesture on his throat.

A brilliant flash of light filled the narrow street. The blast's force was intensified by the buildings on either side, breaking windows and covering everything in a fine gray dust that drifted down in the moments afterward. Ghostlike faces covered in ash were everywhere, and from inside the toxic cloud came the moans of the wounded. The bomb's aftermath was revealed as the smoke settled. The Pajero was a twisted metal heap, and a debris field radiated from the driver-side door, where the packed explosive had concentrated the outward blast. Qassem's decapitated body was being covered with gently falling debris. His head lay nearby.

Analise slid backward, pushing away from the grievous carnage. She stared at the bloody torso and struggled to move away. She looked for Rami, but didn't see him. Stunned men crawled in the street, others stumbled, and everywhere was a tentative awakening to the scope of the violence. She pushed back to the safety of a recessed doorway. Her ears rang and she coughed a milky pink saliva. Ash in her hair made her look like an old ghost. Blood leaked from under her dirt-caked tunic. An eerie quiet settled on the patch of earth. The suddenness of the explosion, and its force, froze everything. Then the entire world rose up in mad confusion. Men in keffiyehs and carrying guns poured into the street, and behind them she heard the hysterical wail of sirens. Frantically shouted orders mixed with the soft moans of the wounded.

Bauman was at Analise's side. She had slumped against the door and held her side with a limp hand. Her face had lost color, her eyes were dim, and the pleasant sleep of death lay over her body.

"Get up." He pulled her to her feet, placing her arm over his shoulder, and helped her walk away through the debris and confusing chaos. "We need to leave. It's not far."

PART III

29

Hospital

It should have been easy for Analise to accept a visit from the man who, in pulling her from the carnage, had saved her life, but she had complex feelings toward Bauman, and whatever gratitude she felt was poisoned by what she knew about him and what he had done.

She spent five days in the hospital, recuperating from the shoulder wound and blast trauma, nursing various parts of her aching body. Helen camped out in the hallway to guard against the dangers that followed from being identified at the site of the blast. Ordinary existence, if there was such a thing in Beirut, went on. Dull routines of her day helped her through the difficult physical therapy and moments of depression. Helen's brusque humor also helped.

Analise thought a great deal about what had happened and the role Bauman had played. She prepared herself for his visit, and was glad he stayed away. She knew she would find it difficult to thank the man she had come to view as her enemy. It was easier to hold on to a course of action if she was spared his convenient denials and explanations. It was who he was. The least transparent men reveal themselves through their dissembling.

Analise had time in the hospital to listen to the quiet voices that spoke to her. The clamor of work had silenced them, but long days in bed gave them an audience. Qassem was dead. It took a day for that fact to settle in, and when it was firmly planted in her consciousness, her thoughts roamed across the collateral consequences—the wound, Rami's anger, her departure from Beirut. All the little details presented themselves for consideration in the enforced confinement of her recuperation. She was obedient to Helen's instructions and rested, and her thoughts wandered to her other life and to her husband. A resourceful UN courier had delivered the note he'd sent addressed to her real name. How many times had she warned him not to put her at risk? He complained that she hadn't called and hadn't answered his texts. She tore the note into halves, quarters, and eighths before dropping it in the wastebasket. Her marriage was dead, but it had not yet been memorialized with an obituary. Another casualty of her tour in Beirut.

Analise's depression came in waves, but like the tide, it also receded. No good came from dwelling on what had happened. She felt responsible for Aldrich's death, although she knew that she was blameless, but the inner workings of guilt didn't assuage her pain. She admired his faith; his noble, hopeless idealism; and she had no problem reconciling that to do good required the diligent exercise of evil. The number of men she'd killed, or had a hand in killing, had doubled. She had done what was required.

In the confinement of the hospital bed, she began dreaming in Arabic. And from dreaming, she found herself in quiet moments thinking in Arabic. Thinking and dreaming in another language gave her distance from her old self. English contained her and preserved habits and behaviors, but Arabic allowed her to discover the possibilities that came from forming thoughts with different words. Arabic's expressive sounds helped her embrace her anger and frustration.

At times in the hospital bed, she thought it might be pleasant to invite Bauman, her savior and nemesis, to dinner when she got out so they could share stories of their work together—the clandestine meetings, Gal's van, the exploding Pajero, and her fear of beheading. But most of the time she couldn't face the idea that she and Bauman might enjoy a bottle of wine and argue the merits of Condoleezza Rice's brokered cease-fire. She couldn't bear looking at him across the table, listening to his confection of truths, half-truths, and lies, thinking that he had been willing to let her die.

Inspector Aboud questioned her about the bombing, but the refusal of people in the neighborhood to cooperate with the ISF left him with only a vague account, and Analise added nothing useful to his investigation. Qassem's assassination was just another unsolved murder in Beirut.

The sudden end of the thirty-four-day war created a new set of challenges for UNHCR that placed a claim on her. The chaotic evacuation from Beirut harbor was now a struggle, among those who had left, to return home. It was impossible to say that her life, or life in Lebanon, was getting back to normal. The only things certain for Analise were her departure and the dead: Aldrich, Ibrahim, Qassem. More vague and unsettled was her relationship with Corbin, who had arranged to meet her when she was released from the hospital.

⁙

"Can I join you?" Corbin asked.

Analise looked up from her breakfast of almond crescent rolls in the Commodore Hotel's pool area, largely empty that morning. The opening of the airport had let stranded businessmen fly home, and the arrival of peace meant the departure of Beirut's war correspondents. Well-dressed Lebanese men moved among the few guests at the pool, pitching their contraband of hashish, watches, and nude photos. Every city, she knew, had a smell, and the smell of Beirut was graft. If she looked closely, she would find diamonds stolen in Sierra Leone making their way through the souk to Antwerp and pornography from Amsterdam offered to visiting Gulf Arabs.

Peace had also changed Corbin. Gone were the dusty cargo pants and days-old beard that he'd worn since they'd first met at the Beqaa Valley border crossing. He wore pressed slacks and a linen sport jacket with the uncomfortable formality of a man who preferred a war correspondent's fatigues—who flinched when a nearby truck backfired.

"You look like a store mannequin," she said, having seen his two sides—the grubby war correspondent who now dressed like a polished copy editor. "The tie is tight. It's strangling you." She stood and loosened it for him.

He went to kiss her mouth, but she offered her cheek. She sat again and leaned back, putting distance between them. She had debated whether to meet him, but her apartment was off-limits and she needed a place to stay.

"You look good."

"What did you expect?"

"You almost died." He nodded. "Your sweet tooth is back."

She picked at a crescent roll and didn't bother to answer.

"They have opened the Syrian border. Damascus is a three-hour drive again. I'm headed that way for my next assignment."

After a beat, Corbin added, "Inspector Aboud thinks you lied to him."

"The Shia woman? He visited me in the hospital. He said he found her."

"He's still looking for Bauman." Corbin paused. "He disappeared after he brought you to the hospital. A hard man to find has vanished again. Aboud thinks you might know where he is."

"He shouldn't assume that. I'm not his caretaker."

"In his mind, the two of you are connected. How's the shoulder? I heard that he saved your life."

"Collateral decency. Nothing he's proud of."

"I never liked him."

"A convenient symmetry." Analise was vaguely fond of Corbin in a way she didn't totally understand, and sometimes she thought it was the obviousness of his probing questions. The dance they did in conversations, holding back and never saying exactly what they thought, was mildly entertaining. She wondered about him.

He pointed at the two flutes of champagne mimosas. "It's early to drink for two. Celebrating? Commiserating?"

"Both." One flute with vodka chaser was nearly empty and she pushed the full one toward him. "Join me." He waved it off and she centered both flutes on the table. Not wanting to laugh, she did.

"What's so funny?"

"I could say it's all too much for me, or I could say nothing, and let you figure it out."

"That would be you."

"Maybe it's not me."

"Then you've got me fooled."

She threw back the second flute of champagne. "I'm alive. That's worth two glasses of this shitty champagne. How's your wife?"

"It's over. She wrote a letter. It was short and not sweet, but it was what I expected, so I wasn't surprised."

"Sad?"

"I'm glad it's settled. Disappointed maybe, but not sad."

"Leaving Beirut?"

He shrugged. "What about you?"

She smiled. "What I like about you is the same thing I don't like about you. You're predictable, but then sometimes, you say something or do something that makes me think I don't know you at all."

He looked at her across the table. "That doesn't sound like a compliment."

"It's an observation. I have a question for you."

"Go ahead."

"Why did you look through my bag that morning? You weren't looking for matches."

He frowned, but then he leaned forward. "I was curious about your friendship with Bauman. He was surprised to see us together in the bar, and then there was his call. The only people who call that early are close relatives and lovers. I looked in your bag to satisfy my curiosity."

She listened skeptically. She went to drink from the empty flute but set it down, remembering. She clasped her hands on her lap and tapped her foot, agitated.

"Are you back in your apartment?"

"Off-limits."

"Stay here. My invitation still stands. Are the ISF looking for you?"

"It's not the ISF."

"What haven't you told me?"

"I've told you what you need to know."

"I think I will have a drink." He got the waiter's attention and ordered a scotch and soda. He pondered her sitting across from him, legs crossed, quiet. "You really haven't told me anything about yourself. What I know about you I've managed to dig up, others have told me, or I've observed."

She uncrossed her legs and leaned back in her chair.

"Do you know what I've discovered?"

"Go ahead. Maybe I'll learn something about myself."

"Analise isn't your name. There is no Analise Hahn Assad."

The smile on her face disappeared. "Okay."

"There is a woman with a different name who's your age, Lebanese-American, who graduated from Georgetown. She looks like you. Her brother died in the attack on the World Trade Center. She came to the attention of the CIA because of a master's thesis psychologically profiling the men who carried out the attack on 9/11. She was recruited by the agency and shipped off to Iraq a few months after her wedding."

Analise remembered what the agency recruiter had said. "We don't recruit happy people. If you're going to join us, you have to be angry at something." Analise sipped her drink and contemplated him. "You think I'm her."

"Same face. Different names. Who am I talking to?"

"You're talking to me. Does it matter what my name is?"

"Yes, it matters to me. Two names. One person. One real and the other a wholly made-up person with fake interests, fake kindness, and a fake smile. Do you know who you are?"

"I'm the person sitting across from you. That's enough." She was aware of the danger that was attached to honesty. She knew she had come face-to-face with a man as dangerous as she was.

"You're quiet," she said. "What are you thinking?"

He looked at her, trying to look inside her mind. "You might want to look at this." He pulled a glassine envelope from his sport jacket and carefully removed a piece of shrapnel. The jagged metal lay in his hand like a saint's relic and he presented it to her as an offering.

"Do you recognize it."

"Where did you get it?"

Corbin pointed across the pool at two ISF officers who had approached the Lebanese man engaged in negotiation with a Western businessman, removing photographs from a leather portfolio. "They work for Inspector Aboud. He tracked me down and asked a lot of questions. He said I might have interest in it."

She lifted it to the light and rotated it, matching it to the fragment she remembered. There were faint alphanumeric markings, but the carbon casing was a unique signature. It was similar to what Aldrich had shown her at the St. Georges Yacht Club—dull tungsten gray, misshapen.

"A precise weapon," he said. "Two people were killed. The concentrated blast came from a parked Honda Civic."

"Who died?"

"Aldrich."

Her eyes came off the shrapnel.

"It's from the wreckage of his SUV. Aboud found more in other car bombs." He paused. "I've never seen you look so shocked. Say something. Your tongue is a stringless instrument."

"I need this."

"I'll keep this for now. There is a story here. My editor doesn't care if Bauman is Mossad, but knowing who killed Aldrich is big news." He held up the shrapnel. "It's news if it points to the ones responsible. You know who placed the bomb, don't you? I can see it in your eyes, Analise Hahn Assad"—he paused—"or whatever your name is."

She hesitated and then slapped his face hard.

His hand touched his cheek, still hot from the sting. His drink arrived and he sipped it without speaking. They sat like prize fighters in their corners waiting for the bell to announce the next round. Corbin touched his face again. "That was unnecessary."

She placed money on the table for the waiter.

"That's it? No questions? You were close to him. He was murdered."

She put on her dark glasses and head scarf.

"You haven't eaten."

"I've lost my appetite." She felt an urge to lie, but she knew that he would use whatever she said against her. Their whole fraught relationship was fraying in an unpredictable way—their first meeting, the sex, their games of give and take, and now an accusation. Nothing made sense to her in that moment. She felt an awakening rage that frightened her, but inside she was also miserable and human. There was an absurdity to the moment, sitting across from an on-again, off-again lover who didn't know her real name, who had handed her the carbon casing of a tungsten explosive used by Mossad to kill the CIA station chief. A wave of nauseating doubt drove her onto the rocks of anger. She understood what it meant to kill another human being, but she did not understand the cynical murder of a colleague. In her wildest flights of paranoia, she never imagined Mossad would do that.

"Bauman had something to do with this, didn't he?" Corbin said.

Analise stared. It was the way he said it, a rhetorical question to test what she knew.

When she stood, he rose from his chair. A man and a woman close together in the heat of the day surrounded by the laughter of a few swimmers in the pool. She started to leave but stopped and turned to him, observing surprise on his face and eagerness for her answer. Approaching him, her lips touched his, kissing him. She pulled back and she saw that she had confused him. Leaning forward, she kissed him again, a longer kiss, that he was returning.

She gently pushed him away but looked in his eyes and tried to imagine the game he was playing. Seeing what she wanted to see, she walked away from the pool.

"It's a big story," he called out.

She looked back. "You don't know what you're dealing with."

30

Drop It

Nothing had changed in the safe house in the time that she had been away. On her way to the bedroom, she saw the desiccated mouse by the refrigerator. The bedsheets were crumpled on the floor where she'd left them and she sat at the small wood table, opening Aldrich's laptop.

She entered the numeric code from her digital fob, and the screen opened into the encrypted router communications network that connected country stations to Langley Headquarters. Security protocols didn't allow agency computers to be used in insecure locations, but Aldrich did business his own way, and for that he'd paid the ultimate price. Secure servers directed her message to the duty officer of the Middle East section of the Counterterrorism Center.

Her note began "Operation HANNIBAL. Deliver Immediately." Using the code name for Qassem's extra-judicial execution was a way to ensure that the note got high-level attention. In spare prose, she laid out her accusation, adding enough detail to make it credible. She signed it with her cryptonym, a word randomly selected from a sterile list that had no relationship to the work she did. The note would arrive in the agency secure network but she added a crude but effective authentication. She misspelled several words—*able* with a *d*, *kind* with an extra *i*, and *public* with an *e*. The desk officer who read the message would recognize the routine misspellings and assemble the sequence of errors as "die," a high-priority code. Her message would light up buttons on telephone consoles of senior intelligence officers. Men schooled in caution would approach the drumbeat of treachery with skepticism, so she described Technical Services' assessment. Facts ruled in a world where opinions were the unwanted dross discarded at the end of a meeting. Her inflammatory accusation would make the agency's bosses fidget, but everything pointed to the conclusion, and nothing pointed away. Mossad had murdered Beirut's station chief.

Analise prepared herself for an inconclusive response, or a request for more confirming details, or even a phone call. Her extraction was set, but she was prepared to stay if the agency needed help with an investigation. The baldness of her report was clear to her but she didn't know if it would seem blunt or careless. Or both. She stepped away from the computer and poured herself a glass of water to wait for the duty officer's response. Upon walking back from the balcony, she happened to glance at the computer and saw the message icon had incremented.

Fifteen minutes. Nothing happened that fast in the agency—nothing with the importance of her allegation. The response startled her:

"Drop it."

She stared at the two words on the screen. The speed of the response and its biting definitiveness baffled her. There it was: *Drop it.* The second surprise came when she recognized the man's alias—a man high in the agency but not high enough to have a public face. The alias was one of several he employed. An entire artifice inside the agency shielded intelligence officers' true identities from each other as a way to prevent the agency's highly confidential human resources information from falling into illicit hands. The commitment to aliases created a hard problem for the IT department, which had to keep a master list of who was whom and how to securely route emails addressed to one person using different names. But she knew the name on the screen. A lax note once, a connection made that she wasn't supposed to discover. No man was more important in counterterrorism than the chief of staff to the deputy director of operations.

Analise sat back in the wood chair, exciting a squeak in the joinery. Her palms were flat on the table and she stared at the screen. There were only two reasons for the wicked speed. What she had reported had already gone up and down the vetting pole, and somewhere in the labyrinth of intelligence operations, this fact—the murder of a station chief by an ally—had been forgiven. Or, the incendiary accusation had been buried by someone inside.

Analise got to the Commodore Hotel late. She slipped out of her sweaty blouse and slacks, placing them over the back of a chair. A tepid breeze came in the open window and provided meager relief from the evening's sweltering heat. She slid under the thin bedsheet in her panties but had removed her bra.

"Where were you?"

"Out."

She turned to Corbin, who had rolled over to look at her. Her poolside kiss had brought peace and she didn't have to endure the awkward silence of an unfinished argument. Lies and lying gave

Analise a way to take control. The advantage of the logic was simple—she was never going to be surprised by betrayal, only by loyalty.

Corbin was propped on one elbow, and his eyes were patient but sleepy. The glow from the full moon coming in the window washed him in silvery light, deepening his August tan.

"Everything okay?"

"I'm fine." She drew the covers over her chest and lay quietly, avoiding his eyes. She heard an abrupt grunt and he flounced onto his side, putting the pillow over his head.

"We can talk in the morning," she said. "When does the helicopter leave?"

"Ten."

She heard irritation in his voice. Her feelings were raw and she considered how she might have offended him, and then it irritated her to think that way. Her husband had used the same sullen behavior to try to make her feel bad. He had never accepted the demands placed on the marriage by her career and he resented her long hours doing work she couldn't talk about.

Analise gazed at Corbin beside her. She appreciated their casual intimacy, but she resisted taking the small steps to open up to him. The war and their marriages had been awkward complications.

Analise touched his shoulder tenderly, and when he didn't stir, she caressed his arm, moving her fingers to his stomach.

"I'm okay," he said, shifting away.

She lifted the pillow and looked into his eyes, surprising him. Her leg swung over so she lay on him, and she gently caressed his cheeks, letting her fingers play with his hair, encouraging him. In a moment, she propped herself on her hands above his face and lowered herself, touching his lips in a passionate kiss he returned.

Using one hand, and a minimal amount of contortion, she removed her panties.

She lay on her back listening to Corbin's heavy breathing until she was certain he was asleep.

She moved to the window. The image of Aldrich's mangled SUV was alive in her imagination, and his face came too—a bloodied, ghostlike apparition, his arm reaching out to her in a plea for help. She shook the horrible images from her mind's eye.

Beirut was alive with nightlife, but the southern suburbs were still dark from war damage. The full moon laid a false peace on the city. Loud, drunken conversation in the hotel's garden was an unpleasant chorus to her troubled thoughts.

What in God's name was a young intelligence officer operating under non-official cover to do with an inconvenient truth? What was a loyal officer who believed in the agency's mission to do now? She had joined the agency to wage peace, but she had only seen war. Should she sound the alarm on the agency's complicity to alert the seventh floor at Langley Headquarters? She remembered the mysterious note she'd found in the drafts folder of the Hotmail account she'd shared with Aldrich, and her thoughts became a tangled web thinking about who benefitted from the chaos.

31

The South

Analise's final reconnaissance mission to the battlefields on Lebanon's southern border had been arranged by UNIFIL, but Corbin had helped advance the date of the tour, so she invited him to accompany her. He'd schmoozed the Ukrainian pilot with crude jokes and a carton of Marlboros. She'd always felt excluded by that particular type of male camaraderie but didn't particularly resent it. Corbin moved over when she hopped on board beside him.

"Two dicks waving in the wind," she said.

"You're jealous."

She tapped her forehead. "My intelligence is in my head, where it belongs." She turned and saw Simon Bekker on the other side of the aircraft. "What's he doing here?"

Bekker raised his camera and pretended to press the shutter release button. "Parting shots of this little fokken war."

Israeli Air Force overflights had ended with the cease-fire, and the absence of war planes in the sky reduced the likelihood they would be mistakenly shot down. The pilot saw her nervousness and laughed. "Drones are still flying. Keep your zipper up."

She thought the joke was probably funnier in Ukrainian. She had no fear of flying, but she knew there was always a luckless soldier in every war who died after peace was declared.

Analise looked for drones during the twenty-minute ride toward the war zone. A merciful God wouldn't save her from Qassem's knife only to deliver her to a meaningless death. Odds were against that unlikely outcome, but she had become a dust bin for cruel absurdities.

"For a frightened person, you're pretty fearless," Corbin said.

She relaxed her fingers gripping the armrest. *Never let them see you sweat.* "He's the frightened one."

Bekker wore a tightly cinched seat belt and had preemptively put on a yellow life vest. She passed him the vomit bag. "Lean away." It amused her to see that underneath his obnoxious personality he was a coward.

"Down there," the pilot said.

The Apache helicopter was flying over terrain south of Beirut, dry hills scorched by summer heat and fierce battles. They had passed miles of blasted highway and had come upon a village of stone homes shattered by bombs and close combat.

The pilot's thick accent and the high-pitched engine noise made it difficult to follow all that he said. She tuned in and out of his shouted communications, understanding what she could, and staring out the window at the scarred landscape. Scattered family groups sat beside stalled cars, and the helicopter's approach got their attention. A young man raised a gun. A woman raised a dead child.

The pilot banked in an evasive maneuver and the bullet fired by the militia man harmlessly passed through the helicopter's aluminum skin.

They continued south. Corbin's banter with the pilot was a pleasant soundtrack to the depressing sights of war. She thought their dark humor was an unconscious defense against the horror on the ground. She saw the Ukrainian's somber face. *The saddest men have the best jokes*, she thought.

"The neocons in Washington are happy," the pilot said. "But Israel didn't need encouragement." His hand waved in a dismissive judgment. "They were waiting for the right excuse. The IDF saw what America did in Iraq. They thought they could do the same here. In and out. Declare victory. Mission accomplished. A cheap war."

She listened to Corbin chime in.

"I have nothing against war. I make my living from war, but I am against stupidity. The winners here are the ones who watch from the sidelines."

Analise admired how he reduced subtle political complications to sound-bite speculation that passed for news. She could never be a reporter. But people listened to him and ignored her.

The pilot banked sharply and made a slow approach to a blasted Merkava tank tipped over in a roadside ravine. Next to it lay a dead cow bloating in the hot sun. Several Lebanese villagers stood over the IDF tank crew, stripping them of clothing and personal belongings, desecrating the bodies. Bekker raised his camera.

Seeing Bekker's interest, the pilot flew low over the tank, scattering the scavengers. The pilot's crackling voice came over their earphones. "They make a distinction between the dead, but the flies don't see the difference between a carcass and a corpse."

"A righteous convocation of worms," Bekker said.

The pilot looked at Analise, nodding at her notebook. "Did you get what you need?"

"I'm done," she said.

She gazed out the window on the return flight. The view gave her time to consider what she would do. The response from Langley pulled at the threads of her conscience and she kept coming to the dumbfounding words. *Drop it.* Her loss of faith didn't come all at once, but slowly, like a gentle dusk.

Analise stuffed her notebook into her backpack and hopped off the helicopter into the rotor wash, following Corbin. She held the backpack close against her chest and lowered her head, moving toward the waiting vehicle. It was the same pier where Aldrich's transport case had been carried to the Chinook. She passed the spot where she'd sat with Gal in the Land Rover listening to the rank hypocrisy of his eulogy.

The Apache helicopter lifted off and dust swirled in the air. "Some war," Corbin yelled.

His words were lost in the turbulence and the screaming pitch of the straining engine. She waited for the helicopter to lean into its flight pattern and move out to sea. They walked side by side and she endured the conflict that had metastasized within her; in the helicopter, she had come to a view of things—an ugly conclusion that she did not want to embrace, but it was there in front of her. She walked with her head bowed. When they reached the chain-link fence, she stopped.

"I have something for you."

"What?"

"The story you're looking for." The decision to break her oath of secrecy had been made through the slow accumulation of uncomfortable details that moved her to a threshold, but it was Corbin's encouraging demeanor that pushed her over. She knew it was a grievous mistake to confuse high-ranking men who spoke for the agency with the agency itself. Men corrupted by disloyalty and ambition operated in the dark anonymity of the secret world.

"It involves someone in the agency." She looked at him. "It goes to the seventh floor at Langley."

"Why are you telling me?" He looked at her. "What's changed?"

"Does it matter?" She looked at him. "You're a reporter. You'll know what to do with it."

"I'm being used."

"The story will excite the fevered imagination of your editor."

"What is it?"

"Be patient. I'll get you what you need."

Corbin's eyes narrowed. "I have nothing but patience. And a deadline."

32

Cleaners

A nalise didn't think of the visit to her old apartment as a pilgrimage, but she had left it abruptly, not knowing whether she would ever see it again, and now she was back. She reached high on the doorjamb and searched for the strand of hair, and not finding it, her hand moved up and down the jamb. It was gone. The locks had not been forced. The intruder had a key.

When she opened the door, she was startled by the apartment's emptiness. Furniture was gone, the floors swept and mopped, shelves and cabinets were empty, windows washed. The photo of her brother removed. No trace of her. She had been effaced.

Agency cleaners had entered and done their work, and she saw the expert way they had removed all evidence of her life. Analise Hahn Assad did not exist in the apartment except in her memory of the space. She had the unsettling feeling of being in a twilight zone.

She sat on the windowsill and pondered the circumstance that had brought her to this precipice. Officially, she didn't exist inside the agency, and now someone in Langley had decided that she didn't exist—period. She had been cut loose. Erased. The fastidious cleanliness of the empty space was perversely humorous—the idea that she would leave an apartment broom-clean. *Corbin would approve*, she thought. Order and regimen were the agency's way of managing unpredictability and chance. When she came to that realization, she understood the extent of her jeopardy.

She found her personal journal in the hidden recess behind the kitchen's electric panel. She had left it behind for safekeeping, and the agency cleaners hadn't found it. It was against agency policy to keep a private journal that contained compromising operational information, but a voice inside her had decided she needed a record to protect herself. Her entries had moved from Aldrich's vague concerns to his specific accusation: there was a traitor inside the agency. She had put down on paper what Aldrich suspected. There were also notes about Gal and Bauman, and telling details that would prove the authenticity of her entries to a skeptical reader. Dates, places, code names, the nature of the DIME, and a lengthy explanation of the use of RFID tags to establish the kill site. She raised another possibility. Had the CIA killed one of its own? She pondered the question and then dismissed it. Agency officers stayed behind Awkar's concertina wire and it was only Mossad that moved through Beirut's streets. She had written most nights and always with a plain, black ballpoint pen. Clandestine training had taught her to remove anything that could be used against her by alert adversaries, and to make the point, her grumpy instructor at the Farm had told the story of a covert officer compromised by his taste for branded pens filched from five-star hotels. *Be every man and no man*, he cautioned.

She replaced the panel and stuffed the journal in her backpack.

Analise stood at the balcony's sliding glass door and took in the view one last time. The world she had encountered each morning from the balcony was her own. She couldn't take it with her, but it was a part of her. All the little things that she'd observed and watched. Beirut's street sounds rose up—car horns, motor scooters, conversations on the street that drifted up to the balcony, a baby crying somewhere. Fragrant jasmine. Roses on the street that drooped in the heat. The predictable arguments of the neighbors two floors below. She breathed it all in and then turned away.

Analise was at the door, hand on the lock, when the telephone rang. She stared at the handset on the kitchen wall, letting it ring twice and then a third time. She moved to the balcony to see if anyone in the street was on a cell phone.

"Hello."

"I've been trying to reach you."

Bauman. "What's up?"

"Your agency babysitter is looking for you. Langley has doubts about you. I said I didn't know where you were."

"Now you know."

"Can we meet? I never got to the hospital. It wasn't safe. I don't like to talk with walls and telephones around."

A beat of silence. "Of course." She rubbed her forehead. "You're the person no one can locate. Not me."

"Mossad has a job if you're interested."

"That's how you think of me?"

"You're good at what you do. A lady assassin attracts less attention."

She almost laughed. Without any conscious effort on her part, she was now considered an accomplished killer. Anger rose in her and she hung up. She saw his text come through on her Nokia. *Name the spot.*

Analise calmed herself and considered his request. Dinner with a bottle of wine so he could offer elaborate apologies, weaving a web around her—to recruit her. She pondered the shrapnel, his role in Aldrich's death. She knew him better the more he lied.

She glanced around the apartment with an acute sense of time—past time, the time of the call, what she had to do, and future time that would swallow her. The day would end, another day would follow, and another, and the moment of her leaving would become an old memory. To be cautious, she removed the battery from her Nokia. No one would know her whereabouts.

She paused outside the apartment and listened. Voices in the circular stairwell. Several people were climbing quickly and speaking English. She left the door ajar and looked over the banister into the sweeping circularity of the old French staircase. Within the gracious architecture she heard the urgency of footsteps running up the marble treads.

Helen moved from one floor's landing to the next and happened to look up. Analise saw the false pleasantry of Helen's smile, and the quick movement of her hand behind, when a companion stepped into view.

"I thought you might be here," Helen said.

It was the tone of Helen's voice that alerted Analise something was wrong. The man who joined Helen on the landing held a pistol in two hands. He had the grim expression of a security officer looking for a fugitive.

"We need to talk," Helen said.

Analise saw the full dimensions of her peril. Telephone consoles in Langley had blinked red alert, and the rapid response to her note had been matched by a furious conviction that a Lebanese-American NOC was in possession of a terrible state secret. Analise's hand gripped the balustrade and she felt a stitch of terror. There were no friends in the agency. Helen was moving upstairs like a hunter advancing on cornered prey. There was no charity in the world of non-official cover. Her apartment had been effaced. She didn't exist. She couldn't unwrite her note or unknow her claim.

In one swift movement, Analise stepped back into the apartment and locked the door. Her decision to run came instinctively, without reason or forethought. There wasn't the luxury of time for a considered choice; there was only escape.

Analise knew Helen had keys, so she clipped the chain to get a few extra moments. When she first took the apartment, she had searched for a way to leave quickly if she needed to.

Her bedroom's casement window opened wide enough for her to squeeze through. Her feet moved slowly along the building's narrow cornice as she slid sideways above a narrow gap in the buildings until she reached the end and dropped down the short distance to the adjacent roof. She heard excited voices behind her, but she was already hurrying down the neighboring building's bulkhead staircase.

33

Café l'Étoile

Analise waited behind the glass counter while the pleasant sales-clerk brought several inexpensive, prepaid cell phones from the cabinet and amiably described their features. Without looking at the others, she chose the plain black phone and paid with bills that she removed from a neatly wrapped wad. The money had come from a bank account she'd set up when she arrived in Beirut and it held enough money for an escape, if she found herself in danger.

The travel office on Hamra street sold her a plane ticket to Paris on a flight that left in two days, and the travel agent help-fully reserved her a week's stay at a Paris hotel on the Left Bank, using the false name on the black diplomatic passport Helen had provided. She paid in cash. She knew the place from her college semester in France, and she was certain the agency's security offi-cers would make the connection. It was the hotel where she'd spent several lovely months with her estranged husband. They'd been expats in France, and had shared a taste for late-night romance, but he always left in the morning for his embassy job, and she held on to her habit of blessed solitude.

It was still before dawn in Virginia when she left a short voice message on his cell phone. Her tour in Beirut had ended and she would be flying to Paris and hoped to see him that weekend. She apologized for not calling sooner and added a few tender details. When she finished the call, she removed the Nokia's battery and SIM card, dropping them in the trash. Agency intercepts would transcribe the message and record the location of the call. Security officers in Paris would be alerted to her arrival and they'd be prepared to grab her when she arrived at the hotel.

She had one day, maybe two, before Helen and her colleagues recognized the diversion.

It was late afternoon and pedestrians strolling through the old square enjoyed the cooling breeze. She spotted Hammadi as she entered Café l'Étoile. A man with habits was easy to find, and his routines made him predictable, but she hadn't left their meeting to chance.

Analise arrived at his table wearing Prada sunglasses and a head scarf.

Hammadi stood. *"Marhaba."* He kissed her on one cheek and then the other, three times. His light touch on her elbow was an invitation to sit. He pressed his hands on hers in a brusque handshake and she didn't object to the new familiarity. Because of all that had happened in her life, and the experiences they'd shared in Beirut, she felt an intimate connection to a man she didn't trust.

"Please join me." A bowl with three flavors of ice cream was on the table in front of him. "The best ice cream in Beirut."

"You've said that before."

"I can't be expected to remember everything I once said." He pointed to a table where the French woman sat with a boy. "Her kidnapped son was returned. There was no news of the abduction in the papers and then he showed up at the hotel. I'm sure it was a large ransom. And the boy still has his ear. Kidnappers harvest body parts from morgues to facilitate negotiation."

Hammadi took a spoonful of chocolate but stopped before he tasted it. "There is another spoon."

"In a moment. Thank you for coming."

"I was told you had left Beirut. But sometimes when I think a person has left, they are still here. Hiding. Beirut is a city in which it is easy to hide. You asked me here to talk about Aldrich?"

"Bauman."

"I believe he is still here." Hammadi smiled. "Perhaps he's waiting for the next war to start."

Hammadi savored the ice cream and then placed the spoon exactly where it had been. "We haven't become friends, but perhaps we can be friendly because we see the same evil." He looked at her. "You may not know where Bauman is, but I suspect you can help me find him. His van is missing. His apartment is empty. We have checked the hotels, but he isn't registered. I have a score to settle with him." He looked at her. "You're nervous. You keep looking behind. Do I make you uncomfortable?"

She smiled politely, lying. "I parked my car illegally."

He pointed at the gay evening crowd in the Place de l'Étoile. "See the effect that Madam Secretary Rice's surprise visit has had on the city. Two weeks ago, we cowered in our basements. Today, you can't find a parking spot. May I share a thought with you?"

"About Bauman? The war? Ice cream?"

He laughed. "My wife complains that I tell too many stories and I bore my audience. Hopefully, what I'm going to say won't bore you. It's about Bauman."

He sat back in his chair. "Often when my day's work is done, I sit at this table with coffee and dessert and wonder if my life has been as successful as it might have been. I have four children, all in good health, thank God, a devoted wife, many friends, but I looked the other way when I saw corruption. I was ambitious, and to succeed I ignored crimes that I witnessed because the criminals had money, influence, and held important positions as journalists, or prime minister. But it is that singular vision that made me a man of importance, which is also the problem with Lebanon. Our weakness comes from the triumph of personal success over the common good, and our weakness is exploited by Syria, the PLO, by foreign agents from Iran, and by men like Bauman. A member of parliament is murdered and I am elected to fill the vacancy. I mourn my friend's death but I rise up into the void that is created. I know this sounds terrible, but we live in difficult times, and if it isn't me, it will be someone else. Someone worse."

Waiting for Hammadi to go on, Analise wondered if she had ever before met a man so cynical. His honesty was seductively reassuring, but offering a truth about his venality didn't in any way redeem him. It was incredible to her that he was confessing his unscrupulousness, yet he obviously was. In a way, it was his honesty that made him so appalling. He had no remorse, no shame, no guilt. She watched him without any expression whatsoever and was irritated by his candor, but at the same time, his confession confirmed her judgment.

"You may dislike me. I see it in your face." He folded his hands on the table. "Do I have doubts about how I have lived? Yes, at times. With doubts come regrets."

He paused. "I was born the same year as Bauman's father. He had a different name. I didn't make the connection for some time, but then I did. His father and I went to school together, we spoke Arabic to each other.

"I knew Bauman as a boy. A good child, studious, respected, and popular among his school friends. It was the same school that my son attended. They were friends. Bauman visited our home many times. I thought he would become a banker, a lawyer, or a merchant. He had a good mind for negotiation and he read widely, even at his age.

"Something changed in him when his father was killed. He became withdrawn, angry, which was understandable, but he went to an extreme. We all suffer tragedy and disappointment. Who doesn't? But what distinguishes one sufferer from another is the way that he is able to rise above misfortune."

Hammadi paused. "He thinks I betrayed his father. He twists facts to make his claim and he invents his own history of Lebanon to justify his actions. I have family in Aley, where Jews lived peacefully with Druze, Orthodox, and Muslims. Have there been incidents of anti-Semitism? Yes, but there was also anti-Muslim sentiment among Christians and anti-Christian sentiment among Muslims, and from that intolerance came civil war."

Darkness had fallen slowly, and with the passing of the day's heat, the city had come alive and couples walked the streets. Traffic in the roundabout was chaotic and everyone walked with a revived humanity. The setting sun washed upper floors of high-rise buildings in golden brilliance that reflected on Hammadi's somber face.

He sipped his coffee, which had gone cold, and he put down the cup. "I am not interested in Bauman's virtuoso explanations or excuses. He forfeited sympathy and a claim to justice with acts of revenge that are more wicked than the score he wants to settle."

"What would you do if you knew where he was?"

Hammadi raised an eyebrow. He looked off but then met her eyes. "We have a saying: if you play with a cat, you'll get scratched."

She put a hand on her heart. "*Shukran.*"

34

St. Georges Marina and Yacht Club

It was Corbin's conversation that provoked her imagination and began a fitful process that advanced her thinking. Her mind was a tangle of complications, but the concentrated act of listening to him deliver a simple message brought clarity to the situation. A plan visited her like a dream.

Corbin had called her to say that he'd bumped into Bauman at a hotel bar and that he wanted to speak with her. "I think he wanted to annoy me," Corbin had said. "He wanted to remind me that he also knows you. I didn't insult him but he looked unhappy with me. Like I was a threat. He said his calls to your cell weren't going through, so I agreed to pass along the message."

Corbin added, "He saw me and made a point of coming over. We talked about the war. I told him he'd crossed the line. A journalist's job is to report the story, not become the story. He didn't think that was funny. I didn't tell him what I thought of him."

Analise picked a small secluded café table at the St. Georges Yacht Club close to the marina's boardwalk, seeking the privacy that Bauman wanted—a meeting place without walls or telephones. It was the in-between hour of the day when sunbathers departed chaise longues to escape the cooling breeze, and Beirut's late-night party crowd was still hours away from arriving. There was a pleasant serenity to the hour. Children had left the pool, and even the casual strollers along the boardwalk were gone. Tall glass towers rose over the squat St. Georges Hotel, which was wrapped in a huge fabric sign, STOP SOLIDERE. One corner had pulled from its anchor and flapped in the breeze.

She removed her dark glasses and head scarf, letting her hair fall to her shoulders, and sat. The Mediterranean stretched into the distance like an interminable highway toward the molten sun dying on the horizon. The flutter of a canvas umbrella disguised the waiter's approach.

"For one?"

"Two. He'll join me shortly."

The waiter placed a small vase with a single red rose on the table and left cloth napkins rolled around cutlery.

"Drink?"

"Vodka martini straight up. Two olives. No ice." She ordered Aldrich's favorite drink to honor him. "When do you serve dinner?"

"Dinner starts at seven. May I offer chips? Mixed nuts?"

Analise saw him first. Bauman descended the stairs from the Corniche to the St. Georges pool area. The boarded-up St. Georges Hotel was a sulking remnant of the old Beirut and a symbol of the city's new chaos. Sleek powerboats and more genteel sailing sloops were boastful prizes moored alongside the boardwalk.

"I tried your phone, but the call didn't go through."

"Corbin told me. Did you get my text?"

"I'm here. It's a new number."

"It's dangerous for me. For you. For us."

He looked around. "Less dangerous here." He turned to her. "The war's over. What are you concerned about?"

"I almost died."

"I saved your life."

"Hezbollah was waiting for me. I was set up."

"Your plan didn't work. The stitching wasn't good. I saw him throw the gloves to the ground."

"You came up with your own plan. It's taken me a few days to understand what happened. You never liked the tags. They knew I was bringing the SUV. I was your bait."

Bauman dropped his cigarette to the grass and ground it in with his heel. "You were never in danger. We had a sniper on the roof. We couldn't rely on the RF tags."

Analise heard his admission, delivered as a convenient exculpatory lie. The car bomb. The sniper. The ugly treason of mistrust was dangerous when your life depended on another, and for that reason she had ignored her doubts, believing—hoping—there was a good explanation for the chilling indifference that he wore like an ugly rash.

"It's not safe for you now in Beirut," she said.

"I have a few old friends. I move from one to another."

She recognized his confident swagger, charming in its own way, but old and tired.

"Gal?"

"I work for him, but he goes where he chooses. He got what he wanted."

"Inspector Aboud wants to question you. Hammadi wants to know where you are. He met with me and he is convinced you're still in Beirut."

Bauman pointed at a nearby sleek powerboat. "Bribes have been good to him." He paused. "A lot of people want to talk to me."

Bauman snapped his fingers to get the waiter's attention. The waiter arrived, smiling solicitously, and Bauman gave his order. "One Almaza. Cold."

They sat quietly facing the marina and the sea beyond. The surface of the Mediterranean shimmered in the late afternoon light, and the sound of the sea's wind was tender and exhilarating, like the hollow whisper of a wood pipe.

"Did Hammadi tell you that he knew my father? He likes to tell the story that they were good friends, but he doesn't say that he forgot his old friend when it became inconvenient to acknowledge they knew each other. He misremembers that part to cover up his betrayal." Bauman pointed at the powerboat. "He's wealthy, corrupt, and a hypocrite."

Analise had not come to argue. "Why did you want to see me?"

"I heard Corbin's writing a story."

Analise had rehearsed what she would say. She had formed her own opinion, but she wanted to judge Bauman's face when she made the accusation. "He has a piece of shrapnel from Aldrich's SUV. It's the same tungsten explosive that killed Khoury and Siniora." The facts came effortlessly, as did her lie. "He's made the connection to Mossad."

Bauman disdained her comment. "He's heard a rumor, but it's not true. He should be careful with the rumors he spreads."

"He says he has proof."

Bauman grew quiet.

"He said that it will look terrible when the *New York Times* runs the story. Mossad assassinates CIA station chief."

Analise watched his expression. His silence confirmed her suspicion.

Bauman took his beer, finished it in one long draught, and placed it on the coaster, centering it. "Do you believe him?"

"He's full of himself."

Bauman smiled. "He's a war correspondent."

"When are you leaving Beirut?"

"Shortly. When I'm done."

"More killing?"

He leaned forward. "The world doesn't understand what we do. Smug attitudes of indignant men who decry our actions but are happy with the results. They prefer the pleasant fabrications found in novels. Life isn't that simple. Corbin is as dangerous as Qassem."

"Truth is dangerous."

Bauman laughed. "That is a stupid thing to say. Truth is dangerous. Whose truth? My truth, the truth of my father, your truth. There is no truth. There are only the things you'd like to believe, and they become your truth, but *the* truth? You're smarter than that."

Bauman reached for his beer but put it down when he realized he'd finished it. "Where is he?"

"He's meeting me tomorrow night."

Bauman considered her. "Where?"

"Here. He wants me to confirm his suspicion. I told him I would have something for him." She looked at Bauman. "You should join us. Maybe you can talk him out of it. Nothing on earth can compete with your indignant outrage. I've stopped believing you, but he might listen."

"We need to put this behind us."

She stood. She hesitated, but then she shook his hand in a friendly gesture. "The dead survive." She met his eyes. "To remind the living." She planted a Judas kiss on his cheek, surprising him, and she walked briskly to the stairs, taking them two at a time, disappearing along the Corniche.

35

Clock Tower

She felt no outrage and none of the brutal anguish that she had expected to feel. She had accepted her fate—to punish evil, she had to embrace it. It wasn't complicated, and once she made the decision, she felt free from the yoke of wrath. Her choice bound the wounds and healed her. The trail of barbaric slaughter would end.

Corbin proved a predictable friend and let her stay another night in his hotel room. His neatly folded clothes made the room familiar, but another woman's underwear in the bedsheets made the room feel foreign. Confined to the room, she felt the lonely sameness of hotel rooms everywhere. She was reminded of the dreary hotel room on the Left Bank of Paris that she'd shared with different boyfriends.

Hammadi answered his cell phone on the third ring. Analise stood at the hotel room's window, undressed in the heat, looking out at the city.

"He will be at a small table at the St. Georges Yacht Club tomorrow at six. By the boardwalk next to your boat. There will be a vase with a single red rose on the table. I told the waiter it was an anniversary."

She had arrived in Beirut one year before, to the day. It wasn't a thing she wanted to celebrate, but the waiter appreciated the occasion and promised the table would be by itself, away from the main sitting. There would be a vase with a beautiful rose.

Analise leaned on the iron railing along the path and looked down at the American University of Beirut's Green Field, where two teams of young boys in colored jerseys played a fierce, scoreless soccer match. It was not dark enough for field lights and not light enough to make out the faces of the young boys racing toward the soccer ball.

"You're restless," Corbin said. He stood next to her in pressed linen slacks and Italian loafers. He looked less heroic in an Oxford shirt and polished shoes—and less interesting.

"Have you changed your mind?" she asked.

"Have you changed yours?"

She looked off at the players on the field. "It's my last day in Beirut. I won't be staying with you tonight."

"Where are you going?"

She didn't answer. She glanced at the clock tower on College Hall. Waiting made time move slower and it seemed like it had been two minutes to six o'clock forever. Her eyes moved off the clock tower and settled on him. The balcony overlooked the field and she watched the group on the sideline cheering on the players.

"I thought we could talk here before I leave." She smiled a vague smile that didn't reveal her thoughts, and seeing his confusion, she added, "Sometimes it's just good to have company. To be with someone you know. Not to be alone. To settle things."

Analise watched the yellow and green jerseys of the opposing team's mix together in the kinetic motion of back-and-forth play.

"You keep looking at the clock tower."

"It tolls for Beirut. For Aldrich." She paused. "For us."

"You're in a dark place." He nodded at the field. "Which one is Rami?"

"In the middle. Long hair. The one with the ball." A thin boy dribbled past a challenger and pressed his attack on the opposing team's goal. "His mother is there. And Halima." She pointed to a clutch of spectators. Fatima wore a hijab and yelled fiercely as her son escaped his challenger.

"Her daughter is on her way back to Beirut. Fatima will be happy."

Corbin watched Fatima encourage her son from the sideline. "She lost her husband, but her two children must be a comfort."

"A good killing ends a bad marriage."

He smiled. "I wasn't that lucky."

The clock on the redbrick tower struck, marking the hour, and the pleasant chime mixed with cries from the field. Analise looked north, along the Corniche, toward the westernmost point of Beirut, where St. Georges Bay was a sliver between tall apartment buildings.

"What about your husband?" he asked.

"Ex-husband. It's over. It's been over a long time. I brought this for you." She handed him pages that she'd torn from her journal and several draft notes she'd transcribed from Aldrich's computer. "What you need is here. It's not everything, but it's enough."

Excited yells from the field took her attention away from Corbin, who studied the pages in the dim light of dusk. Rami had made his way past the last defender and moved the ball with long, reaching strides toward the goalie, who had advanced to meet him. Rami drove his foot into the ball with a swift kick, sending it into the corner of the net. Exuberant cries erupted from his teammates, and spectators raised their arms overhead, clapping and yelling. Players in the field were giddy with victory, chest-bumping each other in an ecstatic display of joy.

Analise observed the youthful innocence among the excited players. For the life of her, she couldn't distinguish the good-hearted ones from the boy who had pointed a weapon at her. To kill her. Perhaps they were all alike, perhaps he was different, but in their moment of innocent joy she couldn't tell one from the other.

She turned to Corbin. "The shrapnel you have is from a new weapon that Israel obtained from the CIA. Powdered tungsten is shaped around an explosive core that directs the blast outward in a cone, limiting collateral damage. No other country in the Middle East has this. Mossad killed the CIA station chief."

Analise noticed his grim surprise and for a moment she saw Robert Redford in *All the President's Men*—the hungry reporter caught up in his role, looking to use the power of his pen to take down men in high office. It didn't give her satisfaction to see him rapidly write down all that she was saying. The attention he paid to her admission made her uncomfortable, but once she began to speak, she had no choice but to finish.

"There are three names that you need to write down." She spelled each of the names Aldrich had left behind on his computer. "One of them is the man responsible. They may be agency aliases or made-up names, but I saw their photographs." She paused.

"One of them doesn't want attention brought to Aldrich's murder and he's convinced others in the agency. It's the other half of the story. A man high up in the agency takes orders from Tel Aviv." She looked at him. "A fox burrowed deep in the agency, but you'll shine a light on his den."

Corbin's writing was slower than her speaking and she paused for a moment to let him catch up, watching him write quickly with his plain ballpoint pen. She looked away, gazing along the Corniche, which curved toward St. Georges Bay. Palm trees swayed in the sea breeze and couples strolled in the pleasant evening, seizing the moment of peace.

Analise's cell phone vibrated with a text. *I'm here. Where are you? Where's Corbin?*

Analise dialed Bauman's number but the call failed. War had destroyed cell towers, and with the peace came overcrowded wireless circuits that made calling unreliable. She tried again but got the same message. She stared at the phone in her hand and glanced again at the slivered view of St. Georges Bay.

"Who are you trying to reach?"

A huge explosion sent a fireball into the sky above the St. Georges marina. A thick plume of black smoke rose between the far-off tall buildings and was followed shortly by the percussive shock wave of a bomb blast.

Corbin turned to look.

"He's gone," she said quietly. The cloud continued to rise, and in the moments afterward she heard the distant sound of car alarms. She had trusted Bauman, but now she wondered if there was any trust between human beings that didn't depend on a willingness to ignore lies.

Corbin's cell phone had gone off while Analise spoke, and in his rush to answer he had not heard her. His short call ended, and standing beside her, witness to the same event, he shared the news he'd just gotten.

"A bomb in the marina. A powerboat exploded."

"He was a dangerous man."

"Who?" Then Corbin saw the answer in her expression. "Did you have a hand in it?"

"His bloody acts caught up with him."

Corbin narrowed his eyes, taking a moment to think. "You need to leave Beirut. They won't stop until they find out what happened."

She turned away and walked down the narrow path toward the rocky shoreline. Streaking light from the setting sun pierced the deepening darkness among the cypress that lined the path. She didn't see Gal's van on the dark street, and it seemed crazy to imagine that he would already be looking for her, but she felt a twinge in her neck—the feeling of being watched. She turned and only saw Corbin, who had come away from the iron railing. She saw him, but no one else. Heard nothing. She wouldn't see them until they were upon her. *You never see the bullet that kills you.*

"How will I reach you?" he shouted.

"I've got your number. I'll call from somewhere." *This has to end,* she thought.

"We can cross the Syrian border at Masnaa. We'll make a plan in Damascus. I'll file the story from there."

She continued without responding and followed the curving path with the slack step of a wary woman, but then she quickened her pace toward the traffic on the Corniche. She had her old passport in her birth name, which would take her out of the country, and she carried the money she would need as the world closed in around her.

"Analise?"

She heard him run after her but then stop. She thought he might continue to follow, and a part of her wished that he would, but another part of her hoped that he didn't. The difficult distance between them, which nourished whatever strange passion they had enjoyed, had closed, and with it came frightening possibilities. She moved past the crumbling ruin of the Roman wall and felt its timelessness mock her. She couldn't think beyond the next hour, the next day, the next week. Her thoughts swirled in the darkness of the moment, trying to imagine what she would do to stay alive.

"Analise." He was at her side, walking in step, out of breath. "I have a car parked nearby."

She saw his pleading eyes, heard his quick breaths, felt his closeness. His hand was on her shoulder and had stopped her so they faced each other.

"You'll need more than luck," he said, lifting her hand with its faded tattoo. "Come with me. We'll make a plan together."

He went on explaining how they would move from one city to another, living in rented apartments under assumed names. He would travel on assignment for periods of time, but he'd return, and in a year or two, it would be safe for her to emerge from his custody.

"Why would you do this?" *Why? Who are you?*

He gave answers that she half believed, explaining that he had never met a person like her and never would, that he felt compassion for her and affection, yes, affection. As he spoke, she was scared, torn between a profound yearning for the protection he offered and her doubts. The more he spoke, the weaker her resolve to hold on to her solitude.

"It's not possible. They'll find me. How will we do it?"

"We'll think of a plan."

She looked off into the night, watching the moths circle lights on the path, and she listened to the rustling cypress branches, wishing there was someone with whom she could share the burden of the evening's horror. A cleansing sea breeze touched her cheek and she saw the splendor of the sky. Everything had gone as she'd planned, but how she wished she could have foreseen the forces that acted on her.

Crimson flames ignited by the explosion licked the sheltering night and tilted in the gentle wind. The evening around them was quiet and the far distance to the marina made the spectacle serene. She gazed at the fire and trembled. It was warm out but she felt cold. Her mind struggled with the strange unreality of all that had happened and she wished she had a faith she could turn to.

In the silence of the moment, she hoped Corbin was right, that a solution could be found and a new life could begin, but it was clear, as they talked, that it was a risky choice, and the most complicated and dangerous part lay ahead.

Acknowledgments

Events depicted in *Beirut Station* are largely fictional, but several are based on historical incidents, including the tragic murder of CIA station chief William Francis Buckley, and the agency's two-decade pursuit of his killers; Condoleezza Rice's July visit to broker a cease-fire between Israel and Hezbollah; and the chaotic evacuation of foreign nationals from Beirut in the early days of the thirty-four-day war. The timeline of certain events has been changed to satisfy the needs of the story. Israeli tanks moved across the Lebanese border after the bombing campaign began, not before. I have no scruples taking these small liberties. This is a novel and not a history book, and its characters live entirely in one's imagination.

My agent, Will Roberts, patiently read several drafts of the novel and his keen editorial suggestions strengthened the book. Beth Parker, my publicist, worked her magic to place the novel in reviewers' hands. I am indebted to my US and UK publishers for the support of the novel, particularly Victoria Wenzel, Pegasus Books' editor, whose persistent challenges guided the novel in important directions. I also want to express my gratitude to Claiborne Hancock, publisher, and the publicity team under Jessica Case. Ion Mills, No Exit Press's publisher, has been a staunch supporter.

Mark Foulon, State Department officer stationed in Beirut in the 1980s, graciously commented on the manuscript, as did Salma Abdelnour and Michael Young, Lebanese writers, who generously read a later draft, corrected the geography, and suggested cultural nuances that would be known only to people who have lived in Beirut. Among the book's early readers were Andrew Feinstein, who has helpfully commented on all my novels, and my fellow writers in the Neumann Leathers Writers Group: Mauro Altamura, Amy Kiger-Williams, Aimee Rinehart, Dawn Ryan, Michael Liska, Erin McMillan, and Brett Duquette. Rae Edelson, Bruce Dow, Stephen Schiff, Fred Wistow, Dwyer Murphy, Lauren Cerand, Kevin Larimer, Jayne Anne Phillips, Elizabeth Kostova, Polly Flonder, Mary Knox, Mark Sitley, Rona Trokie, and Nahid Rachlin have been generous with their support and encouragement over the years. Novels by Joseph Kanon, David McCloskey, and Graham Greene inspired elements of *Beirut Station*.

Several characters quote or paraphrase other works. They are: "No arrests, of course. There never are in Beirut. Warm and gentle Beirut may be. But tough and cruel," Samir Kassir; "Our savage ancient spirit of revenge," Aeschylus, Robert Fagles translator; "It is always better to avenge dear ones than to indulge in mourning," Seamus Heaney.

Many books were indispensable sources of information about Lebanon and the 2006 war. Books that particularly helped me understand Lebanon and the dangers of non-official cover are: *Jasmine and Fire* by Salma Abdelnour; *Breaking Cover* by Michele Rigby Assad; *Pity the Nation* by Robert Fisk; *Life Undercover* by Amaryllis Fox; *Beirut* by Samir Kassir; *Beirut Fragments* by Jean Said Makdisi; *Uncompromised* by Nada Prouty; *The Tragedy of Lebanon* by Jonathan Randal; *House of Stone* by Anthony Shadid; *My War Diary* by Dov Yermiya; and *The Ghosts of Martyrs Square* by Michael Young.

I owe special thanks to my wife, Linda—teacher, partner, muse, soulmate—who introduced me to Aeschylus's trio of Greek revenge tragedies, *The Oresteia*, which planted the seed of an idea.

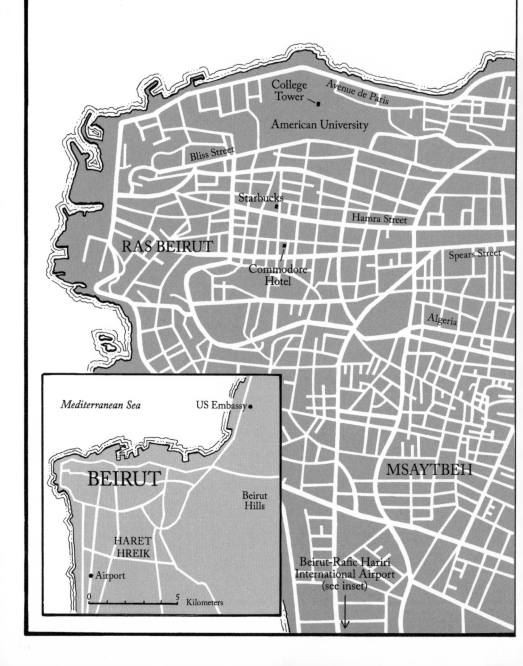

BEIRUT ██ LEBANON

July–August 2006
Hezbollah-Israel War

College Tower
Avenue de Paris
American University
Bliss Street
Starbucks
Hamra Street
Spears Street
RAS BEIRUT
Commodore Hotel
Algeria

Mediterranean Sea
US Embassy
BEIRUT
Beirut Hills
HARET HREIK
MSAYTBEH
Airport
Beirut-Rafic Hariri International Airport (see inset)

0   5   Kilometers